THE
SOULMATE

Also by Sally Hepworth

The Secrets of Midwives

The Things We Keep

The Mother's Promise

The Family Next Door

The Mother-in-Law

The Good Sister

The Younger Wife

THE
SOULMATE

SALLY HEPWORTH

HODDER &
STOUGHTON

First published in Great Britain in 2023 by Hodder & Stoughton
An Hachette UK company

1

A CIP catalogue record for this title is available from the British Library

Hardback ISBN 978 1 399 71356 6
eBook ISBN 978 1 529 33099 1

Printed and bound in Great Britain by Clays Ltd, Elcograf S.p.A.

Hodder & Stoughton policy is to use papers that are natural, renewable and recyclable
products and made from wood grown in sustainable forests. The logging and manufacturing
processes are expected to conform to the environmental regulations of the country of origin.

Hodder & Stoughton Ltd
Carmelite House
50 Victoria Embankment
London EC4Y 0DZ

www.hodder.co.uk

For Alex Lloyd
for all the last-minute changes

1

PIPPA

"Someone is out there."

I'm standing at the kitchen sink, my hands plunged in warm soapy water. Gabe is beside me, supposedly drying dishes but mostly drinking red wine and singing to Edith Piaf. He made coq au vin for dinner using every pot in the house, but if there is one thing to be said for my husband it's that he knows how to create a mood. He's dimmed the lights, lit some candles, even trotted out his best French accent. If not for the kids and my older sister, Kat—who is perched at my kitchen counter—it might have been romantic.

"Where?" Gabe asks.

I lift my gloved hand and point through the window. It is a woman, I think, though it's hard to be sure with the sun setting behind her. In any case, I have a clear view of a figure, twenty-odd meters away, beyond the edge of our property where the lawn gives way to a sandy walking path. *Millionaires' walk*, the neighbors call it, for both its million-dollar views and the multimillion-dollar homes that line this part of the cliff. On the other side of the walking path is a sheer drop down to the jagged rocks and the beach thirty meters below. It's not uncommon for people to stop here and admire the view, particularly at sunset, but when they linger it always gives me pause.

"*There.*"

I keep my voice quiet, steady. I don't have the privilege of hysteria given the proximity of our curious four-year-olds.

"Call the police," he says to me as he heads toward the back door.

Gabe is entirely unflappable. He's your classic *run toward a burning building* kind of guy. He might emerge a hero. He might not emerge at all.

"Where are you going, Daddy?" Freya asks as Gabe reaches for his coat.

"Going to catch frogs, poppet," he says without breaking stride.

I remove my gloves and drape them over the tap. Sometimes I wonder if I should be a little more like Gabe. More of a hero. Instead, I am a *helper*. In times of crisis, I am a creator of meal rosters, a collector of donations, dispenser of information. Last year, when news of the pandemic started to filter through, my entire family—parents, sister, sister-in-law, sister-in-law's parents—all called me with their questions on social distancing, masks, and vaccinations, hanging on my every word and taking notes as if I were an epidemiologist rather than a wills and estates lawyer. I rose to the challenge, dishing out advice gleaned from reputable verified sources and subduing family panic. But the kind of emergency happening outside right now? That is Gabe's domain.

I call the police from the next room—they don't need much in the way of an explanation from me anymore. I've made seven phone calls like this since we moved to the cliff house, a year ago. Now, I merely say, "It's Pippa Gerard—there's someone on the cliff," and it's sufficient.

It's hard to believe that we'd bought this house *because* of the cliff.

"Imagine sitting outside on warm nights and watching the sun sink into the sea," Gabe had said the first time we saw it. "What a dream."

It did indeed seem like a dream. A cliffside home in Portsea, a sleepy coastal town a couple of hours outside of Melbourne, the last in a procession of increasingly exclusive beach towns at the very tip of the Mornington Peninsula? It seemed unfathomable that we'd be able to afford such a place, even if it was a ramshackle cottage rather than one of the sandstone mansions that flanked it. We were shocked to discover we *could* afford it. Being from the city, we weren't aware of the notoriety of The Drop, where the tall cliffs had become popular among those wishing to end their lives. By the time we realized, Gabe was too in love with the place to let it go.

"Do we really want the girls to be around this, Gabe?" I'd asked him. "How are we supposed to explain it to them? And what if they wander too close to the edge themselves?"

"We'll put a fence up. And if they have questions about the people who come to The Drop, we just answer them in an age-appropriate way."

Gabe had been so calm, so pragmatic, that it was hard to argue. And to his credit, he practiced what he preached. The day we moved in, he had a fence erected around the perimeter of our land and warned the girls they couldn't go beyond it unless they had a grown-up with them. And in the year we've been here, they've never gone beyond the fence, and they've certainly never seen anyone jump. They couldn't have, because out of the seven souls who have come to the cliff since we moved in, seven have walked away. Gabe has saved them all.

"What does he say to them?" Kat asks, joining me at the window. She's been working today, and her tracksuit pants and fluffy slippers are oddly incongruent with her fully made-up face. This is the first time Kat has been present when someone has visited The Drop, and she is clearly exhilarated by the drama, while trying to remain appropriately somber.

"He asks if he can help them with anything. Or he might ask if they like the view. Anything to force them out of their thoughts and back into the world. Then he tries to get them chatting."

We watch as Gabe approaches the woman, and she turns to face him. She is farther back from the edge than they usually are, which I hope is a good sign.

"The view?" Kat says. "That really works?"

"Apparently."

But we both know it wouldn't matter what Gabe said. People don't come down from the cliff because of something he says. They come down because of who he is. When people meet Gabe, they feel safe. Seen. I've always thought he would make an excellent cult leader. Or used-car salesman. Last week there'd been an article about Gabe in the local rag—NEW RESIDENT SAVES LIVES AT THE DROP. The article had referred to him as an "angel." Gabe had posed for a photo at The Drop, smiling broadly. With his golden tan, blue eyes, and sandy windswept hair, he looked half surfer, half mountain man.

I've often wondered if his good looks play a part in his ability to convince people to live. I'm reminded of his good looks daily—not by Gabe but by everyone else.

"How'd you land *him*?"

"Is *that* your husband?"

"He is *gorgeous*."

It's not that I'm *un*attractive. In high school, a group of boys ranked me 7/10 for looks (which got them ranked 10/10 for ass-holery), but I think the 7 was accurate. I have a nice smile, wavy blond hair, a well-proportioned figure . . . and I also have a larger than average forehead and smaller than average eyes. I do my best with what I've got, and with makeup and heels I could probably get as high as an 8.5. Still, the fact is, most mornings I wake up looking like Shrek while Gabe wakes up looking like Chris Hemsworth, and there is no use denying facts.

Gabe and the woman appear to be talking animatedly. Gabe is using a lot of hand gestures. Admittedly, he's partial to a hand gesture, but there are even more than usual today.

"What happens if they don't want to look at the view?" Kat asks.

I shrug. "Thankfully we haven't had to face that problem yet."

The first time we saw someone on the cliff, it was midafternoon on a Sunday and the girls were on the grass playing in the blow-up paddling pool because Gabe and I couldn't be bothered walking down the zillion steps to the beach. We'd just moved into the cliff house. It was a sunny day, with a gentle breeze off the water. Gabe and I had gin and tonics and were in the midst of congratulating ourselves on our clever sea change.

"Mummy," Asha said, "that man is very close to the edge. He might fall."

I looked in the direction of her pointing finger. The man was indeed very close to the edge. His toes were *over* the edge, and he held the flimsy branch of a moonah tree in his right hand. It wouldn't save him. If he stepped off the edge, he'd take the tree out by the roots.

"Girls, I think I saw some ice cream in the freezer," Gabe said, understanding before I did. "Maybe you and Mummy should go and get some?"

The quiet that came over Gabe made me feel safe and panicked all at once. I took the girls inside and sat them in front of the television (one of the benefits of minimal screen time is that when you do turn it on, no natural or unnatural disaster can tear their attention away) and stole glances at the scene through the kitchen window. Gabe sat way back on the grass, I noticed, at least ten meters away. After a few moments, the man turned around. Gabe's body language was relaxed, as if he had nowhere to be. Five hours later, Gabe was in the same spot. So was the man, except his back was to the cliff now and he was talking, sometimes passionately, sometimes despondently. Around hour six, he was crying. When it got to hour seven, Gabe stood up and opened his arms. The man walked right into them. Later, Gabe told me the man had got so far into debt with his gambling problem that he couldn't face his wife and kids.

"What did you say to him?" I asked.

"Not much. Mostly I just listened. When he finished, I told him I was sorry."

When the police arrived, we'd been reprimanded for not calling earlier. They'd also praised Gabe's efforts. It was nothing short of miraculous, they said, for a layman with no experience to talk someone down. A couple of the cops even asked Gabe for tips. Now we always call the police immediately, but it's still Gabe who coaxes them away from the cliff, while I watch anxiously from the kitchen, my stomach plaited, wishing we'd never bought this damn house—just like I'm doing now.

The sun has set in the short time they've been out there. It happens quickly at this time of year. Under the lamplight, I can see that the woman has a dark ponytail and is wearing a black knee-length puffer jacket. She throws her arms up, the way Gabe does when his footy team loses.

"Has Daddy catched the frogs yet?"

Kat and I both startle, look down. Asha is standing at our feet holding, randomly, a fork. Freya stands worriedly beside her.

"Oh," I say. "Not yet, poppet."

"Does he need a fork?" she says, aggressively stabbing the air with it.

I wonder sometimes if I should be concerned about Asha's mental health. I remember doing an online survey "Is Your Partner a Sociopath?" and answering the question "Have they ever caused harm to animals?" I felt smug as I reported that Gabe adores animals. (Well, most animals. He has a strange set against llamas—something to do with an incident at the zoo—but he wouldn't cause harm to them, and that was the point.) As for Asha, I'm choosing to believe that even if she would harm a frog now, she will grow out of it. Surely! According to Mum, "All little kids are psychos. It's a necessary, important phase of growth." Except for those who don't grow out of it, I suppose.

I look back through the window. Gabe is standing much closer to the woman than he usually would. Closer to the edge, too. This is against the rules—his own, and the police's. The cliff is precarious enough for one person. Chunks of it fall into the ocean all the time. And on a day like this, the wind alone could force an unsuspecting person over the edge. Gabe has always been diligent about following the rules, despite his *run toward the burning building* mentality. I wonder if this is a sign of how it's going. If so, it's unlikely to be a good sign.

I glance briefly toward the street to see if the police are near. They won't have sirens or lights on. Like Gabe, they prefer a more subtle approach, not wanting to surprise or crowd anyone.

"Mummy," Freya says, "Asha is looking at me."

"Asha, stop looking at your sister," I say, my eyes still on the window.

Gabe takes a step toward the woman, which is also against the rules. "Don't advance on them," he always says. "Persuade them to come toward you, toward safety."

When Freya screams, I think I might faint. "For heaven's sake," I say quietly, as I see the prongs of the fork pressing into Freya's thigh and Asha's huge brown unworried eyes. I grab the fork. "Asha!"

"Come on, girls," Kat says. "I'll read you a book. Let's go pick one out."

I turn back to the window. In the dark it takes me a moment to locate them. When I do, I don't understand what I'm seeing. The space where the woman had been standing is now vacant. Gabe is alone at the cliff's edge now. His arms are outstretched, palms facing the empty air.

2

PIPPA

I throw open the sliding doors. It's bitterly cold, and the wind is wild. I jog across the grass in my Ugg boots and let myself out through the gate. Gabe hasn't moved from the edge, though his hands are now in his pockets.

"Gabe," I say, when I'm close enough for him to hear. "Baby, it's me."

When he turns, his face is eerily pale. He's almost certainly in shock. The air feels charged and fragile, like we should whisper.

"She . . ." He points over the edge as if he can't believe it. He rakes his hands through his hair.

"I know. Come away from there."

He doesn't move, so I take his forearm and guide him toward me. It calms me, taking control like this. *This* is why I'm a helper, not a hero. The world needs helpers for moments like these. And I'm already making a plan. I'll get him back to the house, get a hot drink into him. Something sugary. I'll wrap a warm blanket around his shoulders, like they do on TV. I'll google all the other things you're supposed to do in this situation.

We start toward the house, but we only make it a couple of steps before Gabe sinks to his knees and vomits on the grass.

I drop to my knees beside him. This is the exact situation I'd worried about. I'd worried, of course, for the poor soul who wanted to end their life, but even more than that I worried for Gabe, the poor soul who wanted to save it. The thing about Gabe is that he is a beautiful contradiction, as fragile as he is brave. What makes him a hero is also what compels him to run toward danger, and what threatens to break him.

For over a year, I'd watched with bated breath each time someone appeared on the cliff, wondering if this would be the one that ended badly. But person after person came, and person after person walked away. And as crisis after crisis was averted, he started to change. His eyes became clearer. A new confidence radiated from him—not the false bravado he'd once sported, but a true happiness and comfort in his own skin. It was clear that he had found his calling. I got so caught up in it, I thought he could save everyone. I suspect Gabe had started to think that too, even if he'd never admit it. But now this.

A light mist of rain coats us. Through the window I see the police have arrived. Kat is in the kitchen talking to them and pointing outside at us. Heaven knows what the girls are thinking.

Gabe has stopped vomiting, at least temporarily. He looks up at me.

"Are you okay?" I ask.

But my question is lost in the crash of the ocean, and the sound of the sliding doors as the police and paramedics file outside. I recognize them all. Johnno and Aaron; Fiona and Amir. They're not my friends, exactly, but definitely acquaintances. We've drunk countless cups of tea together at the end of evenings like this. I even purchased a packet of English Breakfast tea after Johnno turned up his nose up at my Lady Grey. But on those nights, there was never a body at the bottom of the cliff.

Johnno and Aaron walk directly to the cliff's edge with torches. They know as well as we do that there is no point, but they go through the motions anyway. No person who's jumped from The Drop has ever been retrieved alive (I'd read that in the news article, but having seen the cliff I would have known that anyway). Still, I suppose they need to be sure.

"Have you called out?" Aaron asks.

Gabe and I shake our heads. Gabe is trembling visibly now.

"Tide's in. We'll have to call Water Rescue," Johnno says.

"Hey, Gabe," says Fiona, one of the paramedics, kneeling beside him and wrapping a blanket around his shoulders. "Why don't we go inside and get you something warm to drink?"

Gabe allows her and Amir to help him to his feet.

As we step inside, I hear the bath running. There is no sign of Kat and the girls, and I thank my lucky stars for my sister. Knowing Asha, she's likely to be dishing out some tricky questions and there's no one I trust more to field them than Kat.

Fiona and Amir settle Gabe on the couch, still wrapped in the blanket, and I bring him a glass of water and wet facecloth to clean up. I flick on the kettle, then find a large plastic bowl in the kitchen and put it at his feet, just in case. Gabe nods his thanks, even smiles a bit, but he's still worryingly pale.

After a few minutes, Johnno and Aaron come inside.

"No signs of life," Johnno says. "Water Rescue is on their way. They'll have to retrieve her via the beach."

"Anything we can do to help?" I ask.

He shakes his head. "The crime scene team will be here soon. They'll do as much as they can tonight: photographing and finger-printing—if there is anything to fingerprint. They may have to come back in the morning when it's light."

We all nod soberly. I wonder what the girls will make of it, having the house swarming with police.

"We'll need to get a statement from you, Gabe," Johnno says after a moment. "Are you okay to do that now? It's better to get it sooner rather than later."

Gabe nods, and Johnno pulls out a chair from the dining table and sits. Aaron also drags out a dining chair. Gabe stays on the couch. I deliver cups of tea to everyone.

"So, what happened?" Johnno asks. "In your own words. Take your time."

"We saw a woman on the cliff. I don't know what time it was, but Pip called you as I headed outside." Gabe is gazing straight ahead, at the coffee table, and his fingers are steepled together. "As I got near, I asked if I could help her with anything."

Johnno picks up his tea and blows on the top to cool it. "Can you describe the woman?"

"Dark hair, in a ponytail. Clothes were all black. Black pants. A black puffer jacket."

"Young or old?"

"Youngish . . ." Gabe says. "Maybe thirty-five? Forty? Maybe even fifty. She was . . . well looked after. Seemed young at first but then you realize she's older than you thought, you know?"

Johnno nods his understanding. Sweet Johnno. I think of all the times he must have showed up on doorsteps in much worse circumstances than these. Situations where he has had to give people bad news, telling them that they have lost a loved one. It reminds me that someone is going to be getting bad news soon about this well-maintained woman aged thirty-five to fifty. A husband, partner . . . maybe even a child?

Johnno makes a note, then looks up. "Did you get her name?"

Gabe shakes his head.

"Then what happened?"

Gabe looks at his own cup of tea but doesn't pick it up. "She said her husband was unfaithful."

Johnno writes this down. "Did she say his name? The husband?"

"No." Gabe goes on: "It was hard to hear her, because of the wind. I think she was mostly ranting about her husband. I came closer, to see if I could talk to her. And she just turned and . . ." He inhales, closes his eyes. "It was so fast. She was there and then . . . a scream . . . and she was gone."

There's a quiet moment, a respectful silence. Johnno writes furiously on his notepad. After a few more seconds, he looks up again.

"She screamed then, did she?"

Gabe frowns, then appears to reconsider this. "I mean . . . I think so. It might have been the wind. To be honest, it's all a little blurry."

"Why?" I ask Johnno. "Is that unusual?"

"Not necessarily. Just worth noting." Johnno duly makes a note of it. When he looks up, he says, "Anything else that might be important?"

Gabe frowns as he appears to think about this. After a moment, he shakes his head. His eyes close.

Johnno puts down his pen. "It's not your fault, mate. Frankly, it's amazing that you've saved as many as you have. So don't blame yourself, okay?"

Gabe nods, his eyes still closed. Johnno shoots me a look and I nod as well.

"Well, we better go secure the site," he says, and he and Aaron stand. Johnno takes the notepad over to Gabe. "Have a read over this, and if you're happy it's accurate, sign and date it at the bottom."

The two men make their way to the back door. Just before he slides it open, Johnno pauses. "You didn't see anything, did you, Pip?"

It's an afterthought. His gaze is on me, but light, as if his thoughts are already outside.

The question takes me by surprise. It's straightforward enough, but I don't know how to answer it. The fact is, I did see something. I saw Gabe, cliffside, talking to the woman. I saw her throw up her arms, and I saw him take a step toward her. Then I saw Gabe alone, his arms extended, palms forward. The more I think about it, there's something about his stance that bothers me. I can't get it out of my head. He was holding his hands the way you would if you'd *pushed* someone.

Johnno is still looking at me, waiting for my response. Gabe's head is still hanging; he's clutching Johnno's notepad, his eyes closed again.

"No," I say. "I didn't see anything."

3

PIPPA

I lied to the police. No matter how many times I tell myself this, I still can't get my head around it. *I lied to the police.* Why did I do that?

Admittedly, it's quite common, if police procedural dramas are anything to go by. In every one I've watched, at least the first three suspects are lying about something. Usually, it's an affair. Or another, more insignificant, crime. I'm hiding neither. And yet, here we are.

I'm not the kind of person who lies to the police. I am the epitome of a good citizen. I have no unpaid fines of any sort. I ceased parking my car in the mother-and-baby spaces the moment the girls grew out of the pram. The time I found a cash-filled wallet I handed it to the police immediately, even though I was a student at the time and desperately needed the money. More importantly, I am a lawyer. I understand the importance of being truthful, and I know that providing a false statement to police is against the law.

I could be struck off the register for it, I realize, with sudden horror. I could lose my ability to practice law. And for what? Gabe didn't even do anything wrong!

It's 9:00 P.M., and I'm folding laundry at the coffee table while our garden swarms with cops. The crime scene team arrived an hour ago, along with the State Emergency Service, who set up tents and huge lights. Police Search and Rescue are also here, apparently. As it turns out, retrieving a body at night from the bottom of a cliff during a rain and windstorm when the tide is in isn't easy business.

Kat left once the girls were tucked up in bed, promising that she'd be back in the morning, and Gabe is running around after the police, switching on outdoor lights and offering warm drinks and umbrellas. Which leaves me with laundry. Normally folding laundry is the antidote to anxiety for me, but tonight I find it lacking. I've already put away the toys and vacuumed. The dishwasher is on. I'm running out of ways to self-soothe.

"Are you all right?" I ask Gabe at intervals, as he hurries past on his way to do one thing or another. He nods. I suppose there's nothing to say. It's too soon for him to be all right. It will take time for him to process what happened. My job will be to provide the support he needs. A listening ear. Counseling. Perhaps even yoga? Recently Mum raved to me about a "laughing yoga" group she attended down at the beach on a Wednesday morning. *Bunch of mad ladies wetting their pants,* she said. Maybe not that kind of yoga.

Perhaps we'll take a meditation course together? We could practice that thing that everyone talks about . . . mindfulness! Or maybe we could try adult coloring books. If it doesn't work out, we could give them to the girls. But I've always found coloring quite soothing—all those lovely colors staying neatly within the lines. I go online and order a couple, and a new set of Derwent pencils. It doesn't completely relieve my anxiety, but it helps a bit.

It's nearly midnight when the police confirm they have found the body, and the victim is indeed dead. The rest of the police work has been postponed to the morning, when it's safe to continue, though a couple of "guards" will remain overnight to ensure the integrity of the crime scene.

"Gabe," I say, after waving off everyone but the guards, but before I can continue he holds up a hand.

"Can I just . . . take a shower?" he says. "Then we can talk."

I nod, because after everything the poor man has been through, how can I deny him a shower? He trudges wearily toward the master bathroom, and I make my way around the house, locking doors and switching off lights. Outside, I hear the great crash of the ocean. Gabe always talks about how calming he finds that noise, but I've always found it ominous. Tonight, it is the most horrible sound in the world.

I check on the girls, who both lie horizontally across Freya's bed, their tummies rising and falling in unison. Asha's arm is outstretched across Freya's face and their legs intertwine in such a way that I can't tell which belong to whom in the dark. It never ceases to delight me that each night we put them to sleep in separate beds, and each morning they wake up in one—a habit Mum tells me they inherited from Kat and me.

My phone pings, once and then again, and I know without looking that it's Mum and Dad. Kat will have texted them the news. They are night owls both, and they'll be worried.

I glance at the screen.

Mum: Kat told us what happened. Give Gabe a hug and kiss from me.

Dad: Send my love to the big man. We'll be around in the morning.

My parents' relationship with Gabe brings me great joy. When Gabe married me, they didn't just become his in-laws, they became his *parents*, something Gabe was particularly grateful for, since he had no living parents of his own. Eighteen months ago, when our lives hit rock bottom, it was my parents who supported us through it, who helped us to restart our life at the beach—with me as the full-time breadwinner and Gabe as primary carer of the girls.

"Everyone should have the chance to start over," Mum used to say back then, to no one in particular.

And that's exactly what we did. I shouldn't have been surprised when, in our usual codependent fashion, Mum and Dad, plus Kat and Kat's wife, Mei, joined us in our sea change, finding houses within walking distance of our place. Our family has always taken togetherness seriously, but this was impressive, even for us. As Mum always says, "Family is thicker than water."

Indeed it is. And that's the reason, I suspect, why I was reluctant to offer the police any information that might reflect badly on Gabe, even though I know he didn't do anything wrong. He's been a different man—a better man—since we moved to the beach. Better than I had even allowed myself to hope. He's like a man who has come off drugs, or found God, or both. Only a few days ago, I looked at him and thought, *You're fixed.* I didn't say it out loud, obviously. Believing people can be "fixed" is a dangerous idea; it encourages young women to stay in relationships with men who "just get a little too angry sometimes." And yet, some people *can* be fixed. Gabe is living proof.

So I know there will be a reason why Gabe was holding his hands out in that way. He'll explain it to me and I'll feel that glorious sense of relief spread through me. Then we'll fall asleep holding each other, and tomorrow we'll get through this together. I'm looking forward to it! Which means I'm disappointed when I enter the bedroom and find Gabe, still fully clothed and still wearing his shoes, lying on top of the bedcovers, fast asleep.

4

AMANDA

So, this is it. I'm dead.

The police are retrieving my body. An arduous process, apparently, and they are out of practice to boot.

I've heard it said that the most difficult death to process is that of a loved one who is taken from you without warning. I agree that that is difficult. But I can now confirm that it is equally traumatic to be the one taken without warning. The whiplash of it. One minute you're here and the next you're gone—yanked from one world to the next as if torn with forceps from the womb. Except, instead of being placed into the arms of a loving mother, I'm alone.

The moment of my death was distinct. There was no slowing down, no light at the end of the tunnel, no moment in which to choose. No decision to make at all. There was a crack, like glass breaking, painless and clean. By the time I realized what was happening, it was done. Nothing to fear in death, I realize. No pain or suffering, at least physically. And yet, I feel a feverish desperation to claw my way back. Because unlike the scores of people who have come to this spot before me, I did not come here to die.

5

PIPPA

It's still raining when I wake. I enjoy three blessed seconds of calm before the horror of the previous evening collapses over me. The woman. The cliff. Gabe's outstretched arms. My lie to the police. It's a wonder I managed to fall asleep in the first place.

I reach for the lamp, switch it on. Gabe's side of the bed is empty, his clothes from last night draped over the beside chair. Gone for a surf, probably. This is a regular occurrence for Gabe, and probably exactly what he needs. Still, I worry that the distance he seems to be putting between us is the opposite of what he needs.

I pull on a robe and head out to the kitchen. The half-empty coffee cup on the counter and the muted television (on the Weather Channel) provide evidence that Gabe was here. I check the back deck for his surfboard and wet suit, and find them both missing, confirming my surfing theory. The weather is awful, but that has never stopped him before.

I take his coffee mug, empty the last of it into the sink, and put it into the dishwasher. Usually, I love the quiet of early morning, when the kitchen is spotless, the benchtop is clear of clutter, and the floors are clean. It is my time to take care of household admin before the girls wake up. Sometimes it's the only time in the day when I'm alone, and I've learned to savor it. Today, though, as I book the girls' four-year-old vaccination appointments, and transfer money for a spa voucher for their preschool teacher's birthday, I find myself watching the door, yearning for Gabe to return.

"It's not normal, the way you love your husband," Sasha Milinkovic said to me recently. We were at a trivia night, to raise money for the preschool's new eco playground. Gabe had volunteered to perform in the talent-quest segment of the evening. He played the guitar and sang "Annie's Song" by John Denver, and I cried. It was, most likely, the three chardonnays I'd consumed. Also, I loved "Annie's Song." But as I wiped my eyes, everyone gave me hell.

"I'd cry too if Stew sang," Emily Kent said. "But not for the same reasons."

Everyone laughed. I had to admit, there were moments that I felt on the outer because of my adoration of Gabe. There was something about the camaraderie of women good-naturedly slandering their husbands, each of them competing to have the worst.

"Stew fed them McDonald's? Dave didn't feed them at all for *twenty-four hours!* I came home and found Lenny in the pantry, scavenging for crackers!"

"They got *crackers?* Ours had to survive on fresh air!"

Occasionally, I tried to chime in for friendship's sake—"Gabe forgot to pick up the milk last night," or "He put Asha in two different shoes!"—but it always sounded a bit lame.

It would be arrogant to say that our marriage is better than other marriages. Arrogant and, let's face it, farcical, if you look at our history. But it is, quite simply, the truth. It's the way Gabe looks at me, even when we're in our tracksuits ambling around the garden, as if I'm the most beautiful, most interesting woman in the world. It's the way he touches me—whether I'm unshowered, postpartum, saggy or soft—without hesitation, as if I'm a cherished gift. It's the way he leaps to my defense, almost involuntarily, when he hears someone say something that could be perceived as critical of me. We've been through the fire, probably more than most couples. I think of our marriage as the reward for sticking it out.

I close my computer and check my watch. It's 6:44 A.M. Then I tiptoe down the hall and peek into the girls' room. It's always a struggle to get them to bed at night, but on the other hand, it means they are sleepy in the morning, often not emerging until almost eight o'clock, with great tufts of head hair and smooshed faces. It's not the first time I've taken advantage of this. During the summer, Gabe and I occasionally duck out for an early-morning swim. Other times, we stay in bed to pass the time.

I find the girls sound asleep, their snoring mismatched. When I'm sure they're still out cold, I slip out the back door. I lock the door behind me and take the path to the steps down to the beach. The rain is more of a mist now. There's something about the ocean air—everyone always says it, but since we've moved here, I can vouch for it. *You cannot go to the beach without coming back feeling a little better,* I'd said recently, as if it were a universal truth. But I doubt the woman from last night would agree.

Gabe is standing on the rocks, staring out across the ocean, his wet suit rolled down to his waist, looking like he's stepped out of the pages of a surfing magazine. I'm close enough to admire his smooth, tanned, muscular back, when I notice something small and silver slip from his fingers.

"You dropped something," I say, by way of greeting.

He turns, startled. His face is pink, as if he's been crying.

"Oh, babe." I touch his shoulder. "Talk to me."

He winces, his eyes on the ocean. "I was just thinking about what I should have done differently. I'm replaying it over and over in my head, wondering what I did wrong."

I wrap my arms around his waist. He's warm, even out here in the cold, and I feel his heart beating against me. "Don't do that to yourself," I say.

"She wouldn't listen to me. She was so upset. I couldn't talk her down." He rubs his temple with one hand. "Maybe I should have . . . I don't know . . . tried to get help."

"Help was on the way," I say. "You were right to stay with her."

Down the beach, a man in a raincoat walks his dog. I wonder how we must look, standing on the rocks, holding each other in the rain.

Gabe wipes his face with his forearm, then smiles. "Sorry. I'll be fine."

"It's okay not to be fine, Gabe."

"I know," he says. "But I will be. I'm dealing with it."

I suppose he is, in his own way. He's been for a surf; got some fresh air. Gabe was raised by a single mother who believed that fresh air and exercise were the answer to all the world's problems. And maybe they are, in a lot of cases. Still, given some of Gabe's difficulties, I've encouraged him to do some more work on himself in adulthood. And this is one of those times when I think that fresh air and exercise might not quite cut it.

"Would you like me to make an appointment for you with Thelma? It's been weeks since you've seen her."

Now I think of it, it might have been *months*. When we first moved to the beach, he saw Thelma every week. Thelma is a local psychologist, a lovely no-nonsense woman in her sixties with wild gray hair and purple spectacles on a chain. Gabe really connected with her. But only a few months into their sessions, she moved back to Melbourne and they had to switch their sessions to Zoom. I remember Gabe mentioning that he'd found it harder to connect over the computer. After a while, I guess, their sessions petered out.

"Yeah, sure," Gabe says. I'm not sure whether he's just saying it to placate me.

He takes my hand and threads his fingers through mine. I stare at them, entwined. Seeing his hand up close reminds me of what I saw last night. The way his hands were positioned the moment after the woman went off the cliff.

"Gabe," I say, after a moment. "I'm not sure if it's the right time to ask . . . but I saw you through the window right after she jumped. Your hands were . . ." I untangle my hand from his and hold my arms out, palms facing him. "Like this."

Gabe observes them for a moment, then looks back to the water. The guilt on his face is unmistakable.

"I tried to grab her," he says.

I can't help it—I gasp. "Gabe!"

"I *know* . . . I know I'm not supposed to, but . . . you see someone leap from a cliff in front of you, you can't help it."

("Never try to grab them," said the police officer who came to our house after the first potential jumper. He'd been very clear about this. "If you do, they might grab you and then we'll have two dead bodies." It was the number one rule, he told us.)

"I nearly had her. She was *right there*." He closes his eyes.

I wrap my arms around him and squeeze him tight, trying not to think about how easily it could have gone wrong. At the same time, I can't deny my relief. That's why he was holding his hands out. It makes total sense.

"I'm sorry, Pip. I'm so sorry."

I'm not sure if he's sorry for reaching for her, or for missing. Perhaps both. Either way, I've already forgiven him.

"Come on," I say, resigned. "Let's get back before those girls wake up."

The rain is getting heavy now. Gabe bends to pick up his board. I tiptoe over the rocks and am already on the steps when I turn back, remembering.

"Oh, you dropped something before."

Gabe stops. "Did I?"

"It was small and silver." I peer back at the rocks, but whatever it was has disappeared deep into its crevices.

Gabe shrugs. "Probably a chunk of surfboard wax," he says. "Forget about it."

And as we climb the stairs back to the house, I do exactly that. Forget.

6

PIPPA

I never get sick of telling people how Gabe and I met. It's a good story. A bit shocking, a bit unbelievable. It sounds more like a daydream, or a scene out of a rom-com that somehow transposed onto my life.

It was a miserable, rainy Saturday. I'd spent the morning in bed, crying over a guy called Mark who, it has to be said, wasn't very nice. We'd dated for six months, but he hadn't met a single friend of mine, nor a member of my family, preferring instead to hang out alone, in his apartment. I told myself it was because he was an introvert, and meeting new people was stressful for him. It wasn't ideal but it was something we'd work on, I thought. But then, after two of my friends had seen him at the local bar dancing and chatting up women, he'd stopped returning my calls. It was as though, suddenly, he'd forgotten he was an introvert.

On my third day of dedicated crying, Kat frog-marched me out of the house, ostensibly to walk her new dog. Mudguts was a rescue, a mixed breed, white with a brown streak across his tummy. (He'd been called Mudguts at the rescue home, a name he'd become irritatingly attached to, foiling Kat's attempt at Droolius Caesar.)

"Maybe I should try calling him again?" I mused as I pulled on my coat.

"You were ghosted, Pip. You're not meant to call people who have ghosted you."

"What *are* you meant to do if you're ghosted?"

Kat thought about this. "Honestly, I don't know. Lesbians enjoy talking about our feelings too much to ghost people. But I imagine you're meant to lose weight, get your hair cut, and post pictures of yourself living your best life on Instagram."

"But what if he thinks *I* have ghosted *him*?"

"The three hundred and sixty-seven messages you've left him will assure him that you haven't," Kat said sagely.

I knew Kat was right, but it didn't make me feel any better. And so I wept quietly as we wandered around the botanic gardens.

Halfway into our walk, when it started to rain, I started to weep loudly.

Part of me enjoyed how theatrical it was—heartbroken, sobbing openly in a park. I was wearing pajama pants beneath my puffer jacket and Ugg boots. I was the very image of a person at their worst.

The wedding that came into view as we walked around the pond felt like a particularly harsh blow, even if I didn't envy them the weather. Standing guests huddled under umbrellas, crowded around the three rows of white chairs where, I guessed, more important guests were seated. At the front, under a small awning, a tall, good-looking groomsman and a nervous-looking bridesmaid held large white golf umbrellas over the bride and groom. Kat muttered something about how desperate they must have been to get married outside on such a day, but I was distracted by the groomsman. He was eye-wateringly handsome. And he was staring, unblinkingly, at me.

Given my pajama pants/puffer jacket combination, the chances that he was checking me out seemed reasonably low. I chalked it up to the dramatic crying.

"He's staring at you," Kat said.

"I know," I replied.

For the sake of the wedding, I reined in the tears as we passed them. Unfortunately, Mudguts stopped to do his business just a few meters from the scene.

"Another reason not to get married outside," Kat murmured, pulling a plastic bag from her pocket. "So you don't have to say your vows while a dog shits nearby. You pick it up."

"Who are you, the Queen? In fact, I'm pretty sure even the Queen picks up after her corgis." But despite my grumbling I bent to pick it up.

And that's why I was bent over, with a plastic bag over my hand, the first time I heard his voice.

"Excuse me?"

It sounds dramatic to say the effect that voice had on me. I felt it *in my body.*

Kat and I turned in unison.

It was the groomsman. He was tall, broad-shouldered, strong. With his golden hair and skin, he reminded me of a lion.

Behind him, the wedding guests watched from under their umbrellas. Many of them were smiling or laughing, whispering to each other. It gave the impression that wandering away from a wedding ceremony in which he played an important role wasn't unusual behavior for this groomsman.

The bride was not laughing.

"Sorry," I said, assuming the bride had complained about the dog pooping near her wedding. "I'll just get this, and we'll be on our way."

I cursed the universe for putting this glorious man in my path while I was wearing pajama pants and picking up poop. Although, it had to be said, the glorious man looked a little disheveled himself. His white shirt looked conspicuously un-ironed and appeared to be untucked at the back. The pocket of his trousers was half pulled out, displaying their shiny silk lining.

The rain got heavier.

"No, *I'm* sorry," he said. "Mostly for Lucy, the bride, who will never forgive me for interrupting her wedding. It's just that I noticed you crying and I . . . I felt this overwhelming urge to ask if you were okay. Then I thought: That's stupid, you're with a friend and I'm the groomsman at a wedding while the couple are exchanging their vows. But you stopped, and I thought, well, it must be a sign." He smiled. "Do you believe in signs?"

"Yes," I said.

I didn't believe in signs.

Gabe looked delighted by my answer. Kat disguised a laugh as a cough.

"In that case, I'd like a sign that I should ask you on a date."

Gabe raised his eyes to the heavens, and for a moment we all waited.

What happened next was freaky. If I hadn't seen it with my own eyes, and if Kat hadn't witnessed it, I wouldn't have believed it.

The rain stopped.

A cheer went up from the wedding party nearby.

I looked at Kat. Her jaw hung open. Gabe also looked stunned. I felt a smile come to my face for the first time in days.

Neither of us noticed the groom approaching, but suddenly he was standing behind Gabe. "Sorry, mate, but can you do this later? It's your turn to sign the register."

Gabe ignored him. "I haven't even introduced myself," he said to me. "I'm Gabriel. Gabe."

"Pippa."

"Gabe," the groom said, sounding less apologetic now.

But Gabe didn't take his eyes off me. "I think it's pretty clear that the universe has spoken. So . . . do you happen to be free later? I came stag to this wedding, but I'm sure I could get them to add one to the bridal table. Right, Ant?"

Ant exhaled heavily. "If you sign the register right now, you can bring an entire footy team to the reception, mate."

"What do you say?" Gabe said to me.

"She says yes," Kat said when I found myself lost for words.

I felt like I was floating. Gabe got out his phone, and I keyed in my number then handed it back. The entire time, Gabe kept his eyes on me.

"I'll call you in a couple of hours," he said, before he was pulled back to the wedding. When he resumed his position, the wedding guests broke into a round of applause, and Gabe took a bow. Lucy, the bride, rolled her eyes.

I hurried home and washed my hair, did my makeup, tried on three dresses. Then I waited for Gabe's call.

But it didn't come for three weeks.

7

AMANDA

(AFTER)

Death isn't so bad when you settle into it. In fact, there's something soothing about it; watching everything but having no bearing on any of it. Hurts from life come with you, but they don't sting—like a mosquito bite that has lost its itch, you know it happened, but you don't *feel* it anymore. I wish I'd known this when I buried my mother. It would have helped me a lot. All I wanted my whole life was for my mum not to hurt anymore. To have the happy ending she'd always dreamed of but never got.

My father wasn't a good man, you see. He was hot-tempered, stupid, occasionally violent. He was extremely good-looking and charming, apparently, but that was part of the problem. He swept Mum off her feet, wooing her with promises of happy ever after. Then, like a lot of charming, good-looking men, he never delivered on any of it.

The story goes that my grandmother warned my mother about him.

"A blind man could see that man was a player," my grandmother said. But Mum didn't listen. He was her *soulmate*, she said. She moved away from her family and friends to a small regional town. She gave my father every cent she'd saved, as well as the car she'd worked so hard for. She became pregnant within a couple of months of their wedding, starting the family they'd talked so much about. She tried hard to make our modest house a lovely home for my father—a waste of time, seeing as he was rarely inside it.

Everyone in our small town knew what my father was up to, myself included. I was a child, but I wasn't deaf. I heard people talking—my friends' mothers, the supermarket cashier, the ladies at the hairdresser's. People gossiping about my father's behavior as if it were entertainment. The worst part about it was that most people treated it as Mum's shame—as if his behavior was a reflection on her rather than him. Mum seemed to agree with them, because to my knowledge she never once confronted my father, and if anyone so much as implied that he was less than faithful (like her best friend Sue did once, as gently as she could), she cut them out of her life.

I was ten years old when Mum and I saw Dad's car parked outside my teacher's house on our walk to school. Dad hadn't come home the night before and Mum had told me he was "away on business," which was how she usually explained his absences. I know Mum saw the car too, but she didn't comment and so neither did I. We were about to cross the road when the front door opened and there they were. Their eyes were on each other and they didn't notice us watching. Miss McKenzie was helping Dad put on his tie. Then she gave him the kind of kiss I'd only seen in movies.

"Come on, Amanda," Mum said, tugging my arm. "We're going to be late."

When I arrived at school, I realized we weren't the only ones who'd noticed my father's car outside Miss McKenzie's house. It was all anyone could talk about in the playground. Even my best friend, Avana, asked me if Miss McKenzie was going to be my new mummy.

At the end of the day, the other mothers made no attempt to keep their voices down as I approached the school gates.

"Can you believe it? With the teacher, no less! Why not the nanny?"

"When a husband strays as often as he does, you have to ask: What's the wife *not* doing?"

"Apparently, she never . . . *you know* . . . so who can blame the poor man for finding someone else?"

Mum was standing a few meters away. I'm not sure if the other mothers were oblivious to her, or if they simply didn't care that she was listening. I do remember how small she looked, caved in, as though she was trying to make herself disappear.

That night, when I came into the kitchen for a glass of water, Mum was crying.

"Are you all right, Mum?"

She was startled to see me and quickly wiped her eyes. "Fine," she said. "Just fine."

"Is Dad still with Miss McKenzie?"

Now she sat upright, shaking her head. "Of course not. Why would you say that? He's working and he'll be home soon."

Did she actually believe that? I wondered.

"Your father loves us," she added. "He *does*. He'll be home soon, don't you worry."

My father left us for Miss McKenzie a few weeks later. Mum never recovered. In the years that followed, she never had another partner. It wasn't for lack of interest; Mum had lots of potential suitors. But whenever I asked her about it, she said, "Your father was the love of my life. There will never be anyone else for me."

How exquisitely, stupidly tragic.

That was when I decided I'd never marry my soulmate. From what I could see, marrying your soulmate was reckless. A commitment like marriage was best treated like a contract, with a list of terms and conditions, and the potential to extricate yourself if the terms were breached. If I left love out of it, I would never end up the way my mother had, I reasoned.

Unfortunately, as so many of us do, I turned into my mother.

Max is sitting in front of the television, in his tracksuit and socks, when he hears the doorbell. On the screen, of all things, was that plastic surgery show, *Botched*. I chuckle at that. He used to say he watched it for me, and he always had a thick book in his hands, but I know he enjoyed it too, because he rarely looked at his book and often said things like, "Surely you'd just stop having surgery, wouldn't you?" I wondered quietly what he thought was keeping my face so smooth and taut at fifty-two years old.

He rises from his chair and walks to the intercom, past the dining room table, where my laptop is open, the video still visible on his screen. I'd left it there for him, so he'd know I knew. He closes the lid on his way to the door.

"Do you have news about Amanda?" he says through the intercom before he even lets the police in.

"It would be better if we talked inside," one of the officers says.

Max presses the buzzer and opens the door. Then he starts to

pace the foyer. He'd finally reported me missing last night, after calling and looking for me in every conceivable place, but I assume he'd
expected I'd show up somewhere—the farm, the city penthouse, the
Portsea beach house. One thing to be said for having a lot of houses
is there are plenty of places to hide. Still, the moment he'd realized I
was missing, he'd had to consider the idea that something more sinister was at play. When you had associates like Max did, you always
had to consider that.

"Come in," he says when the police get to the door. But after
closing it behind them, he doesn't invite them any farther than the
foyer. "What is it?"

"We've found your wife's car," the policeman says. His face is
somber. "It's parked near a known suicide spot, and a body that
matches your wife's description has been found there."

Max turns positively gray. He staggers over to the side table and
clasps the edge, as if to hold himself upright.

"Mr. Cameron?" the young officer says. "Would you like to sit
down?"

Amazingly, I hadn't considered how the word "suicide" would
rattle him, until now. Max's mother and brother had both taken their
own lives after struggles with mental illness. The loss of them had
affected him so deeply he'd started a foundation for mental health
and suicide prevention. The idea that I might have died this way, I'll
admit, feels impossibly cruel.

"No," he says. "No. She wouldn't have taken her own life. She
wouldn't."

The police officers exchange a look of pity. "I'm sorry, sir."

My lilac silk scarf is draped over the table in the foyer. Max reaches
for it, holds it to his face. There's no denying the emotion on his face.

"Mr. Cameron," the policeman says again, and Max turns away, holds up a hand. Then he shoves his fist into his mouth and bites down hard, so the officer can't hear him cry. Despite everything, my heart breaks a little.

Ah, marriage, you wonderful, complicated beast.

8

AMANDA

(BEFORE)

It's funny the way memories float through your mind in certain moments. Max and I met, almost thirty years ago, when I was a waitress at his father and stepmother's wedding anniversary party. Max, apparently bored with the company of his parents' friends, was attempting to flirt by trying to take the tray of canapés out of my hands.

Max's parents' house was like nothing I'd ever seen. Marble everywhere. Arched doors leading to more marble reception rooms. It had a fountain *inside* the house and one of those grand sweeping staircases that split in two. The place was abuzz with music, laughter, dancing. There was a champagne tower. A jazz band. Rumor had it there were to be fireworks at midnight.

"You know that I'm being paid to serve food, don't you?" I said when he'd reached for my tray again. I feigned exasperation.

"At least one of us is being paid to be here," he replied, finally commandeering the tray, which he immediately held out to a passing guest with playful confidence.

It was flattering, I'll admit. Max was handsome—tall and broad enough to fill out his dinner suit. But it was the way he carried himself that was truly impressive. Even then, he knew who he was going to become.

"All right! Give me the tray back."

"Forget it!" Max popped a canapé into his mouth. "These are delicious. I'm not sharing them."

I could feel my boss's gaze from across the room. The only thing stopping her from approaching was the fact that she knew Max was the son of the client. "Please," I said. "Give it back. My boss is looking. I can't afford to lose this job."

Max handed the tray back immediately, his expression a blend of remorse and attraction. How funny to think that someone actually *needing* their job could have such an effect. It was curious the way wealthy people found other people's poverty thrilling; often it even morphed into a perverse sort of admiration. And our stocks rose even higher if we insisted our humble existences weren't that bad. Some felt compelled to save us. And why not? Saving us was so easy. They could play God! Our gratitude was like a drug for them, particularly the men.

"Thank you," I said.

I continued circling the room, but all night I sensed Max's eyes on me. At the end of the evening, once we'd loaded the dishwashers, wiped the kitchen clean, and loaded the kitchen trays into the vans, I found Max waiting for me on the front steps. I pretended to be surprised, but I'd spotted him out there while I cleaned the kitchen.

"Hello again," I said.

"I'm sorry to lurk out here like this," Max said, ever polite. "I just wanted to make sure you didn't get into trouble. If your pay was docked, please—"

"It wasn't." I pulled on my coat. "It's fine."

"Okay, well . . . good."

We stood there for a moment. Max smelled like expensive aftershave. He'd taken his jacket and bow tie off, and the top button of his shirt was undone. He looked better like this, a bit disheveled. His gaze traveled over me, but not in a leery way. Like he was considering something.

"What?" I asked.

"I just realized that I don't know your name."

"Oh. It's Amanda."

He smiled, as if my name was pleasing to him. "I'm Max."

"Yes." I smiled back. "I know."

"What is it that you do when you're not waitressing, Amanda?"

"I'm a photographer," I said. "An amateur one. But I've got a few jobs—kids' birthday parties and the like."

It felt lame compared to what Max did for a living, and yet he responded as if I had said I was in training to go into space. He asked question after question, making me feel like the most fascinating person in the world. Later, I realized this was a gift of his.

"Amanda, would it be inappropriate of me to ask you to dinner?" he asked eventually.

It appeared to be a genuine question, like he couldn't quite figure it out himself. I wondered if he was weighing up our relative positions in life, our employer/employee relationship . . . or something else. I was twenty-five. He was in his early thirties. We were adults. It was a free world.

"If you don't mention it to my employer, I don't see why not."

I gave him my number and he walked me to my car. After opening my door for me, he leaned in for what I thought was going to be a kiss but turned into a hug at the last minute.

He told this story at our wedding, describing how he'd "choked." But I'd found it endearing that he'd lost his nerve. If he had gone through with the kiss, perhaps we would never have made it down the aisle. Would that have been a blessing or a curse?

With everything I know now, I'm not quite sure.

9

PIPPA

The police team return just after 7:00 A.M., and a steady stream of people traipse up and down the side of the house all morning: a photographer with a large camera, people with gloves and protective clothing, people with other people holding umbrellas over their heads. Freya and Asha sit cross-legged by the back door in their pajamas, watching them. Asha fires questions at us. "What's that guy doing? What's the camera for? What's happening over there?" Thankfully, by the time she finishes asking one thing her mind has already moved on to something else, so we're not required to provide answers. She is so much like Gabe; so brilliant, so inquisitive. It terrifies and delights me in equal measure.

When the girls tire of watching the police, we turn on the television. I envy the way they are immediately lost to it, their mouths hanging open, their brains suspended somewhere in the ether. They don't even demand breakfast, which is unheard of for Asha.

Eventually Gabe brings them toast, which they eat on the couch, and I don't object.

Mum and Dad arrive around 9:00 A.M., with coloring books and games for the girls. Dad does a coffee run for the police, and returns with raspberry and white chocolate muffins. Kat arrives midmorning with Mei, and they set up their computers side by side at our dining room table and work from there, as if it's the obvious, most normal thing to do. There's something about the morning that feels sacred and jarring—like someone has died. Which, of course, is true.

Gabe potters around the place, doing laundry, playing with the girls, and everyone watches him closely while pretending they're not. Mum is the only one up-front about her concern, approaching him every half hour or so and hugging him tight before carrying on with whatever she was doing.

During a brief gap in the rain, Gabe and Dad help the girls into their raincoats and gum boots and take them to the playground at the end of the road.

Mei and I are in the kitchen, making yet more tea. Kat is filling up her water bottle. Mum is folding laundry on the kitchen counter.

It's soothing being here with the three of them. Mei, as usual, is a particularly calming presence. There's something about her intelligence, her slow movements, that always puts me at ease. She is an ex-colleague of Gabe's; funnily enough, it was Gabe who introduced her to Kat. He said he just knew they would hit it off—and, as usual, Gabe was right. As if my family needed another reason to adore him.

"How's Gabe doing?" Mei asks, flicking the kettle off and pouring water into her cup.

"Oh, I think he's . . . all right."

"I can't imagine what it must be like." Mei dunks her tea bag thoughtfully. "I've seen a few animals die. Both my dogs, when they were put down, and a bird that I ran over accidentally. Never a human being."

"I saw a man get hit by a car once," Kat says. She perches herself on the counter and takes a slug from her water bottle. "A pedestrian. He was cutting between cars, and someone clipped him. He didn't die, I don't think. But I was spooked for weeks."

"I've seen plenty of people die." Mum was an ER nurse, so this isn't surprising to us. When we were young, she'd come home and tell us stories about kids who'd died of drug overdoses—an effective warning, as neither of us has ever touched so much as a joint. "But I never saw one who didn't want to live. Seeing a healthy person take their own life . . . that's something else entirely."

"Maybe they're not healthy," Kat says. "Mentally, at least."

"Good point," Mum says.

"I've never seen anyone die." I pour milk into my tea. "Thank goodness. I'm not sure I could handle that sort of trauma."

There's a short silence. I look up and find Mum and Mei and Kat exchanging a look.

"Actually," Kat says, "I'd say if anyone could cope with it, it's you."

I'm not sure what Kat's getting at, but the three of them are all staring at me now. It gives me a weird feeling, so instead of replying, I lift my cup to my mouth and take a big slurp.

Midmorning, shortly after Gabe, Dad, and the girls have returned from the playground, a police officer appears at the glass sliding door and waves. I recognize her as one of those who'd introduced herself earlier. She is dressed in a white shirt and navy trousers and a pair of gum boots covered in mud.

Our reaction, as a family, is comical. Everyone freezes, even the girls. Then we blink at the poor woman, standing in the rain, as if her presence is bizarre and unexpected, as if the police haven't been there all morning, as if Mum hasn't been out looking for them several times with offers of tea. The difference, I suppose, is that this is the first time *they* have come looking for *us*.

"Sorry to intrude," she says, sliding open the door. "I'm Detective Senior Constable Tamil. Thank you for your patience as we've tramped around your garden. And, of course, thanks for the tea and coffee." She holds up three empty mugs, and Mum rushes over to retrieve them.

The police officer turns to Gabe, who is on all fours giving Freya a horsey ride. "Before we head off," she says, "I wonder if you'd be able to spare a minute, Mr. Gerard? Outside?"

"Of course." Gabe rises onto his knees so Freya slides to the floor. When she protests, Dad jumps in as a substitute horse and saves the day.

"Do you mind if I join you?" I say suddenly. I feel the gaze of the others on me and wonder if I shouldn't have asked. "Just for moral support?" I add.

Tamil looks a little surprised but hesitates only a moment before she says, "Sure thing. The more the merrier."

The Drop is cordoned off with police tape, a crime scene now. I've always found The Drop eerie, but surrounded by police tape in the rain and wind it has an almost repellent energy. For the millionth time, I wonder why I agreed to move here. Gabe and Tamil also appear to eye it with distaste.

"All right," Tamil says, "it's cold and wet out here, so let's get straight to it. I know this is going to feel repetitive, but I need you to tell me what happened, from start to finish."

"Okay," Gabe says. "Well, we were doing the dishes when Pip spotted her through the window. I came outside right away, and Pip called the police."

"Can you show me where she was standing when you first got here?" Tamil asks.

Gabe points to a spot very close to the edge of the cliff. "Over there."

"And where were you?"

He points to the ground where he currently stands, several meters back from the edge. "Here."

As Tamil photographs each of the places, I consider them. They seem a little different from what I saw. Then again, I was watching from the window. Perhaps my perspective was off.

"What happened next?" Tamil asks.

"I approached her," Gabe says. "And I asked if she needed help with anything."

"Did she reply?"

"She turned around. She was clearly upset. She might have been crying."

A powerful gust of wind cuts through us. One of the legs of the police tent comes free and a couple of officers quickly pin it down. We all look at it for a moment; then Tamil says, "And then?"

"I asked her if she was all right. She said her husband had been unfaithful and that she didn't want to live anymore."

"Did she mention her husband by name?"

"No."

"And she didn't give her own name?"

"No."

She makes a note on her notepad. "What happened next?"

"She kept talking, but the wind was so loud. I was only getting every second or third word. I moved closer, but the wind was wild, and I didn't want either of us to get too close to the edge."

Detective Tamil keeps writing, then flips a page on her notebook and looks up. "And then?"

"And then it happened very quickly. One minute she was facing me, and the next she was facing the edge. I lunged forward to try to grab her but . . ." He's overtaken by a wave of emotion that I recognize as real. "It was too late."

Detective Tamil's gaze jumps to her notebook. "Sorry—you said you lunged forward? I didn't see that in your statement. Did you touch her at any point?"

"No," he says. "Well . . . I touched her ponytail. It flew up as she fell. It touched my hand."

"I see." Tamil makes a note of this. Then she looks up. "Can you show me how you lunged? Act it out? Over here."

Gabe nods, moving across the grass to where she has gestured. "She . . . uh . . . started to fall and I . . ." He steps forward, his arms starting wide and then slowly closing until he's nearly touching either elbow. Detective Tamil watches him for a second, and then she looks back at her notebook.

"And I understand she screamed?"

Gabe straightens up. "Yes. At least I think she did."

"At what point did she scream? Before she jumped? During?"

"During," Gabe says. "But again, I may have got it wrong. Maybe it was the wind."

Tamil scribbles some more in her notebook. "All right. Is there anything else? Anything she said or did that you haven't mentioned?"

"No."

"In that case, thank you very much for your time," she says, returning her notebook to her pocket.

"That's it?" Gabe says.

"For now. We'll be in touch if we need anything else." Tamil looks like she's going to walk back to her colleagues, but she hesitates a moment. "I read the article in the local paper. It's pretty impressive, the number of lives you've saved. Focus on that."

She smiles, then moves off to join her colleagues, who are huddled under the newly fixed tent. The mood feels casual, I notice. A couple of them are talking about where to stop for lunch on the way back to Somerville.

No one suspects Gabe of anything, I realize. I know I should feel relieved by this, yet all I can think about is the position of Gabe's hands when he acted out the lunge for Tamil, and how it looked nothing like what I'd seen out the window.

10

PIPPA

(THEN)

"Pippa? You might not remember me. It's Gabe Gerard, from the botanic gardens?"

It had been three weeks since our ill-fated first meeting. After he failed to call, I'd played out every possible scenario in my head, and eventually decided that my meeting with Gabe, and his subsequent invitation to the wedding reception, had been imagined. It made sense. So much about that meeting had felt strange and otherworldly. And so, when the call finally came, I was genuinely startled.

"Pippa? Are you there?"

"I'm here. And I remember."

Of course I remembered. The man had stopped the rain for me! I'd been thinking about him for three weeks.

Wondering if he'd been horribly drunk and forgotten about our meeting.

If he'd met someone else on the way to the wedding reception and fallen in love.

The entire thing—coming to talk to a crying dog walker during a wedding ceremony and asking her on a date—had been a dare that he never intended to follow through on. (Stopping the rain, I had to concede, was a lucky coincidence.)

Eventually, I'd had to put the whole encounter in the same category as my relationship with Mark: things that I had unwittingly screwed up for reasons that weren't clear to me.

"I'm so sorry I haven't called earlier. But I can explain!"

His excuse, of course, was magnificent. He'd been helping an elderly wedding guest across the road to the reception venue when a car had come around the corner at high speed. Gabe had managed to get the elderly guest to safety but he'd been clipped by the car, breaking his leg in two places. His injuries had required a week's stay in the hospital (something that was verified later by the groom as well as by the gruesome scar on Gabe's leg), and the subsequent two weeks had been spent on opiates, falling in and out of sleep and wondering if our initial meeting was something he'd dreamed up—much like I had.

I wanted to say no to the date. I told myself I had *some* dignity. But it turned out I didn't have much at all.

On this occasion, having the advantage of prep time, I looked nice. I wore a short white sundress with sandals, my hair was washed and in a bouncy ponytail. I wondered if he'd comment on my appearance, but he didn't. Knowing Gabe as I do now, it doesn't surprise me. As good-looking as he is, looks are entirely irrelevant to him. He's attracted to something deeper, harder to pin down.

We met at the botanic gardens—his idea, and a sweet one. This time, though it was cloudy, there was no rain. Gabe arrived on crutches, carrying a thermal picnic bag over one shoulder and a blanket around his neck. When I got close enough to him, I laughed and rolled my eyes, taking the blanket from him. Perhaps it was the crutches that made me feel strangely comfortable. As if they brought him down to a more human level, less the unattainable dreamlike man I'd imagined the past few weeks. As I spread the blanket out for us, he said, "It feels like we've done this before, doesn't it? In another life?"

Yes, I thought. *Yes, it does.*

"So, you're a lawyer?" he said. I'd told him as much in our phone conversation. "What kind of law?"

It was a question I answered often. I was aware wills and estates was not the sexiest area of legal practice. It had never bothered me. But now, faced with a gorgeous man, I found myself wishing I'd chosen litigation, or mergers and acquisitions, or even family law.

"Wills and estates," I confessed, then added in mitigation, "It's most recession-proof."

What happened next was the second miracle of our relationship (the rain-stopping being the first). Gabe rested his cheek in his hand, looked into my eyes, and said, "Tell me about it."

No one had ever said that before. No one has ever said it since. The craziest part was that it looked very much like he meant it.

So I told him. I was halfway through explaining escrow when he took my chin between his thumb and forefinger, looked directly into my eyes, and kissed me. Softly. Just once. Then he smiled and said, "Sorry. Carry on. Escrow."

We talked about everything that day. Important things—like the fact that his father had died before he was born and that he still bore a grudge toward his father's family, who never helped his mother out or made any attempt to meet him. We also talked about unimportant things—like what we watched on TV, why IKEA hot dogs were so good, and whether we were going to get that Indian summer everyone was talking about.

We stayed in the gardens until the sky turned dark and the bats began to fly overhead. The air was warm and sweet, and our conversation was punctuated by short silences and shy smiles and comments of wonder (from Gabe) like, "It feels as if we've always known each other."

It was an evening of that feeling you wanted to bottle, the feeling that no drug or orgasm could replicate—the skyrocketing high of limerence. I was delighted by everything: the way he paused to think before answering any question, as if whether or not he liked pickles was worthy of deep contemplation; the way he laughed loudly at my offhand jokes; the way his chest looked in his button-down shirt. And he delighted equally in me. It was delightful to be delighted in.

By the time we made it back to his apartment, which was just a short walk away, it was not a question of whether the night was ending but, rather, where were we going next. The idea of parting was simply unthinkable.

When I gathered my things to return home forty-eight hours later, he seemed adorably confused.

"Where are you going?" he asked.

"Home." I laughed. "I've been here two nights. How long did you think I would stay?"

He looked at me as if it was the strangest thing I'd ever said.

"Pippa," he said, "I thought you'd stay forever."

We went from nought to one hundred in a second, which, I learned later, was the only way Gabe did things. He met my family after a week, we started looking for a house together after two. Three weeks after that first date, in a bubble bath, he asked me to marry him. There was no ring, no champagne. The idea just occurred to him, he said. I told him he was mad, and you couldn't possibly get married after knowing someone for three weeks. He agreed, it was ridiculous. Then I said, "Of course I'll marry you," and we had sex on the bathroom floor.

Falling in love with Gabe lasted an eternity. It felt like I'd never stop falling. There were a million little reasons to love him. He was the person who always rushed to help when someone dropped their bags in the street. He was the guy at the party who offered to hold the random baby. He was the first to put his hand up for anything— even before he understood what it was or what it would involve. He listened to people, *really* listened, and then thought about what they said later. He went out of his way to include people who were left out of conversations.

I realized, even then, that there was another side of Gabe. He got distracted easily. He could do big talk, but not small talk. He didn't sleep . . . or only slept. He was all or nothing.

I often wonder if choosing Gabe was a direct result of my upbringing. Some people choose the safe guy, the stable guy, if they've had an upbringing filled with uncertainty. My family was so stable, maybe it made me yearn for instability? And Gabriel Gerard was a perfect fit.

My parents were surprised—possibly even concerned—when, six weeks after our first meeting, I told them Gabe and I were engaged. But my mother believed in letting people make their own choices, and my father believed in doing what Mum told him. Besides, I knew that once Mum and Dad got to know Gabe, they would fall in love with him too. How could they not?

We got married in the botanic gardens, in the same spot we'd first seen each other. It was a brilliant, blue-skied, happy day. It was a day of joy and contentment. With Gabe by my side, the future was bright.

11

PIPPA

"Do the silly voices, Daddy," the girls cry. "And put on the head!"

I stand in the doorway of their bedroom, watching. Gabe is lying in the middle of Asha's single bed, with a little girl on either of side of him. In his hands is a copy of *The Tiger Who Came to Tea*.

He looks weary. It's well after the girls' bedtime and they are showing no signs of calming down. Even Freya, our good sleeper, is wide-eyed and wriggly. (Asha, our night owl, is practically psychotic with hysteria.) It is, of course, a problem of Gabe's own making. Just a month ago, while reading *The Tiger Who Came to Tea*, Gabe had donned the fluffy tiger's head and peeped around the corner saying he was "very hungry."

When I'm doing story time, the only thing I don is a no-nonsense expression.

Asha thrusts the head into his hands. "Put it on! Put it on!"

Gabe looks like he's going to protest, but that's all part of the act.

Gabe is a father first, everything else second. It's been an interesting transition this year, handing the primary-carer baton to Gabe. It took time, but these days it's him they go to with the important questions, like "Where are the crackers?," "How does that song go—the one about the bird that we sang to in the car that day?," and "Where is my purple squishy thing that I won in the grab bag at Seraphine's party?" Now he is the expert on hair, playing dolls, baking cakes, doing craft. He revels in it. Being a dad is the blood in his veins. If there were a Dad Olympics, Gabe would win gold.

"Put on the head?" he says. "I don't *put on* heads." He disappears under the blankets and comes out wearing the head, roaring wildly. "This is just what I look like!"

The girls roll about in giggles. Asha wipes away tears.

They look adorable, all clean and fresh in their matching rainbow pajamas.

"Are they twins?" people always ask when we're out in public, usually after hearing both girls call me Mummy. It is, they must think, the obvious explanation, even if it doesn't quite fit. Usually by that point I've felt the person watching us for a while, trying to make sense of the situation.

"Irish twins," I always say. "Born less than a year apart."

This is typically followed by the unasked-for information that the other person had barely had *sex* with their partner twelve months after having their first child, let alone birthed another one, and I do my best to deflect their awe with remarks about how "it's had its difficult moments." (An understatement, I'll admit.)

I close the bedroom door, leaving Gabe to story time. There's a half bottle of red wine on the kitchen counter. I open the bottle and pour myself a glass. It's the same wine we were drinking when we saw the woman out on the cliff, I realize. Gabe had been so alive that night, dancing around the kitchen, singing to French music. How quickly things can change.

My laptop is on the kitchen counter. I open it and do another search. "Woman dies at The Drop."

It's the third time I've done this today, trying different word combinations, and there's still nothing. No name. No information about her at all. I've no idea if there will *ever* be information. I have a vague feeling that suicides aren't reported on. Something to do with not wanting to encourage it. It's a horrifying thought—that someone might read an article in the paper and think, *Ah. Good idea. I'll go jump off a cliff.* It's also horrifying because it means I may never know anything about this woman.

It shouldn't matter who she is, of course. Any death is a tragedy. Still, I've always found details to be orientating in these sorts of situations. For example, if the woman had a history of depression, that would be information worth knowing. I'd also be curious to know if she'd made earlier attempts at suicide. *That's* what I'm looking for, I realize: something to suggest that her death was inevitable. Why am I looking for that? What is wrong with me?

I suppose the woman's family have been informed by now. They're probably trying to process the fact that their mother/wife/ daughter/sister is gone forever. Will it be a total surprise? Or have they been subconsciously preparing for the news all their life? It's hard not to imagine what they must be feeling right now, hard not to feel their pain. It makes me think of a conversation I had with Gabe once, when he was at his lowest. It was a weekday and I'd had a call from childcare to pick up Freya because she wasn't feeling well. I'd left the office, collected her, and arrived home to find Gabe lying on the couch, still in his pajamas.

"Gabe?" I said. "Why aren't you at work?"

He gave me the strangest look. He sat up, took my hands in his, and gazed at me with a desperation I will never forget.

"You know how you feel for someone you know who is hurt or sick or sad? Imagine feeling that for everyone. Not just everyone you know, but *everyone*. Every person in the world. All the time."

I wonder if this is what that woman felt.

I close my laptop.

"I'm not sure if we've heard the last from them," Gabe says a few minutes later when he appears in the kitchen. "But I told them if there was any trouble, I'd send the big guns in to deal with them."

I raise an eyebrow. "The big guns?"

He shrugs. "You can be scary."

I get out another wineglass and fill it, hand it to him. Then I look out the window. The Drop is still cordoned off, the police tape flapping in the wind. "Did we make the right decision moving here?"

I expect him to say yes. I expect him to say, *Of course we did,* and then launch into all the reasons why. He is, after all, the one who was so eager to buy this house. But he doesn't. I look at him. It might be the wine, or the fact that we're alone together, but all at once the thoughts that I've been working so hard to push from my mind start to crowd in.

The fact that he told the police the woman was much closer to the edge than she was. The fact that the placement of his hands doesn't quite make sense. The fact that I felt the need to lie about what I saw through the window.

All of it settles on my chest, like a cast-iron weight.

"Gabe," I start, but he puts a finger to my lips. Then he takes the glass from my hand, puts it on the counter, and hovers inches away from me.

I stare into his intense, handsome face. He's wearing jeans and a white long-sleeved T-shirt that sets off his tan. He smells of the ocean. Usually, he tastes of it too.

"Can we . . . not talk?" he says.

With a few lines and gray hairs, he's even more attractive now than when we met. My attraction to him is the one thing that has persistently refused to die, no matter how bad things got. I understand this isn't always the case. Most women I know are always joking about it, or complaining, trying to avoid their husbands' propositions. But for me, when things were bad between us, sex was what I missed the most. With Gabe, sex is always surprising, and always good. We've been married seven years now, and it's only getting better.

He grips the counter on either side of me and slides a knee between my legs.

The thing about marriage a lot of people don't understand is that you don't get everything. Some people get passion, others get security. Some get companionship. Children. Money. Wisdom. Status. Then there is trust and fidelity. They're the two you hear most about. In general, couples will cite trust or fidelity as their nonnegotiable. In a lot of cases, a partner will offer one in exchange for the other. But Gabe and I have always agreed on our nonnegotiable. Loyalty. Gabe has certainly made me work for that one.

"Yes," I say. "Let's not talk."

I let him touch me until I lose myself in it. *You're not involved in this*, I think as he lifts me onto the kitchen counter. *You're not.* I say it over and over inside my mind, hoping that if I say it enough, it will become true.

12

PIPPA

In the first year of our marriage, Gabe had five jobs.

The first one, as a landscape gardener, he enjoyed immensely. There was something about being outside in the fresh air, watching a garden design come to life, that really excited him. In typical Gabe style, he threw himself into it with everything he had, believing everything he touched would turn to gold. I believed him too. He spent evenings researching irrigation systems and sustainable gardening. He had a good eye for the design side too, balancing the beautiful with the practical and low maintenance. Before long he was redesigning our garden, even though it was a rental, and spending each weekend at the local nursery, or outside planting and watering.

The first change came when he heard about an entry-level job that was available at a local newspaper. I was surprised, given his enthusiasm for landscape gardening, but writing seemed like a good fit for him; he thrived under pressure, and his ability to produce fast, concise prose was exceptional. At first, he excelled at it, as he did with most things. He had a couple of stories published and the senior editor praised his budding talent. But only a couple of weeks in, he got into an argument with the same editor and quit on the spot.

"It's all political," Gabe told me afterward. "Everything's political."

The timing of this coincided with a friend opening a franchise handyman business. Gabe gave this a try, but two months later he left, with grand plans to write a novel.

Within three weeks, he'd written three very good chapters.

In week four, he decided he'd been wrong to quit landscape gardening, and he returned to that. It was then, while working in the opulent gardens of a wealthy business tycoon, that he was offered an internship in a media organization, NewZ. It sounded strange to people, a landscape gardener with no qualifications being offered a job after chatting to the executive, but it wasn't strange to me. For Gabe, this was the way the world worked. It was exhilarating. He shone and the world welcomed him.

Media, as it turned out, was the job that stuck. It was all Gabe could talk about; all he could think about.

I'd never seen Gabe so dedicated. He took seminars, he read books, he met people for coffee to "pick their brains." He finished his internship at NewZ and then was offered a permanent role in the investor relations team. As far as I could tell, his department's job was to convince investors to give them money to acquire other companies. It required lots of schmoozing and gladhanding. Since he was the most convincing person I'd ever met, I had no doubt Gabe would be great at it.

I was right. Within a year, he'd traded his check shirts and messenger bags for dark suits and shiny shoes and expensive hair-cuts that we couldn't quite afford.

"Dress for the job you want," he used to say, along with other business-type affirmations. There was something sexy about his commitment. It made me revise the image of him in my mind. He'd always been so disheveled, so devil-may-care. This new, sharp, dedicated side of him was appealing.

He became more handsome, if that was possible. His jawline became more defined. The lines on his face gave him a rugged look. He looked like a film star. People noticed him. Women at work must have noticed him. If I ever teased him about it, though, he became serious.

"You know you never have to worry, right?"

I did know that.

"Do *I* have to worry?" he'd say then, nuzzling my neck. "Is anyone paying inappropriate attention to my wife?"

But he wasn't the jealous type, not really. We were happy. And I was bursting with pride.

"Gabe's working late" became something I'd say to friends and family. "His team is working on a big acquisition."

It felt so glamorous and exciting. Then again, perhaps everything did when you worked in wills and estates. NewZ was in a growth phase, making acquisitions, building the brand. There were a lot of power lunches and after-work drinks. He was gone a lot. I was often in bed before he got home, waking in the early hours to Gabe sliding into bed beside me, his body heavy and warm. I understood. It was about networking, building trust. This was how business worked.

Before long, Gabe had the chance to be the one giving the pitch to investors. He barely slept the night before. He practically fizzed with nervous energy. I made him breakfast that morning, but he was too nervous to eat. He showered and dressed in his most expensive suit. I told him he looked like Don Draper in *Mad Men* and he laughed, but I could tell his mind had already left the building.

I waved him off from the front porch, like a mother waving off a child. He said he'd call me as soon as they knew anything. I waited for the call all afternoon. When I hadn't heard from him by 5:00 P.M., I called his phone, but it was switched off.

I wasn't worried; Gabe was notoriously bad at charging his phone. I tried calling the office, but they hadn't seen him and hadn't had any news. Eventually I had to assume he and his team had gone out for drinks—to celebrate or commiserate.

I finally fell asleep about 1:00 A.M.

When I woke up the next morning to find I was still alone, I started to worry. I called his phone again, but it was still switched off. I checked the spare room in case he'd crept in overnight and hadn't wanted to disturb me. I even checked the front doorstep in case he'd lost his key and slept outside. That's where I was when the taxi pulled up. Gabe emerged looking decidedly less polished than when I'd last seen him. His shirt was untucked, his hair was ruffled. He didn't appear to have his jacket with him.

His face lit up when he saw me. He ran from the taxi and hugged me so hard my feet lifted off the ground. He smelled of booze and cigarettes and sweat. "We got the money!"

Gabe was so excited it was hard to feel anything but excited too. It was a big deal. He just wanted to talk and talk and talk. I made coffee and told work I wouldn't be coming in and we sat in bed all day, rehashing the events of the day before. Gabe was practically levitating with joy.

Later, it seemed silly that I didn't think it was a sign of something. But I took it as confirmation of his brilliance, his charisma, the great choice I'd made in marrying him. Yes, he'd stayed out all night, but he'd never been great at keeping track of time. He was swept up in the energy of the first deal, that was all. It was the same excitement and energy that had helped him to land the deal, so it seemed to me that I couldn't really complain.

13

PIPPA

It's rare that someone studies law with a plan to become a wills and estates lawyer. We are, at best, the colorectal surgeons of law. Ours is not the most glamorous specialty—in fact, it is the butt of many jokes—but on balance it's an important and necessary one. There are those who get into it for practical reasons—job security, work/life balance, and the ability to work for yourself—and those who enter the field because they've seen family members miss out on inheritances or estates get manipulated by greedy individuals. I am one of the few people—heck, perhaps the only one—who *did* go into law to become a wills and estates lawyer. Not because I watched a family member get swindled or because I was worried I'd get swindled myself. I chose it because, in this world where so much is out of your control, it is one time when, with the right person in your corner, you get to play God.

"Have you had any thoughts about your funeral arrangements, Mr. and Mrs. Peterson?" I ask the couple on the screen.

I'm sitting at my laptop at the dining room table, as I often do in the morning when the light is better here. Beside me are a notepad, a glass of water, and a digital clock that beeps when we've reached the end of our allotted time. Obviously, I'm aware of the time, but the loud beep helps the oldies to stay on track.

It's clear Mrs. Peterson hasn't thought much about funeral arrangements, because she looks at Mr. Peterson questioningly. I'd told them exactly what we'd be covering today and asked them to make these decisions in advance. So far, they've argued over their medical power of attorney, their choice of executor, and whether or not to hold assets in a family trust. Now it's 10:50 A.M., and I'm getting the sense this will take longer than the allocated ninety minutes, particularly since the first fifteen minutes were spent speaking to Mr. Peterson's son Nigel, who was trying to set up the Zoom call and was having trouble with the technology. I shouldn't complain, as I have no issue charging for every minute, but today I'd like to get off the phone sooner rather than later.

Gabe and the girls bustled out the door just before 9:00 A.M., in a whirlwind of bags and lunch boxes and scooters. This morning's drama centered around Asha's declaration that she only wanted strawberries in her lunch box. No sandwich. No yogurt. Just the strawberries. Gabe had wanted to oblige, but I'd opted to sneak a sandwich into her bag in a separate container to avoid the judgment that would be forthcoming from their teacher. As they disappeared out the door, I noticed Freya was still wearing her pajama top and Asha was wearing tights without a skirt. "Gabe! Asha needs a skirt!"

He was so confused. "But she's wearing pants." He surveyed her for a moment. "With feet. Why don't they make these for men?"

I tossed him a skirt and rolled my eyes. The girls were going to be late, but it wouldn't matter because *Gabe* was dropping them off. Sarah Punch, the girls' teacher, loves Gabe. Every time I show my face at school, she goes out of her way to tell me how wonderful it is that Gabe is such an involved parent, how he's the only dad who volunteers, how he remembers every special day and activity. She appears not to hear when I point out that 1) he really doesn't do any more than the other mums, and 2) I'm the one who remembers the special days and activities. Most irritatingly, she only answers to Mrs. Punch—and that goes for the mums as well as the kids—but laughs giddily when Gabe calls her "Sares." Gabe is staying on as the parent helper at preschool this morning, which means Mrs. Punch will lose her mind. This is why men rule the world.

"Have you thought about whether you'd like to be buried or cremated?" I ask.

"I'd like to be buried," Mr. Peterson says definitively.

"Fantastic!" I say. "Anywhere particular?"

I expect this will be another twenty-minute debate, but Mr. Peterson answers immediately. "We have a family plot in Sorrento."

Perfect, I think. *We might finish before noon.*

But I've barely finished formulating that thought when Mrs. Peterson's head snaps to look at him. "You want to be buried in the Sorrento plot? With Jilly?"

Jilly, I have ascertained from our discussions, is Mr. Peterson's late first wife.

"It's a family plot," Mr. Peterson says. "You can be buried there too if you like."

"The *three* of us?" Mrs. Peterson looks at me beseechingly. "Together?"

"Why not?" He grins. "It'd be the only threesome I'll ever have."

Mrs. Peterson gasps at the same time as I hear a knock at the door. A moment later, Dad calls out "Hello!" and lets himself in. I peer down the hallway to see him with a newspaper under his arm and a takeaway coffee cup in his hand. Mum must have sent him. ("Go check on Pippa. Make an excuse so it doesn't look overbearing. Take her a coffee and the paper or something!" Dad was excellent at following directions to the letter.) I wave to him and hold a finger to my lips.

"I'm not forcing you to be buried there," Mr. Peterson is saying. "I just said that you'd be welcome."

"You're unbelievable!"

"Calm down, woman—we'll be dead, for crying out loud. Besides, I already paid for the plot and there's room for six!"

Dad puts the newspaper and coffee on the table beside me. I nod my thanks and take a giant slurp. Then he goes into the kitchen and starts unloading the dishwasher. ("And clean up while you're there," Mum must have said. "Unload the dishwasher or something.")

"We can come back to this," I say to the Petersons, "when you've had some more time to discuss it. In the meantime, I think we should move on to the—"

"Everything comes down to money with you, you cheap bastard!"

"And you wonder why I don't want to be buried with you."

Dad chuckles as he unloads the water glasses and puts them back in the wrong spot.

"For all of his foibles," Mum always says, "at least your father does what he's told." I wonder what my marriage would have been

like if I'd married a man like that. Someone dependable. Responsible. I suspect Mrs. Peterson is wondering the same thing.

"What if you get cremated?" Mr. Peterson is saying. He has his
reasonable, mansplaining voice on now, which will irritate Mrs. Peterson no end. "You could be sprinkled somewhere nice. Down at
the golf club, perhaps."

"The golf club? While you're getting cozy with Jilly down at
Sorrento?"

Dad finishes unloading the dishwasher and looks around. He
must have run out of specific jobs that Mum told him to do and has
graduated to "then look around and see if anything else needs doing." I wave at him and point to the door, giving him permission to
leave, which he does with obvious relief. I look back at the screen.

Mr. and Mrs. Peterson are now facing each other, hurling insults.
They may have forgotten I'm here. Outside the window, a woman
slows down at The Drop. *Keep walking*, I will her. *Keep walking!*
Thankfully, she does. I keep an eye on her until she's disappeared
from sight.

"Look, I think we might have reached an impasse," I say to my
bickering clients. "We can either move on, or we can pause things
here and set up another meeting when we have reached some agreement. I will remind you that we have gone over the ninety minutes
now, and while I'm happy to wait for you to work this out, I'm sure
you'd rather not pay me to listen to you argue."

Talk of the hourly rate is usually an effective way to move things
along, and certainly Mr. Peterson seems to snap to attention, but
as Mrs. Peterson is intent on resolving the issue, they decide to end
the session and book another meeting in two weeks. As I end the
Zoom call, Mrs. Peterson is already asking if he'd like to be in the
same coffin with Jilly too.

I close the lid of the laptop and walk to the kitchen to move the items Dad unloaded into the right cupboards. I don't have any more meetings this morning, so I make a cup of tea and flick through the newspaper. Dad brought the local paper rather than the national, which suits me, because I get the national news via podcast anyway. I flick past an update on the latest attempt to fix the beach that was ruined by dredging—the community was up in arms about it two years ago but have become increasingly apathetic—and skim-read an article about how suburban councillors and mayors have voted to pay themselves the highest amount permissible under state government legislation. I am looking for the horoscopes—I do *not* for one second believe in them, but I do like to read them, and it is spooky how sometimes they are very accurate—but before I find them, my eyes land on a picture of a woman who looks vaguely familiar. I scan the article. It's about the unexpected death of a woman, the night before last. There's no information listed about how she died. But when I read her name, the air leaves my lungs.

14

AMANDA

My body has been identified by dental records. It's probably for the best because, unsurprisingly, my body isn't in great shape after my fall from the cliff. Twisted, bloody, broken. Half my teeth have been knocked out and there is some gnarly facial damage. It probably would have been enough to make Max bring up his breakfast.

Although . . . Max hasn't eaten breakfast. Not today. Not yesterday. Usually, he is militant about his All-Bran and peaches and black coffee, but he hasn't been doing well since the police told him about me. I'd like to think it's the grief of losing me. I hope it is. I know it's not *only* that, though. Max is many things, but he's not stupid. He knows something isn't right about my death. He knows that while I would have been upset about what he'd done, I had plenty of ammunition with which to retaliate. Taking my own life isn't something that I've ever talked about, ever considered. It doesn't make sense and Max knows it. It's driving him crazy and I have a front-row seat to his misery.

But I don't enjoy it as much as I thought I would.

15

AMANDA

(BEFORE)

I wouldn't say I was nervous the first time Max came to my mother's house. "Worked up" would probably be a better description.

I was aware how her house would look to someone like Max. An unrenovated single-fronted two-bedroom next to a petrol station in Melbourne's inner west, before the inner west became trendy. I suspect that until he met me, Max thought the inner west was only for factories and industrial estates, not a place where anyone actually lived.

I knew Mum had spent the day cleaning the house from top to bottom. She'd made a roast chicken using a Jamie Oliver recipe she'd found online. When I arrived, I found her in her best floral dress, and she was wearing lipstick. Something clutched at my heart when I saw that. She was on her best behavior. Max had better be on his best behavior too, I decided. If he looked down his nose at my mother's house, the relationship was over.

Max arrived exactly on time, with flowers and a bottle of wine. He greeted Mum with a hug. Before he arrived, she'd worried about whether he'd give her one kiss or two . . . she'd even asked her friend Rhonda, she said. The hug had been disarming and Mum had been surprised.

"I've heard so much about you," Max said.

"Ditto," she said shyly.

It was a surprise, how well the evening went. By that time I'd seen Max dine with businesspeople, but this was something quite different. He appeared invested in impressing my mother. He asked thoughtful questions and gave intelligent answers. He talked about my (still-fledgling) photography career as if I were Annie Leibovitz. After dinner, he told my mum to relax while he cleared the table.

Mum was beside herself.

"He's the one," she whispered, as he carried the plates into the kitchen. "He's your happy ending."

The house was small, and her whisper was loud. When I turned around, I saw Max looking very pleased with himself. But I wasn't pleased. "He's a good choice," I corrected her. "It makes sense."

After dinner, we sat on the couch and ate Sara Lee Sticky Date Pudding with ice cream and looked at photo albums. Each time Mum produced another one, she said, "Look at me—I'll be boring you to tears, Max!," and Max shook his head and insisted she continue. At the end of the night, Mum was the one to hug *him*.

"Do come again, Max. You're welcome any time."

"Just try to stop me."

Dinners with Mum became a regular thing after that. Each time, Max brought flowers and Mum got out the photo albums. After a while, I wondered who was enjoying it more, Max or Mum.

Mum got sick a few years after that. I'll never forget the day the hospital called to tell us to come in quickly. Max dropped everything and we went straightaway, but she'd already died by the time we got there. She was the only family I had left. So it was surprising that Max was the one who fell to his knees, keening. Everyone assumed it must have been his mother who died. I kneeled on the floor and held him while he sobbed into my skirt. I always had a feeling it was his own mum he was crying for. Either way, those are the strange, beautiful, and bizarre moments of marriage that no one tells you about. The moments that, even after everything, still pierce your heart.

16

PIPPA

Amanda Cameron.

I stride along the footpath, reciting the name over and over. Amanda Cameron. The woman on the cliff was *Amanda Cameron*. Not a stranger, as Gabe claimed, but the wife of his former boss, Max Cameron. The media mogul who'd recruited Gabe to NewZ from a landscape gardener.

I'd left the house without even bothering to get a coat. I hadn't even brought my keys or phone. I have that vaguely cold and sweaty feeling I get from travel sickness, the one that precedes vomiting. Why would Amanda Cameron come to our cliff? Why didn't Gabe tell me it was her? What happened that night?

I throw open the gate of the preschool. To my left, there's a washing line strung from the door to the fence with paintings hung with pegs; to my right is the veggie patch the kids have been working on. "We got our first carrot!" the newsletter announced proudly last week. There is a pile of tiny jumpers and hats in a lost-property box, and a little table holding artwork ready to be taken home. Normally this space fills me with contentment. It's a virtual haven of adorableness. Today all I can think about is keeping my breakfast down.

I punch in the code and let myself into the classroom. I find Gabe at a tiny table cutting up slips of colored paper. The children are outside; I can see them through the window sitting at tables, having their morning tea. Gabe looks up, surprised but happy to see me. Until I place the newspaper on the table in front of him.

He glances at it quickly; then his eyes close.

"I'll wait for you outside," I say.

"I'm sorry," Gabe says.

We are sitting on a park bench in a playground adjacent to the preschool. A few meters away, a bunch of toddlers play in a sandpit while their carers gossip nearby, clutching takeaway coffees. Outwardly we look normal. Even our body language is unremarkable as Gabe recounts the story of what happened that night on the cliff, while we sit side by side on the bench, not looking at each other.

"Why?" I say. "Why are you sorry?"

He exhales slowly. "I'm sorry I didn't tell you it was her."

Adrenaline courses through my veins. I'm not sure I'm ready to hear what is coming next. I want to run away and cover my ears. I want to turn back time and stop Gabe from going outside.

"The truth is, I didn't recognize her at first," he says. "I only met Amanda a few times, at office functions. Seeing her at The Drop, I didn't make the connection. Then she introduced herself. She said, 'You don't recognize me, do you?'"

Gabe's face is pale and intense and ravaged. He looks like a character in a film who has just accepted a suicide mission.

"That was when I realized she *did* look familiar. But I couldn't place her. It was on the tip of my tongue, but she was the one to say her name. *Amanda Cameron*. She said she had seen the newspaper article about me, which was how she knew where we lived. When she said that, I was relieved. I thought, *Oh good, she's not going to jump*. I figured it was something to do with Max. That was when I moved closer, and I noticed she was crying. She was . . . devastated."

A sick feeling overtakes me. I didn't know nausea could come on this quickly until I married Gabe. Now, it's a phenomenon I know all too well.

"Why?" I ask quietly. But I already know. Gabe's face is confirmation.

"She knew, didn't she?"

"Yes." Gabe nods apologetically. "She knew about you and Max."

17

PIPPA

(THEN)

"Gabe!"

"*Gabe!* Over here!"

"Gabriel Gerard, just the man I was looking for!"

We were at the office Christmas party—an opulent affair at the National Gallery of Victoria—and Gabe was like a minor celebrity. To be fair, he looked like a celebrity in his dinner suit. Everyone knew his name; everyone wanted a moment with him.

I loved watching him in action. His job brought him to life. It was like watching a performer on stage, and not just at the party. At home, whenever I heard him on the phone to a client or colleague, I'd think, *Wow*. His gift with people was undeniable. He had an ability to cut through the bullshit, to understand who needed to hear what. He knew what excited one person and bored another. It was this instinct that enabled him to rise through the ranks so quickly.

"This is my wife, Pippa," he'd say to everyone we met, and they were polite, but quickly moved their attention back to Gabe. It wasn't just handshakes and small talk. Or maybe it was, but Gabe made it into something more. A moment of connection. A current of electricity. People's interactions with him, no matter how brief, would be the highlight of their evening.

We were seated at the table with the top executives and their partners, including Max Cameron, the boss. I remember being surprised by that. Yes, Gabe was doing well, but Max was a big deal. A powerful Australian media mogul, he owned newspapers, TV stations, and an online media network. Apparently, he even owned a footy team. Despite Max's presence, it was Gabe who owned the table that night. He was in one of those moods where he seemed to be lit from within. Charming, funny, self-deprecating. You could have seen him from space.

"He's an asset to the organization, he really is," Max said to me after dinner.

The dance floor was pumping by then, but Max and I sat at the table, drinking coffee and eating petits fours. There was no denying that Max was an impressive man. Not handsome like Gabe, but *commanding*. Even the way he sat back, relaxed but upright, as if admiring his empire, which perhaps he was. Despite the constant interruptions and people coming to say hello, he made it clear to me that I had his full attention. It was rare that a man other than Gabe turned my head, but I had to admit, there was something about Max.

I'd discovered over the course of the evening that Max didn't have children of his own. I wondered if, perhaps, he'd wanted children and couldn't have them. In his pre-dinner speech, he'd discussed his passion for mental health—fueled, apparently, by the loss of his mother and brother to suicide. It was now his mission, he said, to prevent as many needless suicides as he could.

As Max and I chatted, Gabe was telling Max's wife the story of how we'd met. He told her about the broken leg, and how it had taken him six weeks to call (it had only taken three, but Gabe never let the truth get in the way of a good story).

"I don't know where he gets his energy," Max said, observing him.

I laughed. "Honestly, sometimes I wish he had a little *less* energy. I fear one day it may send me mad."

I meant it as a joke, but Max appeared to take it seriously. "Some of the best creatives have that problem," he said. "It's definitely something to watch." He reached into his breast pocket and pulled out a shiny white business card. "If you ever find that you're worried about it, don't hesitate to get in touch. I mean that."

I was disarmed by his kindness, even though I reasoned that it was likely tied up in his passion for mental health and suicide prevention. But as he pressed the card into my hand, it felt like a strangely intimate moment—and I felt an unmistakable frisson of electricity.

18

PIPPA

I told Gabe about Max and me immediately after it happened, eighteen months ago.

"I understand," he said, when he'd recovered from the shock of it.

After everything he'd put me through, what else could he say? He had one job, and he knew it. It was the same thing he'd asked of me, time and time again. Loyalty. If he didn't give it, how could he ask for it? And to his credit, he did. We'd put it behind us. Until now.

"Amanda knew about Max and me?"

There's something acutely familiar about the bodily sensations I'm feeling. The racing heart. The clammy hands. The velocity of my thoughts, so fast and strong it brings on an instant headache.

"Yes."

I turn toward Gabe. Bizarrely, he looks apologetic. As if *he* has a reason to be sorry. Preschool will be finished for the day in a few minutes, and parents are starting to line up at the gate with babies in tow. I hear Alice Williamson reminding people to contribute to Mrs. Punch's spa voucher.

"How?"

"She found a video on Max's computer."

"A video?"

Gabe scratches at a piece of peeling paint on the bench. He is staring straight ahead at the playground. "I guess he must have filmed it."

It takes me a moment to process this. Filming without consent sounds like something a teenager would do, or a pervert. Max, on the other hand, always seemed like a gentleman.

"*Seriously?*" I say.

It is, I realize, not an important detail, given what we are discussing. And yet my mind remains stuck on this ill-fitting piece. It causes a sudden shift in my entire recollection of that night, making it slippery and out of focus.

Gabe shrugs. "That's what she said. Apparently, she had the footage on a USB stick. She brought it with her because she didn't think I'd believe her."

I'm still trying to untangle this. "So she came to The Drop to tell you?"

"Actually, it was you she wanted to talk to. She said that the video cut off at a crucial moment and she wanted to know what happened. If you and Max actually . . ."

A sick feeling builds in my belly.

"And what did you say?"

"I said you did."

I think I might throw up. Amanda discovered a video of Max

and me, then had her worst fears confirmed by Gabe. Moments later, she was at the bottom of a cliff.

And it's all my fault.

Emily Kent hurries past on her way to pickup. "Am I late?" she asks. Gabe and I shake our heads, and she slows down. "Phew! Mrs. Punch would kill me."

We sit in silence till Emily is out of earshot.

"What happened then?" I ask, even though I don't want to know.

"She was so upset," Gabe says. "She said that fidelity was one of the foundations of their marriage."

I think of the woman's arms flailing. Suddenly it makes sense.

"She said she couldn't go on." His face twists in an ugly, silent sob. "When she leaped, I tried to grab her. My hands shot out. But there was nothing to grab. She was gone."

The bell rings, indicating preschool has finished.

"I didn't want you to have to live with that, Pip," he says, as the singsong voices of children start up. "I hoped you'd never find out."

The gate opens, and kids burst out of the gates and run toward their parents. Asha and Freya look around, then, spying us near the playground, launch themselves at us at full speed. The timing is perfect because, after that, I can't talk anymore.

19

AMANDA

It's true, I hadn't anticipated that Gabe already knew about Pippa and Max. What sort of couple could know this about the other and then move on with their lives as if it were inconsequential? Then I realized it should have tipped me off about the kind of people I was dealing with. The pair of them pride themselves on loyalty, as if it's all they could possibly need for a good marriage. They forget the most important thing about loyalty: Sometimes it's warranted . . . sometimes it's not.

20

AMANDA

"Before I ask you to marry me," Max said, "there's something we need to discuss."

There was no ring. No kneeling. He said it in between bites of his medium-rare steak.

We were in a lovely restaurant, but then we ate at lovely restaurants most nights. Why cook when we lived near some of the best restaurants in the world? We never needed to book ahead of time. Reservations just appeared for Max, as did window tables and dishes that weren't on the menu but that Max had a hankering for.

"All right," I said, setting down my cutlery.

I had understood that things were going in this direction. We'd been dating for over a year, I'd met all the key people in his life and passed all the tests. I knew the role I needed to fill, and I did a good job of it. Max needed someone to accompany him to functions.

Someone to organize his social life. Someone to attend to his physical, mental, and sexual needs. Someone he could *trust*.

Max filled his role equally well. He was a gentleman; the kind of man who looked into my eyes rather than at my breasts, who spoke to me respectfully, never mocked me or put me down. He was considerate of my needs sexually and provided for me financially.

It was time, not just for the outward appearance but because it was practical. Max's business was poised to explode. At work, he was hiring manager upon manager, staffing up teams, delegating. But he needed someone to manage his home life. I knew Max's first love would always be his business, and I was fine with that. Unlike my mother, I was going to marry with my head.

"So what do we need to discuss?" I asked.

As Max put down his own knife and fork, he looked as close to nervous as I'd ever seen him. His cheeks were flushed, though later he would blame the red wine.

"I don't want children, Amanda."

I'll admit, that surprised me. While I hadn't known Max to show a lot of interest in children, I'd assumed he'd be the old-fashioned type—happy to have as many as his wife wanted as long as he only had to pay them a cursory interest. I knew enough to know he wouldn't be the type of father to get down on the floor and play or change dirty nappies, but the strength of his assertion—that was puzzling.

"All right," I said. "May I ask why not?"

He shrugged. "You know about my mum and my brother."

I nodded, even though I knew very little. Both had died by taking an overdose of pills, but even that I'd only gleaned from Max's speeches at suicide-prevention fundraisers.

"These kinds of mental health issues can be hereditary. I don't want to take that chance with my own child."

I sat back in my seat as I digested this. I wasn't a woman who desired children particularly, I had just assumed they'd probably come along. To be told suddenly that they were off the table took some adjusting, if only to alter some of the fuzzy-edged visions of the future—the first words, the family holidays, Max walking a daughter down the aisle.

"You're disappointed," he said, after a few moments.

Was I? Maybe I was, a little. But it wasn't a deal breaker.

"If you decide to accept my proposal, and I sincerely hope you do, we will have a good life. Travel, art, music, food. I will support you in anything you want to do. I will be a real partner to you. But I warn you, I will not change my mind on this."

"I need to think about it," I said, even though I'd already decided. As it turned out, I was highly efficient at adjusting my future visions. I'd already replaced them with adults-only resorts, trips to Europe, gala dinners, and lazy Sunday brunches. It would be fine, I realized. It would be great.

I waited four weeks before I told Max I would marry him. But I had a condition of my own.

"I want fidelity."

My condition, I was aware, was perhaps not typical in marriages such as ours. After all, I understood the lay of the land. Powerful men like Max tended to have a mistress or two. Some of them used discretion, whereas others provided their wives with a very nice lifestyle to compensate them for looking the other way.

"My father didn't have a lot of great attributes," I continued, "but infidelity was the worst of it. He humiliated my mother time and time again. I am not interested in a marriage like that. If you want to marry me, I insist on fidelity."

I spoke powerfully, pragmatically, and without emotion. And so it surprised me when Max reached across the table to place his hand over mine. "That works for me."

He handed me a ring he'd purchased; it cost more than the home I grew up in.

We married six months later, and the pictures were in all the magazines. A few months after that, my sad fertility stories started making headlines. In every single story, the reason we didn't have children was attributed to me.

21

PIPPA

No one will ever know.

That's what I'm thinking as Gabe and I walk home from preschool, chasing the girls on their scooters, each of us with a pink schoolbag over our shoulder. I am in activewear, and Gabe is in jeans and a North Face vest and trainers. The streets are bustling with parents pushing prams, joggers, surfers carrying boards. People smile as they pass Freya and Asha, who have their hair in identical pigtails with straight center parts—the only hairstyle Gabe has mastered and one he is very proud of.

No one will ever know.

Gabe and I keep our eyes forward and our heads down, like a pair of criminals being bustled out of a courtroom, past the media, into a waiting vehicle.

"She died because of me," I say, so quietly I'm surprised that Gabe hears.

"No," Gabe says. "She made a decision—"

"A decision based on something *I* did."

I'm ashamed to realize that the night I went to Max's office, Amanda never featured in my thoughts. I knew she existed—indeed, I'd met her at the Christmas party where I'd first spoken to Max—but she was like background noise. Even now I find it hard to conjure an image of her. Things were so messed up at the time. *I* was so messed up.

"What is *wrong* with me?" I say out loud.

"It was her choice to jump, Pip. You didn't push her."

I understand Gabe is trying to make me feel better. I know, because that's what I've always done for him. It's our own strange brand of loyalty, one that has worked so well for our marriage. The problem is, I don't buy it. I may not have pushed her, but it *is* my fault.

"This is what I wanted to avoid, Pip. This is why I didn't tell you it was Amanda on the cliff."

We walk in silence for a while. I see now how this secret must have been haunting him. Gabe is a good person. He would have been aware of every ramification of keeping this secret. For so long I have been the person protecting him. It feels so strange now that the shoe is on the other foot.

"Asha!" Gabe yells, as she nearly takes out an elderly man on the footpath. "Slow down." To the man he says, "Sorry!"

Asha is half a block in front of us, flying along on her scooter, so fast the tail shakes. She stands up on her tiptoes, her hands flat on the handlebars, barely holding on. Like this, I see the magic of her and the danger simultaneously. It brings on a wave of love and worry so strong it takes my breath away.

At least Amanda didn't have children, I think. But I immediately withdraw the thought. What difference would it make if she had kids? Just because she didn't have children doesn't mean she wasn't beloved. It doesn't make her death any less sad.

Max must be brokenhearted. Bereft. Or maybe he isn't? My whole radar for Max feels off now that I know he filmed us that night in his office. When I'd gone there that night, I thought it had taken him by surprise. But maybe women go to his office all the time? Maybe he had a camera set up just in case?

"Come on, slowcoach," Gabe says as we catch up to Freya. He grabs the handlebars and runs along, speeding her up. It gives her the giggles. To anyone else, he would look relaxed, like he didn't have a care in the world. But I see the tension in his shoulders, his jaw. After years of close observation, I am an expert in Gabe's mental state. I'm an expert in *Gabe*. I'm not the only one who is going to have to live with this guilt, I realize. Gabe will too.

"What happened to the USB?" I ask when Freya takes off again.

A look of guilt crosses Gabe's face. "Remember when you came to the beach, and you saw me drop something?"

I do remember. It was silver. Gabe had said it was surfboard wax. It makes sense now. Everything makes horrifying sense.

"Hold hands, girls," Gabe says as we reach the road. He takes their scooters in one hand and holds Freya's hand in the other. She chain-links to Asha, who holds out her hand to me. A middle-aged woman smiles as we cross the street, a wobbly line of children, scooters, and schoolbags. On the other side of the road Gabe puts the scooters down again, and the girls take off.

"How are you doing that?" I say. "How are you operating like a normal, responsible human being?"

Gabe takes my hand in his. "You've been strong for me so many times, Pip," he says. "Now it's my turn."

. . .

Mr. and Mrs. Hegarty are in their front garden. The Hegarty house faces ours, so they don't have the ocean view, but their front garden is almost as spectacular. Several times I've noticed people slowing their cars to admire it. Mrs. Hegarty waves at the girls as they scoot past, then rests her forearms on the fence, settling in for a chat. Mr. Hegarty remains kneeling, holding a trowel.

"The garden is looking great, Mrs. Hegarty," Gabe says as we stop outside their house. Even under these circumstances, he can't turn off his charm.

Mrs. Hegarty practically levitates with pride.

"We decided to get some weeding done while the sun is out," she says, removing her floral-trimmed gardening gloves. "Who knows when we'll get another chance, with all this rain!"

The Hegartys are gold-star neighbors—no loud parties, always keeping an eye on things, happy to take our rubbish bins out or collect mail if we go away. They have a flourishing lemon tree, and we regularly come home to a bag of lemons on the doorstep. They adore the girls and have admired many a "street performance" the girls have put on, as well as having regular chats with them at the fence.

Mrs. Hegarty has told us many times how pleased they were when we bought the cliff house.

So many weekend homes around here, she said. *It's nice to have permanent neighbors. And ones with children!*

To society, there is nothing purer than a family with small children. Except, perhaps, being elderly and enjoying gardening. We trust people based on the strangest, most arbitrary things, none of which have any bearing on whether or not you are inherently good. The Hegartys have no idea what we are capable of. No one does.

"How are you both holding up?" Mrs. Hegarty puts a hand to her chest. "It's tragic, what happened to that woman. And the paper said she was only fifty-two. So young! What on earth would possess her to jump?"

The newspaper hadn't said Amanda Cameron had taken her life, but the Hegartys would have seen the police and rescue operation last night and it didn't take much for people around here to put two and two together.

At first, I think Mrs. Hegarty's question is rhetorical, but when she says nothing more, I realize that Mrs. Hegarty is wanting an answer.

She discovered an incriminating video of me and her husband, I imagine saying. *When she realized what I'd done, she decided her life wasn't worth living.*

Gabe's eyes dart to me for just a second. Then he says, "We don't really know."

"But you were with her, weren't you, Gabe? Surely she must have given you some indication of why she jumped?"

He hesitates a moment. "She said her husband had been unfaithful."

Mrs. Hegarty tuts. "Well, I hope it was worth it. Now he'll have to live with guilt for the rest of his life."

She looks over her shoulder at Mr. Hegarty, as if in warning. He keeps his head down. After a moment, she turns back to us. "Pippa? Are you all right, dear? You look unwell."

"Actually," I say, "I don't feel well."

Gabe puts an arm around my shoulders. "I'd better get her home."

"Yes," Mrs. Hegarty says. "Go. Just sing out if you need anything."

She gives us a wave and Gabe and I shuffle off.

We've almost reached our driveway when she calls after us: "I'll bring you some lemons!"

22

PIPPA

"I'm pregnant."

We'd been married two years when I became pregnant with Freya. It was a good time for us, in a lot of ways.

After two years in the job, Gabe had gone from promotion to promotion, pay rise to pay rise. We could finally afford those suits he'd been buying. We had saved a good deposit for a home. I was even starting to buy nice things for myself. Now he was running the investor relations team and apparently, he'd single-handedly brought in more than fifty percent of the company's investors that year. If they'd used a broker to find those new investors, he told me, it would have cost the company hundreds of thousands of dollars in fees.

Still, I was nervous about revealing the pregnancy to Gabe. Not because I thought he'd be unhappy. After all, when I'd suggested we try, he was the one to ceremoniously empty my birth control pills into the toilet. My anxiety stemmed from another issue I wanted to talk to him about, something I'd been increasingly worried about over recent months.

"Now that we're having a baby," I said, "I've been thinking about these late nights. I don't see you a lot."

"You're right," Gabe said. "I'll dial it back. Time to focus on family."

"The other thing is," I said, gaining courage, "your drinking."

I wasn't sure when alcohol had become a fixture in Gabe's life. It wasn't necessarily a huge cause for concern. He didn't drink every day; he didn't hide bottles around the house. But when he did drink, he drank to excess—usually when he was out with work colleagues. Several times, he'd come home so drunk after a night "working" he couldn't get his key in the front door.

Gabe was quiet as he contemplated my comment. One thing I'd learned in our marriage was that some topics had to be broached delicately. During the year that he kept leaving jobs, for example, we talked about it—even just between the two of us—in terms of "opportunities." It wasn't that he couldn't hold down a job; rather, he was lucky to have these new opportunities. Gabe took the same care with me, though he really didn't need to. In that way, I was far less fragile than he.

After a moment, he nodded.

"Yes," he said. "You're right. With the baby coming, it could be better to stop the drinking."

Gabe stopped drinking the same day, just like that. Overnight he developed a new interest—and it was preparing to become a father. The late nights ceased, too. Thus began the evolution of Gabe from young partying executive to family man.

. . .

Freya's arrival, on her due date, was the conclusion of the metamor-
phosis for Gabe.

For him, it was love at first sight. He was besotted with Freya. His
patience was endless. He paced the hallway with her at night, pat-
ting her and cradling her little head and marveling at her existence.
He came to her pediatric appointments and listened intently to the
nurse's suggestions. Whenever he saw another baby—in the street,
on TV, in a commercial—he said he felt bad for the parents that their
baby wasn't as beautiful as Freya.

Admittedly, Freya was a pretty baby, petite and delicate with
a heart-shaped face and piercing blue eyes. She was also a placid
baby: content if she was being held, happy to observe. From day
one I felt like she was watching me. Often, I wondered if I was
meeting her expectations.

I was certainly prepared for motherhood. I'd read the books
about the first three months, the "wonder weeks," the eat-play-sleep
routine. Gabe and I took a class in baby first aid. I'd set up a nursery
with everything I might need. I'd purchased bottles and formula
in case breastfeeding didn't work out. I was ready for anything. I
assumed I'd excel at it. Maybe that was the problem? Motherhood
wasn't really something you *could* excel at. You did the same thing,
day in and day out: feed, sleep, change. Hold her while she cries.
Visitors came and went, and I acted the part of loving mother for
all of them. I even performed it for Gabe. *Yes, I feel so much love. It's
mind-blowing. What did I ever do without her?* But the truth was, I
found it hard to feel much of anything. To me, Freya was a prop in
a pointless show I had to perform in, over and over, to no audience.

We lived in a tiny inner-city town house at the time, near a strip of coffee shops and restaurants. Before long, Gabe and Freya were known by everyone. He was the sexy dad in the puffer vest, proudly striding the pavement with the adorable rosy-cheeked baby in her pram. He was the dad who chatted to other parents about sleep times and feeding schedules and came home to me with suggestions like: "We should stop letting her sleep so much during the day." He was the dad who laughed out loud when she yawned or smiled or farted, because his daughter delighted him that much. It was almost enough to compensate for the fact that I felt nothing for her.

I tried to force a connection. I held her skin-to-skin and stared into her eyes. I breastfed. I recited affirmations. I sniffed her head. I tried to recall all the reasons I wanted her, but I came up blank. If I'd had any—and I was sure I must have—they were gone now.

Once, while Gabe was at work, I dressed her in one of her most adorable outfits and just stared at her for hours, willing myself to feel something. When nothing happened, I put her into her crib in the nursery and left her there for the afternoon. If looking at her didn't work, maybe absence would.

Gabe's new zeal for fatherhood only made me feel worse about my lack of attachment. He was always thinking up something to do with her, to get us out and about.

"It's beautiful outside!" he said one day, when the weather was average at best. "Let's go have an adventure."

Freya was only a couple of months old, and I was about to take a nap. By that point, I'd developed an unhealthy attachment to my bed. I sat around the house in sweatpants, living from feed to feed.

I glanced out the window. "It looks like rain."

"A drive then," he said, unperturbed. "Down the coast."

If I'd said I was too tired, or I just wasn't up for it, Gabe wouldn't have minded. He would have taken Freya alone and told me to stay home and rest. But I wouldn't have been able to rest. I'd have spent the day chastising myself for not going, for not taking part in my life, for *not being grateful*. After all, what more could I ask for than a day at the beach with a good-looking man and a cute baby?

What was wrong with me?

I started to cry. And once I started, it was impossible to stop.

Gabe dropped to his knees in front of me and I told him everything I was feeling. Every little wretched thought. I told him how I hated him for being so happy. How I hated myself for being so sad. I even admitted to the most shameful thought: that sometimes I even hated Freya for what she'd done to me. I told him I was dead inside.

Gabe listened to me the way he always did, with undivided attention. He didn't interrupt, or tell me I was just tired, or suggest something to cheer me up. When I finished talking, he put his arms around me and said, "I didn't know. I'm so sorry I didn't know."

When I finished crying, he put me to bed, and looked after Freya around the clock, only bringing her to me for feeds. The next day, he took me to the doctor, and I was prescribed antidepressants. The doctor said it would be two weeks before I would feel an effect, and that until I did it would be advisable to always have someone with me.

Until then, I'd always been the organized one, but now Gabe did me proud. He organized a roster so that I was never alone. Usually, Mum, Dad, or Kat or Mei came during the week, when Gabe was at work, but one Saturday Kat turned up when Gabe was home. He told me to get dressed and we got in the car. I didn't ask why. I assumed we had another doctor's appointment, but my mental state was such that I couldn't even be bothered to ask the question.

When we pulled up at the beach, dread set in.

"What are we doing?"

He handed me a wet suit. There was a tent on the beach where you could rent a board. I thought he was joking. Surfing was the *last* thing I wanted to do. The weather wasn't great. I had a bulge of baby weight around my middle. But Gabe had made up his mind.

We rented a board for an hour. Gabe helped me change into my wet suit in the beach tent and led me into the surf. Then he stood there, waist deep in the water, while I lay on my stomach on the board. If I'd had an ounce more energy, I might have been able to protest. But I had nothing. It was easier just to go along with it.

The first time he pushed me onto a wave, I floated a couple of meters and then stopped. The same thing happened the second and third time. On the fourth, I caught a glimpse of Gabe looking back for the next wave as he held the board. There was something about his face. The determination of it.

The fourth time I used my arms to paddle, like he'd showed me. Given the effort he was making, the least I could do was go through the motions, I reasoned.

The fifth time, the wave was more powerful, and I rode it all the way to the shore. Gabe cheered so hard I felt something come undone inside.

He put me on the board again and again, until his teeth were blue and chattering. After forty-five minutes he suggested I try to stand and, more for his sake than mine, I did. And as the wave propelled the board forward, I found my footing—a lucky accident— and I rode that wave all the way the shore. The feeling was visceral. Sensual. It was flying.

Gabe lost his mind. He cheered so hard people on the beach all looked to see what the commotion was about. For the first time in a very long while, I smiled.

"Again?" he said.

I nodded. That was the thing about Gabe. Yes, he could hurt me. But he was the only one who could make me fly.

23

PIPPA

I spot my parents from the end of our driveway. They are sitting side by side on the bench on our front porch, next to the boot rack where the girls' tiny pink gum boots sit beside Gabe's and my larger ones. I don't remember them saying they were coming for a visit, but it's not unusual for them to show up unannounced. They're at our house a lot, even when we're not having a crisis. Part of it, I think, is guilt, because last time they'd failed to realize the extent of what had been going on with Gabe until it was too late. Now, I think they are determined to make sure it doesn't happen again.

Unfortunately, it's too late.

Mum waves wildly at the sight of us, but Dad continues looking at his folded newspaper; he is almost certainly completing the cross-word. His glasses are perched on his nose, and he holds the news-paper in an outstretched arm, both for more effective pondering and to see it better. Mum jabs him with her elbow, presumably to tell him that we're approaching, but he ignores her.

"Nana!" Asha cries, dropping her scooter to launch herself at Mum.

I feel an overwhelming urge to do the same, to feel the soft warm comfort of her, for my problem to be of a size and shape that my mother can fix with a hug. *I killed a woman, Mum. Not directly, but indirectly. Do you still love me?*

Freya takes the time to return her scooter to the shed before greeting her grandmother.

By the time Gabe and I reach the house, both girls are sitting in Mum's lap, interrupting each other as they talk about preschool, about how it was their friend Liam's birthday today, about how their friend Isla burned her hand on the stove at home and you should never touch things that are hot. Mum appears riveted by each new subject as she toggles back and forth between the girls.

"Conspicuously and tastelessly indecent," Dad says without looking up. "Six letters."

"Vulgar," Gabe replies. He's always been freakishly good at things like crosswords.

Dad frowns at the newspaper a moment, then nods and starts penciling it in. "Good man."

When he finally looks up, he's smiling. But immediately his grin falls away. "Are you feeling all right, Pip?"

Mum, Gabe, and Dad look. I do, in fact, feel unwell. Clammy and cold. My stomach feels off. "I don't feel the best actually."

Mum stands, letting the girls slide off her lap. She puts a hand to my head. "You're not warm. But there is something going around at the moment. Off to bed with you. We'll look after the girls."

I have nothing like the strength to fight her. She is right: I need sleep. I am tired. Bone-tired.

She follows me into the bedroom, turning on the lamps and pulling down the blinds. She kisses my forehead. Then she leaves.

I change into my pajamas and climb into bed. But sleep doesn't come.

I wrap the comforter around myself more tightly. I am wearing a T-shirt, pajama pants, underwear, and socks, but I feel cold. I wonder if I might *really* be coming down with something. I feel ill—not in my stomach or my throat or my head; it's more of a full-body ache, an overwhelming heaviness that pins me to the bed, renders me unable to lift so much as a finger.

How many times have I been thrust into this kind of situation? Well, not exactly this kind, but a situation that felt impossible, like something I'd never get beyond. Each time felt acute and breathtaking and, without a doubt, like things couldn't possibly get worse. But this time it was true.

The walls in the house are thinner than I'd realized. As I lie in bed, I hear the familiar domestic noises with startling clarity—arguments between the girls, negotiations between Mum and Asha about what healthy food she must consume before she's allowed to eat one of the Freddo frogs that Mum always keeps in her handbag. (At first, those Freddo frogs used to be accepted with delight and gratitude, but now they've become a noose around her neck. Recently Mum called me while I was at the supermarket, and when I asked if she needed anything she said, "Better get a bag of Freddo frogs to leave in your house. I live in fear of Asha's wrath if I arrive without one.") Dad and Gabe are still doing the crossword. It's soothing to listen to.

"Edmund Hillary's sherpa, seven letters," Dad says.

Silence. I imagine them pondering it.

Tenzing, I think.

"Tenzing," Gabe says.

Once again, I wonder how he is doing that. Sitting with my parents, doing a crossword. Pulling facts from his mind, facts buried below the immediate, the pressing, the horrific knowledge of what his wife has done. Yes, Gabe has made his share of mistakes, but that was when he was unwell. I don't have an excuse. My involvement in this wasn't an accident; my intentions were not noble. I made a choice without considering who I was hurting. That choice started a chain of events. Now Amanda is dead. Max has lost his wife.

I hear a cheer from the girls and deduce that the Freddo frogs have been distributed, and that's when something occurs to me—something so obvious I can't believe I hadn't yet considered it.

Max.

Max is going to find out that Gabe was the one on the cliff with Amanda. In fact, he might already know. After all, the man does run a media organization. No doubt he'll go to the police with this information, and it won't look good for Gabe: a former employee of NewZ who'd left in disgrace. Plus, Max had slept with his wife! And Gabe failed to disclose any of this when he was questioned by the authorities. Things are so much worse than I thought, I realize. Gabe could go to jail.

I hear the thud of little feet jumping for joy and then scampering around the house. I imagine chocolate melting in my little girls' warm sweaty hands. In a normal situation, I'd insist they sit on their stools and wrap a tea towel around each of their necks (Gabe called this "Mummy's straitjackets") and I'd stand by with a damp face washer to clean their hands when they were done.

Freya will feel rattled by this sudden freedom. Asha will revel in it. When I get up, there will be chocolate on the couch and God knows where else. And yet, as further proof of my malaise, I can't bring myself to care.

Gabe is good. He is a man who marches for causes, gives to charities, is brought to tears by a feeling that he *isn't doing enough*. A man who spends hours on the edge of a cliff in the bitter cold trying to convince strangers to choose life, for heaven's sake! A man who'd saved the lives of seven of those strangers! He can't go to jail. If anyone should go to jail, it's me.

The door to my room bursts open and the girls stand there with huge, chocolate-covered grins and sticky brown hands. Their eyes are glazed with sugary delirium. Even Freya looks slightly maniacal. I wonder how many Freddo frogs they've eaten.

"Mummy," they cry, leaping onto the bed. They plant chocolate kisses on my face and make tiny chocolate handprints all over my pressed white comforter.

Freya notices the destruction first. "Asha's making a mess!" she cries, her eyes wide and horrified. She points a chocolate finger at Asha, desperate to distance herself from the trouble.

Asha bounces on the bed, either oblivious or uncaring. I love them both so much in that moment, I think I might die.

"Mummy doesn't care," I say, grabbing Asha's foot so she collapses onto me. Freya clambers on top of me too. There are fingers and heads and legs everywhere. I breathe in their sweet chocolate breath. "Mummy doesn't care one little bit."

24

AMANDA

I never got used to the wealth. Perhaps I would have, if the wealth had stayed at the same level as it was in the early days. Back then, we had a lovely house in a sought-after area of Melbourne. Two cars. A kitchen with a butler's pantry and wine fridge. A holiday overseas every year—flying business class. But Max's wealth was growing almost daily. Business class became first class. Tables at expensive restaurants turned into private rooms.

Having money hit me daily in ways I didn't expect. Getting places was faster now that I could park in the most convenient location, regardless of the cost. Getting ready to go out was easier now that I'd shopped for "outfits"—including shoes and a bag—rather than having to piece things together to see if they worked. I started ordering what I felt like when I went out for a meal regardless of cost. I caught taxis instead of trains. I bought myself a camera that cost more than my first car and was invited to photograph all the hottest events—fashion shows, design launches, architecture. I'd had no idea how many doors opened to you simply because of who you were—or, as in my case, who you married.

For the most part, Max and I were happy. I knew what Max needed from me at any given time and I supplied it: trust first and foremost, but also a listening ear, a home-cooked meal, sex, time to unwind. What surprised me was how much I enjoyed giving him what he needed. Charming the relevant people at dinner parties. Challenging him just the right amount. Being playful or serious, as required. Max also gave me what I needed: good company, a nice lifestyle, and, most importantly, his fidelity. I couldn't say I was in love with him, but as far as I was concerned that was a good thing.

But one night, a year or so into our relationship, things changed. We were hosting a dinner for some of Max's colleagues and their wives. The dinner had been catered and served by staff in aprons, as usual. My role, as I'd come to understand, was to be fabulous, effortless, comforting.

The evening started much like they all did. I chatted with the wives about Botox and face-lifts, the latest place to go skiing, the most exclusive new villa to book for a holiday in Tuscany. Conversation at these functions was achingly repetitive, but it meant I could contribute without having to try too hard. Usually, I was more interested in what the men were discussing. To be clear, those topics were also achingly repetitive, but the subjects tended to offer more opportunity for a discussion beyond getting the name of a new aesthetician or travel agent.

The men's conversation tended to be louder and more aggressive. They stood with their legs spread and their arms crossed, determined to tell you what they thought. Max was the only one who didn't stand that way. He didn't talk over the top of anyone or argue his point belligerently. He waited for a natural pause in conversation before he offered his opinion. If someone started to speak over him, he stopped and listened to them before responding. Perhaps on a different person this would have conveyed weakness, but with Max it was the opposite. In any room or situation, it was clear that Max was the most important, the most powerful person present.

At these dinners, it was only when the staff invited us to be seated at the dinner table that the men's and women's conversation merged. Usually at this point discussions moved into more personal matters, like people's health, their children, perhaps a scandalous news story that had caught people's attention. This night, though, the men brought their pre-dinner conversation to the table; they were speaking of the plight of the unemployed. It wasn't an unfamiliar topic. The wives were often involved in some sort of charity fundraiser that the men had been roped into attending. Typically, the conversations were sympathetic, if empty, trotting out someone's sob story, mostly to affirm the speaker's own privileged place in society and express gratitude for their individual circumstances. On this night, however, the conversation took a different turn.

"But this is Australia!" Steve said, nodding for a waiter to fill his glass. His cheeks were already pink with passion, or maybe with red wine. "This is the land of opportunity. People need to stop looking for handouts and pull themselves up by their bootstraps, am I right?"

Steve had inherited his very successful industrial cleaning business from his parents and been appointed CEO on his thirtieth birthday.

"I've always hated that expression: 'pulling yourself up by your bootstraps.' It gives the idea that anyone can do anything with hard work." My voice was quiet, my tone polite. I wasn't drawing attention to the antagonism or prejudice of Steve's comment. Although I felt the energy of the room change as our guests absorbed the comment.

"You don't agree, Amanda?" Steve looked amused.

"No. There are a lot of reasons people can't help themselves. Mental illness. Disability. Criminal records. Language barriers."

I was thinking of my mother, of course, who'd spent a large part of her life unemployed despite attending hundreds of job interviews, each position more menial than the last. Her pelvis, which had been shattered in a car accident when she was twenty, meant she couldn't work in a job that required her to be on her feet for long periods of time, and considering the kind of jobs she was qualified for, this made her virtually unemployable.

"And that doesn't even take into account the people who are working hard but just can't get ahead because they are supporting their entire family," I added.

"I'm not saying it's easy," Steve said. "But opportunities are there, if you work hard enough."

I couldn't help it; I rolled my eyes. "And how would you know?"

A hush fell over the room. Steve's expression became slightly less jovial. I felt Max's gaze on me, but I couldn't quite read his expression.

"Oh, please. You're not one of those bleeding-heart lefties, are you?" Steve said. "All I'm saying is that handouts aren't the answer."

"I disagree," I said. "In many cases, handouts are the difference between people feeding their children and not feeding their children—even for hardworking people."

Steve held up his hands in mock fear. "All right, all right! I don't want to offend the lady of the house. Let's agree to disagree."

Agreeing to disagree was the last thing I wanted to do, but it was clear that I wasn't going to change Steve's mind, and I could see our exchange was making the other guests uncomfortable. I was about to let the matter rest when Max spoke up.

"But you didn't answer Amanda's question, Steve," Max said. "How *would* you know? When was the last time you had to pull yourself up by the bootstraps?"

Everyone turned to look at Max. His expression was calm, considered . . . and something else. Perhaps faintly amused?

Steve looked abashed. "All right. Why don't we get off this topic and—"

"Why? Because you're not as qualified to speak to this complex issue as you suggested? Because you're afraid that adding nuance to a bullish, one-sided commentary will diminish your argument?"

"With all due respect," Steve started.

"Actually," Max interrupted, "nothing about this conversation has showed Amanda the respect she is due. So I'd suggest you think carefully about what you're going to say next."

Everyone looked at Max as he sat back in his chair, resting his arm around the back of my seat.

That was the moment I fell in love with Max.

25

PIPPA

"I'm going to tell the police about my connection to Max," Gabe says at 2:00 A.M.

He paces the room in his boxer shorts. His thoughts on the matter have suddenly become infuriatingly, intensely clear. He wants to confess. He *must*. It's so Gabe of him. But my thoughts are not clear. They are slippery and suffocating, flipping from one conviction to another so fast I feel dizzy.

"You can't, Gabe! You concealed the fact that Amanda was the wife of your former boss—a man who fired you. Do you really think that if you go to them with this information now, they'll believe you had nothing to do with her death?"

"It's the truth," he says. Gabe's voice sounds scratchy and hoarse. It reminds me that while I've seen Gabe in many different states— angry, manic, depressed, overjoyed—I haven't seen him like this. I haven't seen him afraid.

I'm afraid too. Afraid of losing him. If I'm honest, this has been my fear since the moment we met. Something about him has always felt fleeting, even after marriage, even after children. "But what if they don't believe you?"

He sits on the edge of the bed. "Then I'll go to jail."

"No," I say. "No. That can't happen."

I've always been a visual person. All over the house I have pinboards and blackboards and whiteboards decorated with brightly colored Post-its or whiteboard markers. When something is coming up—a birthday, an event, a deadline—it is right there, displayed for everyone to see. Gabe is not a visual person. For a while, I put his important dates on my boards too. It didn't work, but I derived a perverse sense of pleasure from pointing out the occasion he'd forgotten.

"It's right here," I'd say, pointing.

For me, if I could see something, it would happen. And I can't see a world without Gabe. That must mean something. Mustn't it?

"I'm not saying it *will* happen," Gabe says. "Just that it's a possibility."

I force myself to imagine Gabe going to jail. On a superficial level, we'd manage. I am the breadwinner anyway. Mum and Dad and Kat and Mei would rally around to offer emotional support. The initial flurry of activity after his arrest would help. I could turn my mind to logistics. Lovely, clear logistics. I would need to arrange for childcare. The girls would need to see a psychologist, which would involve getting a referral and a mental health plan. I'd probably need one too.

There'd be the shame to deal with, of course. Both the internal and, of course, the external. News would travel fast. We live in a small coastal town. For the past year we've been cruising on our reputation of being good people. Lifesavers! But small towns are notoriously difficult when you aren't popular. I wonder, suddenly, what the Hegartys would think. "They seemed like such nice people. They have *children!*"

We'd probably have to move again. To a city, where we could blend in. We'd need to make new friends, ones who didn't know Gabe and me before. But ultimately, we would get through it—physically, at least. Emotionally is another story. Because I can't let Gabe go to jail for a crime he didn't commit—a death for which *I* am responsible. I can't. I *won't*.

The night ticks on, but we don't sleep. At one point, we have sex. A bizarre thing to do, maybe, but not for us. Even in the most terrifying moments of our relationship, we've been able to connect this way, with our hearts in our throats and dread in the pit of our stomachs. Sex has been our escape, our distraction, our apology. And over the last year, when we haven't needed an escape or a distraction or an apology, it's been our comfort, our pleasure. It's something I've had tucked in my pocket of self-satisfaction. Gorgeous husband. Adorable little girls. Great sex. Soulmates, with a connection that I've never seen in another couple.

"Why didn't you just tell the police in the first place?" I ask him at one point. "If you'd just told them, they would have been more likely to believe you."

Gabe appears tortured by this. "I know! I wasn't thinking. It never occurred to me that either of us could be suspects in her death. Amanda made the decision to jump. You didn't push her and neither did I. I thought it would be written off as any other suicide . . ."

"But surely you realized word would get out that it was Amanda Cameron on the cliff?"

"I hoped it wouldn't."

"And the suicide of Max Cameron's wife isn't an ordinary suicide."

"I know."

And this, of course, brings us back to why *he* must confess. The reason our conversation has traveled in circles all night. There is no other conceivable option. Max *will* discover that Gabe was with Amanda when she died. Either Gabe goes to the police with the information . . . or they come to him.

"I'll go to the police station in the morning," he says.

This time I don't argue; I just slide into his arms and begin to sob.

26

PIPPA

Freya was six months old when I fell in love with her. We were in the doctor's waiting room when it happened. She had been fussy for a few days with a runny nose, and it seemed like a good idea to have her checked out. I was holding her upright against my chest when she let out a long, sleepy sigh. I inhaled her sweet milky breath and, just like that, my heart moved in my chest.

By then, I'd clawed my way back from postpartum depression. I attributed this to medication and exercise—as well as the Gabriel Gerard rehab center, which regularly took me on excursions and provided opportunities for me to feel. No matter how resistant I was initially, every time Gabe took me out on a new adventure he helped me to connect with some part of myself that had been dormant. Little by little, I felt myself come back to life.

"I feel better," I said to Gabe one day. "I feel . . . *good.* You fixed me."

The wonder of it was indescribable, a confirmation of what I already knew about the power of my connection with Gabe. I was the fixer; we both knew that. Gabe was the dreamer. And yet, when I'd needed him, he rose to the challenge.

I was intoxicated by it, the yin and the yang. Unfortunately, as with yin and yang, there was a cost to my recovery. As life returned to me, it slowly leached out of Gabe.

It started with sleep.

In the past, I'd always been shocked by how little rest he needed. He was always so full of energy! But suddenly he was yawning all the time, turning in at 8:00 P.M.

We laughed about it at first. Blamed parenthood. *Look how wild we are now that we're parents!* Quietly, I was grateful that he was home at night, going to bed early. It beat the days when he stayed out all night.

When the tiredness persisted, though, I told him to stop getting up to feed Freya during the night. But even after nine hours' sleep, he would wake exhausted. Dark circles appeared under his red-rimmed eyes. One Saturday, he slept the entire day, and when he got up around 6:00 P.M. he still looked awful. It made me think of the "black periods" he'd described suffering from as an adolescent.

"I think you should see a doctor," I said eventually.

I made an appointment for him with Dr. Withers, our local GP, who tested his iron levels. When the tests came back fine, Dr. Withers decided Gabe must have a lingering virus. I suggested that he get a second opinion, but Gabe told me not to worry so much.

He took so much time off work I worried he might lose his job. But, perhaps due to his relationship with the boss, he managed to get by doing the bare minimum. I still had Max's business card. Several times I'd picked up the phone to call him, then I'd put it down again. After all, the man was a media tycoon! He had enough to worry about without the wife of one of his executives calling him. I almost threw the card out a couple of times, but I always ended up tucking it back into my wallet—just in case.

One night, while watching a British police procedural on Netflix, Gabe started to cry.

We were tucked up in bed with cups of tea. Freya was sleeping soundly. It was the first time Gabe had stayed up late enough to watch a movie in weeks, and I had been thinking how remarkably normal I felt, like the other new mums in my mothers' group, watching TV with their husbands.

"What is it?" I asked him. "What's wrong?"

He didn't answer. The tears weren't alarming in themselves; Gabe was a crier, especially at movies. What disturbed me was the fact that it wasn't a remotely sad film, combined with the fact that the crying continued after the credits had rolled and went on for four days after that.

"I think you're depressed, Gabe," I said. "It happens to a lot of people. I think you should see a psychologist."

In fact, I'd started to wonder if I should see a psychologist too. I was battling the sleep deprivation of new motherhood and Gabe's moods simultaneously. The littlest things had started to annoy him. As he lay on the couch, he'd complain that the cars outside were too loud. Freya's sweet snoring was too loud. It was all interfering with his sleep and that's why he was so . . . damn . . . *tired.*

All day long the curtains were drawn, the windows were closed.

I forgot what natural sunlight looked like; it felt as if we were living in a cave. If I tried to let air and light in, Gabe recoiled like he was in pain.

More and more, I felt trapped by Gabe's moods. I mourned our old happy life, and I had no idea how to get it back.

"Let me make you an appointment," I suggested.

But he was adamant in his refusal. "I just need to ride it out, Pip," he said. "I will come good again. Trust me."

But he didn't come good, apart from the odd proclamation of love for me or Freya that felt worryingly incongruent with his mood. "I'm so grateful to you," he'd say. "I'd do anything for our family. I really am the luckiest man alive."

Freya was my solace. I built a little world just for the two of us, structured around Freya's naps and mealtimes and evening routine, her playdates, doctor's appointments, first words, and first steps. I made friends with other mums and we met in parks and libraries and play centers, where we talked about breastfeeding, baby-led weaning, gross motor skills—new, interesting, distracting things that required a lot of my time and attention. At night, if Gabe had fallen asleep on the couch, I'd bring Freya into our room, bathed and sleepy, and fall asleep to the sound of her rhythmic, steady breath.

The days were full and, for the most part, fulfilling. It was surprisingly easy to forget for hours or even days at a time that there was something very wrong with my husband. Besides, what was the point of thinking about something I was so powerless to change?

Once, I came home at midday to find Gabe at home. It was a Wednesday, and he should have been at work.

"What are you doing here?" I asked. "Why aren't you at work?"

"I couldn't stay there," he said. "I tried, but I couldn't. It was too loud."

The noise was becoming more of a problem. The day before he'd told me he'd unplugged the photocopier because he couldn't bear hearing it outside his office all day long. He'd also complained that the lights were too bright. Recently he'd petitioned to HR to get dimmers in the offices. I hadn't heard how that campaign had gone.

"Was it the photocopier?" I asked.

"It was the voices. All day long, voices. They reverberate in my brain." He sat on the couch and dropped his head into his hands. "I can still hear them."

I sat beside him. "You hear them now?"

He nodded. "In my head."

"What do the voices say?"

He threw up his hands. "You know. *You're not good enough. You're not working hard enough. Your ideas are crap.*"

I relaxed a little. "I think everyone hears those voices. When I hear them, I just remind myself that they aren't real. And I tell myself that I *am* good enough."

His eyes were narrowed, and he was leaning in as if he was listening hard. But when I finished speaking, he seemed dissatisfied. And I started to suspect he was hearing a different kind of voice.

27

PIPPA

We get up just before 6:00 A.M. Neither Gabe nor I has slept. My head aches and I feel that slightly surreal, off-balance feeling I used to get after a rough night with Freya when she was a tiny baby. The girls are still fast asleep, so we stumble down the hallway in darkness toward the living room. Halfway down the hall I crash into our fiddle-leaf plant, upending it and cracking the terra-cotta pot. It lands on my toe.

The pain is breathtaking.

"Fuck," I shout-whisper. "*Fuck.*"

The floor is covered in dirt and shards of the pot. The sad-looking (and surprisingly expensive) plant that I have nurtured for months lies on its side, its roots exposed. It feels like a metaphor. Particularly since, like my life, I have no idea how to clean it up. Gabe turns on a lamp, then drops to his knees, gently manipulating my toe in his fingers. Yesterday's frenetic energy is gone, and suddenly he seems almost Zen-like in his calm.

"Don't think it's broken," he says. While I hop to the couch, he goes to the kitchen and returns with a bag of frozen peas wrapped in a tea towel. He kneels before me, places it on my toe. "You okay?"

I nod. But I'm not. A tear slides down my cheek.

"What happens if I stub my toe and you're not here?"

Unlike the broader vision of life without him, there's something about this specific situation that fills me with loss. Gabe is the first aid man, always has been. He's not squeamish about blood or pus. When the girls hurt themselves it's Daddy they run to. Daddy, who is calm in the face of chaos and distress. But if Gabe is in jail, the girls will shout for me when they have a bloody nose or a grazed knee. I'll be the one to get out the first aid box, the frozen peas. It'll be up to me to bandage them up and send them on their way. And I will do it. But I'll do it with a broken heart.

Gabe is quiet for a long while. "What if I didn't go to the police?"

It feels like a trick question. "But you have to."

"Maybe not. I've been thinking: If the police discover the connection, I could just say I didn't recognize her. We'd only met a couple of times; it's plausible. The rest of my story stands. She came to the cliff because Max cheated. She jumped."

I try to work through the ramifications of what he's saying, searching for gaps in his logic. But my thoughts are so tangled I don't know which way is up. "But—"

"The thing is," he continued, "we're assuming that if Max knows, he'll tell the police. But I'm not sure he will."

"Of course he will," I say. "Why wouldn't he?"

"Max Cameron isn't the nice guy everyone thinks he is, Pip. He has another side to him. You don't get to where he is without making a few deals with the devil."

I'm reminded that Max filmed us. It felt out of character with the Max I thought I knew. What else don't I know about him? Maybe Gabe is right. Maybe Max won't pursue this.

"Think about it. Amanda was furious with him. This has saved him a messy, expensive divorce. He might not be interested in where she died or who she was with."

"But what if someone else makes the connection? The police?"

"Like I said, I didn't recognize her. I'm as surprised as they are to find out who she was. Besides, Max and Amanda have a beach house here and it's a well-known suicide spot; it's not unfathomable that she would come here to take her life. It's a coincidence, pure and simple."

I've never wanted to believe anything more. And yet I'm afraid to believe that it could be this simple.

Down the hall, a door opens and two little girls in pajamas scurry out, teddies in hand.

"Daddy!" they cry as they break into a trot. We turn to face them, pasting false smiles on our faces.

"Can I have strawberries for breakfast?" Asha asks.

"Okay," I say to Gabe quietly as Asha runs headlong at me. "We won't say anything."

28

PIPPA

"Dada."

Freya was a year old. It was 7:30 A.M. She was in her high chair playing with a piece of toast that I'd put on her tray. That was when she said it. Two clear syllables. Da-da. But Dada wasn't here.

It had been twenty-four hours since I'd seen him.

When his energy had started to return a few weeks earlier, I'd allowed myself to hope that things might be getting better. And indeed he *had* stopped sleeping around the clock. Unfortunately, things quickly went the other way. Now, as far as I could tell, he wasn't sleeping at all.

The speed of the transition was what alarmed me. One day, out of the blue, he mentioned something about going out for drinks after work. He went out the next night too, and the one after that. I knew he was drinking on these nights; it was impossible to hide it. I began to wonder, though, if that was all he was doing. I knew some of his younger colleagues did cocaine, but Gabe was in his thirties, he had a child. He also had an addictive personality, I realized.

I started to nag him about it. "Gabe, it's nearly six in the morning," I'd said to him last Saturday morning when he crawled into bed after a night out. "Where have you been?"

"We don't have plans today," he said testily. "What does it matter?"

"I was worried."

"You worry too much."

Now, as I listened to Freya's first word, the question came to me: *How long will you live like this?*

It felt like a betrayal even to think it. Obviously, I could never leave Gabe. The idea was as ridiculous as leaving Freya. Eventually, he'd come back. After all, his adolescent black periods had ended. This phase would pass too. I just needed to wait it out.

After Freya finished her breakfast, I glanced out the window, checking again for Gabe. It was a workday for me, and Freya was going to child care. I didn't need his help. I had our routine down pat. Each morning, we showered together and got ready for the day. I packed our bags, while she sat on the kitchen floor and banged the pots and pans. It wasn't terrible. We had a roof over our heads, money in the bank.

When we were ready, I picked up Freya and our bags and headed out the door just in time to see Gabe pull up in an Uber.

"Off to work?" he asked cheerfully, taking the steps up the porch.

He kissed Freya's cheek, then mine. He reeked of whiskey. He was wearing his suit from the day before, but his shirt was buttoned up wrongly and untucked. One trouser leg was rucked up and his sock was missing.

"Why are your clothes like that?" I asked.

He looked down and, seeing the state of himself, chuckled. "I'm a mess, aren't I?" He reached for Freya, but I yanked her away.

"What's wrong?" he asked.

My gaze was still caught on the missing sock. I couldn't look away from it.

"Have you been with a woman?"

At first, he looked confused, amused even. Then he looked down at himself.

When he looked up again, his expression was blank. It was as though he couldn't think of another explanation for his missing sock, even though there must have been one, surely. After everything I'd put up with, every blind eye I'd turned . . . he couldn't have been with another woman. He couldn't because I didn't have the capacity to withstand it.

Gabe still hadn't spoken, but his expression had become re-signed. *Resigned.* The most hateful of all emotions.

Freya put her arms out toward Gabe, and I pulled her away. How long had it been since she said "dada"? How long had it been since I wished that Gabe were here with us? It was astonishing how much your life could change between locking your front door and getting into the car.

Gabe dropped to his knees. "Oh God, Pip. Oh God."

"Oh God *what*?" I demanded. "Were you with a woman?"

Like a fool, I was still hoping desperately it wasn't true. Part of me wanted him to lie to me, so that I could keep lying to myself. Perhaps all of me wanted that.

But he nodded.

I thought of all the other nights he'd stayed out. When was the last time I'd asked him about it? *Why* hadn't I asked him? What was *wrong* with me? Was this my fault?

It was strange, then, the way we snapped into our roles. There was no emotion, just an exchange of facts. For two emotional people, perhaps it was the only way we could get through it.

"Who?"

"A bartender. At Young and Jackson."

"Do you love her?"

"No."

"Then why did you . . . ?"

"I don't know." He went quiet and still. Then, suddenly, he smacked himself in the face with his hand, once, and then again. He made his hand into fist.

"Stop it," I said. And he did.

I closed my eyes. It felt undeniable. That this was *it*. All the problems we'd had—all the nights out, the drinking, the ups and downs—they had been terrible but, ultimately, they hadn't broken our vows. They hadn't breached our marriage contract. But this . . . this was different. Our one nonnegotiable had always been loyalty. And what was infidelity if not a lapse in loyalty?

Still on his knees, he grasped the hem of my shirt. "It will never happen again, Pippa. I swear. I will kill myself before I'll let that happen."

It wasn't the first time he'd used that kind of emotive language. It worked to throw me off balance.

"You were right—I need help. I haven't been okay for a while now. I need to see a psychiatrist. Something is wrong with me; I know it is. Normal people don't cheat on the woman they love with a bartender they don't care about."

He knew the buttons to press, the things I needed to hear. It was cruel and comforting and humiliating in its mind-fuckery.

"Let me prove how sorry I am by getting help and becoming the man you deserve. The father Freya deserves."

It's shocking how easy I made it for him. How, despite what he had told me, I actually felt hopeful. He wanted to get help. He *needed* it. And so, at what should have been the lowest point of my life, I felt my heart lift. This was what I'd been waiting for.

I made an appointment for him within the hour.

29

AMANDA

I am starting to wonder where I am. It's not heaven or hell. Not even purgatory. I'm still on earth, but removed; everywhere and nowhere at once.

It makes me question . . . what's next? Or is this it? Will I spend eternity like this, suspended between life and death? I wonder if it's to do with the suddenness of my demise. The unexpectedness of it. Perhaps someone upstairs is scrambling to complete the paperwork? Or maybe I won't be going upstairs at all.

I am, after all, no angel.

Max is in my wardrobe again. It's the second time he's been in there today. I'm not sure what he's doing, and judging by his uncertainty he feels the same. He opens a drawer, pushes my underwear to one side, closes it again. What does he expect to find? Then he just steps back and stares at my dresses, my jeans, my neatly folded T-shirts.

He's already looked through the photographs on my camera and those I saved to my computer recently. Clearly he hasn't found what he's looking for.

He hasn't been in the office all week. Not surprising, some might say, given his wife's unexpected death, but it is surprising to me. The office, after all, is Max's church. His yoga studio. His place of work, but also his place of equilibrium. In the past twenty-five years, the only time I've seen him spend this long away from it was when we were on holiday and after his hernia operation. I wonder if I should be flattered.

It's the visit from the police that's got him rattled. The young officers, a man and a woman, arrived a couple of hours ago with my wallet and jewelry and other personal effects. They told Max my car would need to be collected, and they provided its location.

"It's on a small residential street, but the residents have been informed that it is there, so there's no rush. And there are car collection services you can use if you don't want to do it yourself."

They handed him my keys, a heavy bunch made heavier by the brass penguin-shaped key ring I'd added to make it easier to find them in my handbag. Max always laughed at my keys.

"One day the ignition will fall out under the weight of those things," he said, even though it had been years since I'd driven a car that required me to insert keys.

As he took them from the police, he turned them over in his hand. It must have looked like he was examining them with sadness, but I knew better.

"Where is the data stick?" he asked. "The USB?"

The key ring USB had been a present from Max. It was silver and engraved with my name and had enough capacity to store all of my photographs. USBs had always eluded me; they were impossible to find when you needed them and then lost a moment later. How many times had I stridden around the house, asking Max where my USB was?

"Now you'll always know where to find it," he'd said when he gave it to me. "And everyone will know it's yours."

The ladies at tennis had laughed at the gift. *That's what you get for your birthday when you're married to Max Cameron?* I understood the joke. It *was* funny. But it was also perfect. I never took it off my key ring, unless it was plugged into my computer.

"This is all we were given," the young police officer said. "But I'll make a note to ask about it."

"I'd appreciate that," Max said.

After they left, he'd gone to my study and opened my computer again. Apart from the photographs, which he'd already seen, there wasn't much there that would interest him. Mostly I used my computer to edit photographs, google handbags, and search for exercise workouts. He'd tired of it quickly, and that's when he went to the wardrobe. Eventually he tired of that too.

"Why did you take the USB with you to jump off a cliff?" he says out loud.

In the master bedroom, he sits on the bed and picks up the framed photograph on my bedside table. It had been taken the Christmas before last. We'd spent it in the Whitsundays on a yacht, just the two of us. In the picture, I am wearing a red caftan and we are each holding a glass of champagne. He closes his eyes for a moment and rests the photograph against his chest.

He returns the photograph to the bedside table and then, as if on a whim, he opens my top drawer. It is there, next to some bobby pins and a bottle of multivitamins for perimenopause, that he sees the article about "the hero of The Drop" with a picture of Gabe Gerard's handsome face.

Max pulls the article out of the drawer. He recognizes the picture, of course. He was the one who'd showed it to me a few weeks ago. He'd been pleased to see that Gabe was doing well, and so had I. But that didn't explain why the article is now in my bedside drawer.

Max puts a hand to his temple as he tries to make sense of it.

"Amanda," he whispers, "what did you do?"

30

AMANDA

Falling in love with Max was, at best, an inconvenience. At worst, it was a fucking disaster. People always talk about love like it's a magical thing, a gift from the gods, a sunbeam of euphoria from above! But it's horrible, being in love. The vulnerability it exposes. The person it makes you. It sent me nutty for a while. Made me lose my edge.

It started with little things. The faintly desperate pitch of my voice when I suggested Max make it home in time for dinner. The way I stuck to his side at dinner parties when I knew my role was to work the room. How I found myself thinking about him all the time.

I started making phone calls to his office, just to say hello. Max was unfailingly polite but his mind, I knew, was elsewhere. He had always worked a lot, but while he was growing the business I barely

saw him. His TV and newspaper business was doing well, but online media was the goal. He was so hungry for it. The internet was
still niche, and Max had decided it was the way of the future. He
wasn't wrong, of course; he rarely was. But that meant very little to
me when I was alone at home night after night.

It was only natural that, after a while, I began to question if
Max really was where he said he was. Growing up with a philan-
dering father teaches you to stay vigilant. I adopted the expected
rituals. I checked his phone while he was in the shower. I eaves-
dropped when he left the room to take a phone call. I scanned his
emails when his computer was left open and unlocked. I never found
any evidence of infidelity. But there *was* one thing I often wondered
about.

It was midweek, and I'd woken in the dead of night to find Max
hadn't come to bed. On my way to the kitchen to get a glass of water, I found Max in his study, sitting in the glow of his laptop, fully
dressed, even though it was three or four in the morning. There
were two things about this that caught my attention. First, he was
using a laptop I'd never seen before. And second, his face was crum-
pled, as if he was on the verge of tears.

He looked startled when he saw me in the doorway and immediately his expression changed to one of impatience. "Go back to
bed, love. It's just work."

I did what he said. But I didn't go back to sleep. When he eventually came into the bedroom, I watched in the darkness as he put
the laptop into the safe in the walk-in wardrobe. From then on, I
was obsessed with that laptop. I knew there'd be a time when he
left it out or forgot to lock the safe. And I planned to be ready for
that day.

. . .

I was desperately lonely. The kind of loneliness that claws at your insides. I found it hard to concentrate on photography. I still accepted invitations to take photos at events that interested me, but it became more of a hobby than a career. After all, we didn't need the money, and two big careers were a lot to manage. That's what I told myself, at least.

I drank a lot, alone at night. I slept a lot during the day. At functions, we looked like an adoring couple. Max always spoke about me with the utmost respect. He made playful comments about how good I was to put up with him. When he looked at me, even though I knew it was part of the act, it did something to my insides. I wanted the way he looked at me to be real. I wanted the things he said to be true. I yearned for a real marriage, one that was bigger than the exchange of loyalty for fidelity. But that wasn't the deal I'd made.

And so I created a life for myself with Pilates, tennis, taking pictures of beautiful people and beautiful things. I made friends with women I found superficial, and I started to become superficial myself. I bought things I didn't want. I renovated the kitchen and bathrooms and then renovated them again. I hired stylists, for me and for my house and for the garden. I learned to cook at expensive cooking schools that paired the meals with wine and featured celebrity chefs.

Once, after one such cooking course, I re-created a Spanish feast at home—sautéed chorizo, garlic prawns, seafood paella. Max had promised he'd be home on time. I lit candles, put on some music, wore a flamenco-style dress.

Max arrived home fifteen minutes late, which wasn't bad for him. But then he'd looked around as if confused. "What's all this?"

"Dinner," I said proudly. "I told you I was cooking Spanish tonight!"

In his defense, he did look ashamed. He closed his eyes and swore under his breath. He was apologetic when he said, "I have to go back to the office. I'm so sorry. It can't be avoided."

I'm not sure who was more surprised when I threw the paella at the wall. The worst part was that it was very unsatisfying. There was no thud or smash. Just rice and seafood all over my new Shaker cabinetry and marble benchtop.

Careful, Amanda, I thought. *You're following your heart. Look what it's doing to you.*

"Sorry," Max said again, and then he went to the bedroom, changed his clothes, returned with another briefcase. "I'll make it up to you, I promise."

He stepped over the paella as he left.

When I was forty-one, I had a late period. Not very late. Two days. But it was unusual for me. And when you don't have much else to do, you notice these things.

"My period is late," I said to Max when he came home from work that night. It was after midnight, and I'd been staring into the dark for hours. "I'll do a pregnancy test in the morning, and if I am I'll take care of it. I just thought I would . . . should . . . let you know."

Max came around to my side of the bed, sat down, and switched on my lamp. "Are you all right?"

It wasn't the question I was expecting. That's probably why, though my eyes filled with tears as I said it, I answered, "Yes."

He slid into bed beside me that night and held me close. It had been years since we'd fallen asleep like that. And in the morning, instead of heading off to work, he canceled his meetings and changed into casual clothes.

"Shall I go to the pharmacy to get the test?" I asked him.

"How about we just have breakfast together first," he suggested.

So we ate breakfast, talking about everything other than the crisis we were facing. I couldn't remember the last time we'd breakfasted together. I loved every minute of it.

Then, while I loaded the dishes into the dishwasher, Max said, "I'll go get the test now."

When he returned, I went into the en suite while he sat on the bed and waited. When I emerged a couple of minutes later, he stood.

"Not pregnant," I said, holding up the stick showing only one line.

Max closed his eyes, his relief palpable. "Just one of those things, eh?"

"I guess so."

He told me to make a doctor's appointment, just to make sure everything was okay. Then he kissed my forehead, got dressed, and went to work, and I crawled back into bed and wept.

31

PIPPA

(NOW)

Our morning routine is different. It doesn't look different—in fact, to an outsider, it would be conspicuous in its sameness—but I feel the difference and I know Gabe does too. We go about our tasks—making cereal, unloading the dishwasher, cutting up strawberries and placing them in bento-style lunch boxes—with careful precision. We talk to the girls in a louder, more intentional way, as if we are *Play School* presenters rather than weary parents.

"I don't want my strawberries cut up!" Asha cries. "And no sandwich this time!"

The girls are cranky and on edge, perhaps picking up on our energy. There are three sets of tears before 8:00 A.M., all Freya's, mostly caused by Asha (although, in her defense, her crimes were "eating too loudly," "singing," and "looking at me"). As for Asha, she is inconsolable to learn that it is Tuesday, "because words that start with *t* make me sad." Asha's ability to understand and communicate her emotions always arouses equal measures of fear and pride in me. A few months ago, I found her lying in her room with the curtains drawn and the lights off because "I want the outsides to be as dark as I feel on the inside." The whole episode had lasted only thirty minutes, but I'd been alarmed enough to book an emergency appointment with a child psychologist, who declared Asha a "delight" and also "one we need to keep an eye on." Luckily, I'm an expert in keeping an eye on people. I make a mental note to talk to the psychologist about her recent trouble with "t" words, and avert catastrophe in the present by pointing out that Tim Tams make her happy.

When they finally leave for preschool with Gabe, I seek comfort in my regular activities. I organize the buckets of toys, placing like with like, removing the pieces of Lego from the bottom of the basket of dolls, until everything is in order. I go through the girls' closets, removing clothes that are too small or too worn, arranging them in bags by size for donation. Then I make a list of wardrobe deficits—new underwear for Asha, warm coat for Freya, leggings and pajamas for both.

As I perform each task I find myself wondering: What do the police know? What does Max? Are Johnno and Aaron at the station right now, talking about how they can't believe they were duped, that Gabe had always seemed like such a nice normal guy? And what about Max? Is he truly the kind of monster who wouldn't care what happened to his wife? And then there's the inescapable question: No matter which way this goes, will I ever be able to live with myself?

Gabe will be out for most of the day. After dropping off the girls he'll go for a surf; then he's going to help Dad clean out the gutters. "He's a godsend," Mum had said when Gabe offered his services. Mum was, rightly, worried about Dad getting up on the ladder

("He'll do his hip and then who will have to look after him?"), but Dad flat-out refused to pay someone to do the gutters for him. Fortunately, Gabe stepped into the breach. I wasn't the only one who relied on him; the entire family did.

Turning my attention from domestic to paid work, I sit at my laptop and complete an application for probate. Then I sit through a meeting about a complicated will dispute. I am answering an inquiry to my website about my services when out of the corner of my eye I see the figures appear at my back door.

"Surprise!"

I scream.

"Sorry," Kat says, sliding open the door. She gives me a strange look. Mei is with her. They are rugged up in coats, and their faces look pink and flushed. "We're going to the Pantry. Wanna come? Apparently, they've got the clam chowder on."

The Pantry is a new café on the main street, next to the pub—a little shopfront that butts up against a grassy area that, in turn, butts up against the beach. Last week Mum tried the clam chowder and declared it the best she'd ever had. (I pointed out that she hadn't had a lot of clam chowder before, but she said that was beside the point.)

"Come on," Mei says. "We'll have you back at your desk in an hour."

I want to protest, but Mei is already getting my coat, and there's something about the gentle authority of this that I am helpless to resist.

On the short walk to the café our conversation focuses on the light and trivial. Dad and his obsession with crosswords. (He thinks they stave off dementia.) Property prices. Kat's suspected scalp skin cancer that turned out to be a stain from her box hair dye. Asha's decision to consume only strawberries from now on. What surprises me is how easily I play my part in the discussion, as if drawing on muscle memory. It feels like it should be a pleasure, but today it leaves me feeling empty. I am incapable of conversing properly with my sister now that I am keeping this secret from her. Maybe from now on our relationship will be nothing more than this, a series of repetitive brain spasms.

"Table for three?" Dev says when we arrive at the café.

Dev is the proprietor of the Pantry. He took over the premises three months ago. Previously it was called the Lunch Basket and was run by a husband and wife who always looked irritated when you wanted to order something. Dev, on the other hand, is a thirty-something hospitality natural fresh from the city. He remembers customers' names and coffee orders, gives coloring books to cranky kids, and offers free desserts to old ladies who've finished their coffee and have nowhere else to go. The town had lost their minds when he arrived, and now the only complaint is how hard it is to get a table. But today, with the weather being nice, most people are sitting outside at the tables Dev has set up on the grass, and there is plenty of space inside. He shows us to a window table and says, "I'll leave you to peruse the menu."

"So," Mei says, when Dev has left, "we have an announcement."

I notice suddenly that Kat and Mei are holding hands.

"We're pregnant!" they say together.

Kat reaches into her bag, pulls out a small white card, and pushes it across the table. I gasp as I clock the familiar black square, the scratches of white, the abstract blob in the center.

"Kat is carrying," Mei says proudly, and as soon as she says it, I've never seen anything so obvious. Kat's face is rounder. Her breasts are larger. Her hair is shiny and thick and lustrous. She appears both healthier and more tired at the same time.

I slide out of my seat and throw my arms around them jointly, burying my face in Kat's lovely, thick pregnancy hair. I remain there for several seconds, joy washing through me, before returning to my seat. "Congratulations! This is the best news."

"I'm fourteen weeks along," Kat says. "I know you usually tell people at twelve weeks but I'm superstitious. This is the first time I've eaten out in months; the morning sickness has been too horrendous for me to stand the smells."

As if on cue, Dev places a bowl of clam chowder on the next table along. Kat turns green. "Oh God. I think I'm going to . . ." She leaps from her seat and dashes to the bathroom.

"Wow, that's some morning sickness," I say, watching her disappear.

When I turn back to Mei, I'm surprised to find that her expression is serious.

"What's wrong?" I ask.

"I know, Pip."

I don't have to feign my confusion. "You know *what*?"

"I *know*." Mei glances around and lowers her voice. "I know it was Amanda Cameron on the cliff."

The adrenaline spikes in my blood immediately.

"I've been following it, Pip. I read in the paper that she'd died unexpectedly. I used to work for Max too, remember?"

It's funny, but I had forgotten. I hadn't even considered the fact that she would make the connection.

"Yes, it was Amanda," I admit when I realize I have no choice. "But it was a coincidence, Mei. Gabe didn't even recognize her. She came to the cliff to jump, that's all."

"Then I assume Gabe has told the police of their connection?"

I don't reply. Mei nods. It's almost as if she's not surprised. It puzzles me. Mei knows Gabe pretty well. She loves him. She knows he wouldn't harm anyone.

"He didn't mention that he knew Amanda because it would have looked bad."

"Yes," she says. "It would."

The silence between us drags on for several seconds.

"Gabe wasn't involved in her death," I say. "You know that, right?"

But before she can answer, the door to the bathrooms swings open, revealing a slightly less green-looking Kat. Mei leans forward. "I haven't told Kat about this. She's pregnant and having a rough time of it, and I don't want to worry her. But I don't believe it was a coincidence that Amanda was on that cliff."

"Guys," Kat says when she reaches us, "I don't think I can stay inside with the chowder smell. Can we move to an outside table?"

Kat and Mei call Dev over and a flurry of explanations and congratulations ensue. I muster up a smile but I'm too shocked by my exchange with Mei to engage in any of it.

"Right this way," Dev says, taking our menus. "Coming, Pippa?"

I nod and gather up my things.

You're right, I want to say to Mei. *It wasn't a coincidence. But it wasn't Gabe's fault. It was mine.*

32

PIPPA

Dr. Ravi, Gabe's psychiatrist, was a kindly man with a thick gray beard and a pleasantly chaotic office. His vibe, according to the reviews I'd found online, was "old school," but in a good way. After Gabe's first appointment, he'd echoed the reviewers' enthusiasm.

He really listened.
I felt understood.
He made me believe I could be helped.

Gabe and I sat across the desk from him expectantly. It was Gabe's third appointment, but the first time I had joined him. In the lead-up, there'd been a mountain of paperwork to complete, covering everything from Gabe's family history of mental disorders to long-ago school reports, as well as questionnaires for Gabe and me to complete. There was also a questionnaire to be completed by a boss or work colleague, but we had decided to skip that one to maintain Gabe's privacy. Now the psychiatrist was prepared to give us a diagnosis, and I was holding out hope that he might offer a treatment—preferably in pill form—that would fix Gabe.

"Have you heard of attention deficit hyperactivity disorder?" Dr. Ravi asked.

I had, but only in passing. It conjured up an image of a naughty, fidgety little boy in third grade. "You think Gabe has ADHD?"

"I thought that ADHD only affected children," Gabe added.

"It is commonly diagnosed in children, but about half of children with ADHD will continue to experience symptoms into adulthood. And given what I've learned about your childhood, Gabe, it seems likely that your symptoms could have been overlooked due to the lack of close parental involvement while you were young."

The more Dr. Ravi told us, the more sense it made. Gabe had almost every symptom: trouble focusing or hyperfocus; physical restlessness; rapid or impulsive speech; disorganization; trouble with impulse control; periods of prolonged depression. The psychiatrist recommended a combination of medication and therapy, and he referred Gabe to an ADHD coach.

Gabe started taking the prescribed stimulants immediately. I bought every book I could find on ADHD. Gabe was going to be the poster boy for ADHD management, I decided, and I would be the poster wife.

Gabe threw himself into his new identity as an adult with ADHD. He met with his coach, he followed his new routines, he downloaded the apps. It took a while to get the medication right. At first it seemed to make him even more manic than before, but Dr. Ravi adjusted the doses, and eventually he settled down. The change was nothing short of miraculous. He stopped going out all night; in fact, he hardly went out all. He was promoted once, and then again. He was making so much money that we bought a house in a nice neighborhood with plans to renovate it.

Most evenings were spent on the couch, watching home-renovation shows and discussing vaulted ceilings, and weekends were spent at the new house, watching Gabe talk to tradesmen and warning him not to be a pest. He was fascinated by their crafts-manship and peppered the tradies with questions as they worked. Often, after we left the house, we'd wander through the streets of our new neighborhood with Freya riding on Gabe's shoulders.

We never talked about the infidelity he'd confessed to. In those moments when I couldn't help but think about it, I told myself it was a good thing; it had been the catalyst for Gabe getting the help he needed and turning his life—our lives—around. All that mattered was that I had Gabe back. The real Gabe. He was finally fixed, and now we could live in peace.

33

AMANDA

"I'd like to speak to the investigators in charge of my wife's suicide. . . . Amanda Cameron. . . . Yes, I'll hold."

Max is in the kitchen. On the counter in front of him, the newspaper is open to the article about Gabe saving lives at The Drop. He stares at it as if the answers he's looking for will suddenly leap from the page. It's affirming to see that despite our troubles, Max still cares about what happened to me. It's probably born out of a desire to protect himself, but it heartens me nevertheless.

I can tell the moment the person comes to the phone, because Max stands tall again. "Yes, hello, it's Max Cameron here. I have a few questions about my wife's death. Do you mind telling me from where, exactly, she jumped?"

He glances down at the newspaper.

"I see." His eyes close. "Yes. I know the place. And one other question, if I may. You mentioned someone was with her before she . . . Yes. Do you happen to have the person's name?"

He listens a moment. Then the hand not holding the phone clenches into a fist. I wait for him to say something—that the man is a former employee, that Max had fired him. When he doesn't, I'm not surprised. It makes sense, under the circumstances, that Max would want to deal with this himself.

He ends the call, puts the phone down on the counter, and looks out the window. I can practically see his brain ticking. It's amazing how often people underestimate Max. They take him at face value, seeing a thoughtful, intelligent, considerate gentleman. Don't get me wrong—he is all these things. But Max didn't get to where he is by being kind and lovely. When he needs to be, he's as ruthless as the next guy—with one difference: No one ever sees him coming.

34

AMANDA

After the pregnancy that never was, Max and I entered a new season of our marriage. I pushed my feelings for him to the side and, instead of focusing on what I wasn't getting from my husband, I focused on what I *was*: a comfortable life with a good man. Experiences and possessions beyond the wildest dreams of most people. It wasn't so bad.

Instead of nagging Max to come home earlier, I waited up for him. Often, when he arrived home at midnight, I would have wine and a cheese platter waiting for him. Max didn't seem to find this irritating, the way he had with my demands that he be home in time for dinner. In fact, he told me once that he looked forward to our new ritual. Sometimes we sat up until two or three in the morning, just chatting idly.

After a while, he started to open up to me. He described the pressure he'd been under to get the online business up and running.

He told me about the two occasions on which he'd thought he was going to lose everything—the house, the business. One of those times, I discovered, had been the night of the paella. I made him promise that from now on he would share his problems with me, no matter how bad. "Believe it or not," I said, "I can handle it."

Max regarded me for a long time then. "Actually," he said, "I do believe it."

A few weeks later, I came home early from a charity function one evening and found Max sitting at the dining room table with his head in his hands.

"What's wrong?" I asked him.

He didn't even look up. "It's all so much more expensive than I thought."

I pulled up a chair beside him. The online business again, I ascertained. He'd spent months setting it up. I thought it would have taken off by now. Clearly Max had thought so too. "But I thought it was all ready to go?"

"It is. But the bank has cold feet and won't advance the final payment. And I have no money left. There are no more investors. At least, none that I would want to call on."

I thought about that for a moment. "Why don't you call on them anyway?"

Max didn't reply.

"Sometimes," I said thoughtfully, "the road to our destination leads us in a direction we don't want to take. But does it matter, in the end, if it gets us where we want to go?"

It felt like the right thing to say. It was the kind of thing Max himself might have said. Perhaps that's why he lifted his head. After several seconds, he smiled. I wish I could have bottled that smile. It was the way you want the man you love to smile at you.

"You're right," he said.

The next morning, I made coffee while Max showered and dressed. When he emerged, he was bright-eyed and focused. I fed him, pumped him up, and then waved him off at the door, still in my nightgown.

"Go get it done," I said to him.

By the end of the day, Max had the money he needed. In desperate times, sometimes we do desperate things.

The online business moved us into a new stratosphere of wealth. We bought a new house—a mansion. We had a swimming pool, a tennis court, a private cinema. An underground car park with room for twelve vehicles. It was ridiculous. I adored it all.

I filled my days with enjoyable, purposeless things like tennis and shopping and visits to art galleries. I started a "classics" book club. I took photographs of my friends' children and grandchildren and gave them as gifts. And I kept an eye on Max. If he left his phone or computer lying around, I'd take a quick look. I never found anything incriminating—usually it was mind-numbingly boring—but it didn't stop me. I still wondered about the laptop that remained locked in the safe; I had never seen it again.

I'd like to say that I drew the line at spying, but shamefully that wasn't the case. On the rare occasions when I came home and saw Max's car already there, I always took advantage of it. There was one such occasion that stands out in my memory. It was a weekday, around 5:00 P.M. That alone was reason to be suspicious. Max was never home from work by five unless he was ill—or, perhaps, up to something.

When I noticed his car in the garage, I slid inside quietly. It was a mild evening, and he was on the patio, talking on the phone with the French doors ajar. He was in his suit, minus the tie and the jacket. His sleeves were rolled up.

I crept as close as I could and concealed myself behind the curtains. Max's back was ramrod straight, and he was pacing.

"I understand," he was saying, "and I'm grateful for your support, but I'm now in a position to return your investment. I'm sure you can appreciate why I'd want to do that."

Even though it was clearly a business call, and I hadn't stumbled on evidence of an affair, I continued to listen anyway; I appreciated the calm, authoritative way that Max handled himself.

"That may be the case, but as I've delivered great returns for you, I'd like to think that we're even."

It was obvious that the person on the other end of the phone was not happy, which was odd. What kind of person would get angry about someone wanting to *return* their money?

"I'm sorry you feel that way," Max said finally, "but I've already decided. The money will be transferred back into your account at the end of the month."

Max ended the call and looked out over the pool and gardens. I crept from the room and acted as if I'd just arrived home.

"Max?" I called.

Max was in the same spot on the patio, but when he heard my voice he turned around. "Hello."

"You're home early!"

He came inside and greeted me with the customary perfunctory kiss. It was one of those small marital rituals that always brought me immense pleasure. We went to the kitchen, and I opened a bottle of wine.

"So why are you home at this hour?" I asked, pushing Max's glass across the counter to him.

Max lifted his glass and touched it to mine. "Just had a few phone calls to make, so I decided to make them from here. Nothing for you to worry about."

The truth was, I knew what kind of person Max would want to return money to: one of those shady investors. Someone crooked. The kind of investor Max might have turned to when he was desperate, but someone he would definitely want off his books now.

Still, as long as Max wasn't talking to a secret lover, I was going to take his advice and not worry about it.

"All right," I said. "I won't."

35

PIPPA

(NOW)

"Why don't we go out for an early dinner?" Gabe suggests.

He looks weary. It's 4:00 P.M. and we're standing in the kitchen. The girls have been home, as they don't go to preschool on Wednesdays, and Gabe has had a full schedule of imaginative play, craft, and baking.

"Sure," I say.

After lunch with Kat and Mei yesterday, I'd told Gabe that Mei had figured out it was Amanda on the cliff, but I didn't tell him of her suspicion that it wasn't a coincidence. I was still shocked that Mei could think Gabe could be guilty of something. Particularly since, this time, he was the one protecting me.

We arrive at the Pantry half an hour later. The after-school rush is over but it's still too early for most people to be thinking of dinner, so it's just us and an older couple sharing a fancy-looking ice-cream sundae. The girls look at them enviously.

"Why are they allowed ice cream before dinner?" Asha demands.

"I told them they could," Dev says, appearing like a hero before Asha has a meltdown, "but only if they eat a bowl of brussels sprouts immediately afterward. Would you girls like the same deal?"

The girls look appalled and quickly move on from the ice cream, instead focusing on the colored pencils and paper that Dev has placed on the table.

"What can I get you?" Dev asks us.

Gabe and I order a bottle of wine, apple juice for the girls, and a bowl of chips to get us started. As Dev writes down the order, I think again of my visit to the Pantry the day before and what Mei had said. *I don't believe it was a coincidence.*

"Your mother told me that you handle wills and estates," Dev says, as he tucks his notebook back into his apron. "I've been meaning to do a will. Are you taking new clients?"

"Of course," I say. "Give me a call."

Dev leaves us and returns gratifyingly quickly with the chips. Then, as the girls focus on their coloring, Gabe and I enjoy a few moments of precious silence. For the first time in twenty-four hours my mind feels blank. Numb. Under the circumstances, it's the best I can hope for.

"What happened to the woman who was outside our house?" Asha says out of nowhere.

Her voice is loud in the quiet café. Her eyes are on her drawing. I put my drink down on the table. "Which woman, baby?"

"The one that was on the cliff before the police came."

She reaches blindly for a chip, dunking it in sauce and lifting it to her mouth without looking up from her drawing. Freya, on the other hand, immediately looks up.

I glance at Gabe as I try to activate my brain. We've never had this conversation with the girls. I'd thought it was still a few years off. I'd planned to thoroughly research the best ways to talk to kids about suicide, maybe even consult a psychologist first. Trust kids to interfere with best-laid plans.

"Well . . ."

"Did she jump off the cliff?" Asha asks, looking up. She raises her eyebrows, her expression simultaneously curious and uninterested, as if it is something she'd been meaning to ask about but it isn't of much importance either way. "I heard Nana and Papa saying she jumped. And you and Daddy did too."

Gabe puts down his wine. "It was an accident, baby girl. She walked too close to the edge, and she fell. That's why Mummy and Daddy tell you not to go anywhere near the cliff."

It is classic Gabe: the perfect response. He says nothing to alarm her while also reinforcing the importance of staying away from The Drop. Even now, it makes me fall in love with him a little bit more.

"Did she get dead?" Asha asks.

Both girls stare at us. Even Gabe falters for a second. Eventually he answers the only way he can.

"Yes," Gabe says finally. "She did."

Asha nods wisely. "Her family must be very sad."

"Yes," Gabe says. "I imagine they are."

Asha appears to think about this. Gabe and I don't look at each other.

"Where is the lady now?" she asks.

Her gaze moves back to the rainbow she is drawing. I want to ask her about it. Offer to help. Anything other than answer these questions for my beautiful little girl.

"She's in heaven," Gabe says.

Asha looks at me then. Her expression is slightly different now.

Less wise. All I see is her small round face. The vulnerability of it. I want to take her in my arms and block her ears, so she never has to try to understand any of this stuff.

"With my mum?"

I take a breath in, hold it, then slowly let it go. And I do her the respect of looking her in the eye when I answer. "Yes, baby. With your mum."

36

PIPPA

(THEN)

"I have to tell you something," Gabe said.

I pulled two glasses out of the cabinet, set them on the kitchen counter, and looked at him expectantly. It didn't occur to me to be worried, even though, on reflection, the words "I have to tell you something" rarely preceded anything good. Although, on hearing them, my heart rate didn't speed up. I didn't have the faintest idea what was coming.

It was just that things had been so damn good. Three weeks earlier we'd moved into our stunning new dream home—a four-bedroom renovated Edwardian house with a swimming pool and a rich green lawn. Freya was a delight: a busy but thriving almost two-year-old. We'd just put her to sleep in her big girl bed. We'd even been talking about trying for another baby.

"I'm so sorry."

I thought it must have something to do with money. The house had been so expensive. We'd taken out a mortgage that was a challenge to the risk-averse side of me, but Gabe was so confident that we could afford it. I remember feeling a flash of annoyance at myself. Why had I listened to him? Why hadn't I suggested something smaller and cheaper? Perhaps it was because his boss, Max Cameron, seemed to believe that he could do no wrong? It was hard to imagine that he had anything other than complete job security.

But it wasn't the house.

"There's a little girl," he said.

It should have taken me longer to understand. I should have been confused. I should have asked, "What do you mean there's a little girl?" But I knew. Perhaps I'd been primed for it since learning about the night he spent with the bartender. I assumed it had been more than one, but I hadn't pressed him on it because I couldn't bear to have my fears confirmed.

I broke into silent tears. The kind that fall without effort or noise or even feeling. The kind movie stars cry. It was a strange thought, in among everything else. *I'm crying movie star tears!*

"I got the call a couple of days ago. A woman I used to know . . . she died of a drug overdose."

I closed my eyes, unable to look at him as I listened. Gabe told me he didn't remember the woman, though he had memories of sex, shameful memories that he'd tried to push down. She'd certainly never got in touch to let him know of a baby. The little girl was six months younger than Freya. His name wasn't on the birth certificate. The woman's friend had been the one to identify Gabe as the father. The baby's name was Asha.

There had been a DNA test, of course, but when I finally saw her I realized that we needn't have bothered. Her mother was of

Indian descent, and Asha's eyes were brown and her skin too. But she had Freya's mouth, her chin, her smile. She was Gabe's daughter. Anyone with eyes could have told you that.

I considered leaving him. I considered slapping him. I cycled through every emotion, once and then again. There was a rhythm to it, the way they spiked and settled, spiked, settled. Anger, I realized, was the least painful, so I concentrated my efforts there for a time, but eventually my rage dissipated. Because, unlike the other times Gabe had disappointed me, this time there was another person to consider. A little girl who had just lost her mother. A girl who was currently being cared for in a foster home. Whether or not she stayed there was up to me, Gabe said.

"All right," I said, a week after I'd found out about Asha's existence. "I'll meet her."

The foster home was a modest brick bungalow in a quiet street. There was a swing set in the front yard, and a boy who looked to be around three or four played in a sandpit.

Asha sat between an older woman's legs. She was wearing a yellow polka dot dress and yellow leggings, and she held a blue plastic shovel and ball. When we walked into the garden, Asha looked up at me and smiled. Was it strange that I immediately felt a connection with her? I put it down to the fact that she bore such a strong resemblance to my own child. I didn't look at Gabe. In that moment, perhaps oddly, he'd never felt more irrelevant.

I kneeled, collected the ball that had rolled away from her, and handed it back. She held up her shovel as if to show me.

I'd already decided we were taking her home, but if I hadn't, I would have decided then. *Of course* she was coming home with us.

It was as if she was always destined to be part of our ragtag crew. After we'd played with the ball and shovel for a bit longer, Asha reached for me with her chubby little arms. It was so typical. Gabe created beautiful things, and I took care of them.

37

AMANDA

Max is in the back seat of the Mercedes, his driver, Arnold, up front. For once, he's not looking at his phone. He hasn't opened his computer. A couple of times on the journey he wipes a tear from the corner of his eye. That's the funny thing about Max. He is capable of bad but also good. I forgave him for all of it, loved him for all of it. There was only one thing I couldn't forgive. He knew that. But he did it anyway.

The newspaper on the seat beside him is folded open to the page with the article about Gabe Gerard. It's the only thing he looks at on the whole two-hour drive.

What are you going to do, Max? I wonder, as the car pulls up in the Gerards' street.

He picks up the newspaper, tucks it under his arm, and gets out of the vehicle.

38

AMANDA

(BEFORE)

Max was always a self-confessed security freak. It took some getting used to. The deadlocks, the security systems, the CCTV cameras. The alarms that went back to base. Every time I got used to a new system, he'd install something new and more high-tech. I thought of it as a "man fetish." Some men had car fetishes. For others it was grass or tools or golf. Max lusted after security systems. It never occurred to/me that his obsession with security might spring from a fear for our safety. Until the day that it did.

It was a Tuesday. Max had left for work an hour or so before and I was in the house alone, doing some stretches before my 9:30 A.M. Body Pump class. The first hint that something wasn't right came with the knock on the door. Not the most ominous thing in the world, but this was not how people signaled their arrival at our house. Usually, visitors pressed the intercom at the gate. I would examine their face on a screen while they told me what they wanted, and then I would decide whether or not to open the gates to let them in.

I'll admit, the knock unnerved me, but I was a nervy type. I froze right there on my yoga mat and listened.

There was another knock, this time louder. As I made my way to the door, I remembered that the intercom hadn't been working and Max had said someone was coming to fix it.

I walked through the living room to the foyer. "Who is it?" I said through the door.

"Mrs. Cameron? Sorry to bother you—it's Adam. I work for Max's security team. We're installing a new intercom system today. I just need access to your unit so I can connect it, and then I'd like to run some tests, if that's okay?"

I'd started to open the door even before he finished talking. By the time I saw the two giant men, it was too late to close it again. A boot thudded into the door. It flew backward, taking me with it. My head hit the wall. I was still seeing stars when the door closed again, and the men were inside.

"Please," I said. "Don't hurt me."

The men wore black jeans, T-shirts, stockings over their faces. One was tall and muscular. The other was shorter but wider, like a bodybuilder, with veins bulging from his biceps. They had hands like baseball mitts, with fingers covered in gold rings.

"Don't be scared," the shorter one said. But his unsmiling face and dull gaze did nothing to reassure me.

"I have money. Or jewelry. Whatever you want—you can have it."

The taller man said, "We don't want money." He sounded amused.

"We have some business with your husband that we need to sort out," the shorter one said just as the phone in my hand started to ring. I glanced at the screen. Max.

"Speak of the devil," the shorter man said. His tone told me that this was expected. "Answer it."

I lifted the phone to my ear.

"Amanda?" Max said, before I could speak. His voice was strained. "Are you all right?"

"Yes. But there are two men here."

"*Inside* the house?"

"Yes."

I heard him exhale slowly. "Are you hurt?"

"No. They just said . . . they have some business with you that needs sorting out?" My voice rose in desperation. *Sort out the business,* it said. *For God's sake, sort out the business.*

"Okay." Max took a long breath. "Put me on the phone to them?"

When I held out the phone, neither man looked surprised. The shorter man took it.

"Max? . . . Glad to hear it. . . . She's fine, not a scratch on her. Just a minute."

He handed the phone back to me. I lifted it to my ear.

"The men are going to leave now," Max said. "When they're gone, lock the door and don't answer it for anyone. Don't call the police. I'm on my way home, but I want you to wait on the phone with me until they are gone, all right?"

The men were already gone.

"All right."

When Max arrived home ten minutes later with two security guards in tow, I was still sitting on the floor in the foyer with my back against the wall. It was as though my limbs had frozen into position. Max had to put both arms around me and pull me to my feet to get me to move to the living room. There, he helped me onto the couch, even though I was entirely uninjured apart from the bump to my head.

"I cannot begin to tell you how sorry I am, Amanda."

Max looked worse than I did. His skin was gray. I worried he might be having a stroke or a heart attack. He pressed his fingers into his eye sockets. "When they said they had you . . . I went out of my mind. . . . The idea that they might hurt you . . ."

We sat there for a long time, just holding each other, while Max apologized. In the end, *I* was the one comforting *him*.

I'll never forget those moments, sitting together on the couch like that. I remember thinking: *I didn't realize how much you cared.* That's another funny thing about marriage. Sometimes, when you look back on it, the worst moments are in fact the best.

39

PIPPA

The streets are busy as we make our way home after dinner. As usual, the girls are on their scooters and Gabe and I on foot. It's a mild night and it takes forever to get home because people are out and about, riding bikes, scooting and walking. Freya and Asha see half their preschool class. Gabe and I wave at the parents, but we keep our heads down and don't engage further. I'm not sure I'll ever be able to make small talk with strangers again.

"Interesting that Asha brought up her mother," I say to Gabe.

"I know."

We've always been honest with Asha about the way she came into our family. We talk about it in positive, age-appropriate ways, saying things like, "Freya, you came out of my tummy, but Asha, you had another mummy, and you came out of her tummy before you came to live with us." We read books to the girls about adoption, stepfamilies, and the different ways people become a family. We had framed a picture of Asha's mother and hung it in their room. We told her it was sad that her mother had died, and that her mother had loved her very much. Asha had been completely uninterested, but of course we'd always expected that one day she'd want to know more. It was only a matter of time.

"She pays closer attention than we think," Gabe says. "We need to be more careful about what we say in front of her."

"I agree."

We turn onto our street. Mr. Hegarty is mowing his nature strip. He gives each of the girls a high five as they scoot past. When Gabe and I get close, he stops the mower. The setting sun shines into his eyes, and he lifts a hand to shield them.

"Nice evening for a walk," he says.

We both smile, nod, agree, but my mind is elsewhere and I think Gabe's is too.

"There was a man here earlier asking after you." He squints at us. "Well, technically he asked after Gabe. He pulled up in a fancy black car with a driver. He was probably sixty-odd. Sandy-gray hair. Smart trousers. Collared shirt."

I feel my smile freeze in place.

"Did he say what he wanted?" Gabe asks.

"No. Just asked if I knew Gabriel Gerard and asked which house was yours. I told him I couldn't give out that information, of course. Not that he looked shifty or anything, but you can't be too careful these days, can you?"

I open my mouth to respond, but nothing comes out. My mouth is dry.

"Thank you, Mr. Hegarty," Gabe says, reaching for my hand and squeezing it. "We appreciate your discretion. Especially with our little girls around."

Mr. Hegarty gives us a wave and starts up his mower again. But above the noise of it, Gabe's voice remains in my head. *Our little girls.* Dear God. We have just endangered our little girls.

"It must have been Max," I say to Gabe when we are inside.

He's sitting on the edge of the tub, I'm pacing. The girls, already naked, are streaking up and down the hall, oblivious to the storm brewing around them.

I am both shocked and totally unsurprised. Also, irate with myself. For goodness' sake . . . what did I *think* was going to happen? *Of course* Max had found out. *Of course* he was going to come here. All we've done is make things worse for ourselves by not telling the police. Worse for Gabe.

"It might not have been Max," Gabe says.

"Who else would it be?"

"I don't know." Gabe looks stressed, even though he's keeping his voice calm. "It could have been a police officer. A plainclothes detective, maybe?"

I stop pacing and look at him. "Would that be better?"

He sighs. "I don't know."

"What do we do? What is the plan now?"

I feel like I'm in a Hollywood movie. We're a nice normal couple who find themselves embroiled in something involving the Mob or the government or an underworld gang. The bath, with its floating rubber ducky, is a sickening, bizarre backdrop.

"We do nothing," he says. "Just wait. If anyone knows anything, we'll hear about it soon enough."

As if on cue, his phone rings. He pulls it from his pocket and shows me the screen. The number is withheld. My adrenaline spikes.

Is this what it's going to be like every time the phone rings? Every time someone turns up at the house looking for us?

Gabe turns off the tap and lifts the phone to his ear. "Hello?" We lock eyes. "Yes, speaking."

I watch him, my heart rate climbing.

Gabe scrunches his face up tight, then lets it go. "Damn. Yes. It's my fault. I'm so sorry."

"What is it?" I mouth. I am already steeling myself.

"Yes. Yes, that works for me. I'll be there. Thank you. My apologies again."

He hangs up. "I forgot to take the girls to get their vaccinations."

The flash of rage I feel doesn't completely make sense, even to me. It's wild and furious.

"For fuck's sake!" I scream. "I made the bloody appointment for you! All you had to do was show up!"

It feels amazing to scream at Gabe. It's not something I do. We speak respectfully to each other; we tiptoe around each other's feelings. But there's something about screaming that feels good, particularly given the banality of the subject. This is normal marital irritation. I focus on it.

"I'm sorry," Gabe says. "I had things on my mind."

Like trying not to be imprisoned because of you.

And there it is: the reason I can never yell at him again.

Gabe's gaze flickers to the bathroom doorway. I turn around. Two naked girls stand there, eyes wide. Their parents fighting is something new to them. They appear more curious than frightened.

"Bath time!" I say, in a ridiculously cheerful voice. The stress of the situation has sent me mad.

Asha's gaze travels to the bath and she shakes her head. "More water! And bubbles!" Then she tears off back down the hallway with Freya at her heels.

Gabe picks up the bubble bath and pours it in, turning the bath a sickly pink color. He turns the tap back on.

"I'm sorry," he says again.

I close the lid of the toilet and sit on it. My anger dissipates as fast as it came on. "I don't care about the vaccinations."

"I know."

My shoulders slump and I hold a palm against my forehead. "If Max has been asking around about us, it means he knows you were the one with Amanda before she died. Which means it's only a matter of time until—"

The doorbell rings. The girls squeal. I hear the thunder of feet as they streak to the door.

Gabe turns off the tap again. "Wait!" he and I shout in unison. We grab a towel each and race after them.

"Mummy!" Asha calls as Gabe and I arrive in the hallway. The front door is wide open and Detective Tamil is standing there. "The police are here!"

40

PIPPA

(THEN)

I'd just got out of the shower when I heard the thump. It sounded distinctly like a body hitting floorboards.

It was early, just after 6:00 A.M. Asha had been with us nearly a week. It hadn't been a terrible adjustment, considering. Asha had not been overly distressed. She hardly ever cried. She played with the toys we put out and ate the food we offered. She allowed us to care for her. But there was a guardedness. She didn't smile. I hadn't once heard her laugh.

We'd fallen into a bit of a routine, the way you did with a new baby. Everything was trial and error. We knew that she liked pasta and strawberries. She'd commandeered one of Freya's stuffed frogs, which she carried with her everywhere, and we'd already developed a hearty fear of losing Froggie, the way any parent worried about losing that one toy that would soothe their child. We knew that she hated daytime naps but would fall asleep at 6:00 P.M. and then sleep right through till the next morning. During the day, I was her primary parent, the one she went to instinctively to have her needs met. But this early hour, this short period of time before Freya woke up, had somehow become Gabe's.

When I heard the second thud, I grabbed my robe and raced out of the bedroom.

In the living room, I found Asha sitting up in her high chair. Gabe was on the floor, facedown, his arms and limbs splayed like the police outline of a murder victim. But I barely registered that because of what else was happening.

Asha was laughing.

Gabe saw me. "Watch!" he said.

He jumped up and took a few steps, acting super casual. Then he pretended to catch his foot on the corner of the rug. "Whoa!"

To his credit, it was a good fall. He didn't brace himself or land lightly. He threw himself across the room and landed on his face. I was certain he'd have a bruise tomorrow.

Asha lost it. She thew her head back, slapped her hands against her tray. I'd never heard a laugh like it. It was a dirty laugh, deep and husky and from the soul. She held her stomach. It was the kind of laughter that ends wars, cracks you open, makes everything okay.

Gabe's eyes were glistening with tears. I assumed they were tears of mirth, but then his chin quivered. "She's laughing," he said. "I'm so happy that she's laughing." He pressed his lips to Asha's mop of dark hair and just stayed there for a moment, breathing her in. I forgave him in that moment, as I always knew I would. It was impossible not to forgive this man. Even though I knew that, eventually, this would probably be my downfall.

. . .

Asha's arrival into our family was complicated in many ways. The love part, though, was simple. We all adored her. We adored the crevices in her belly, the pads of fat on the backs of her hands. We adored the way she nestled against my chest when she was tired.

My family knew how she came to be, of course, and they didn't miss a beat. If anything, they worked harder to prove their love for her, to make up for the fact that I was afraid it wouldn't come naturally. They needn't have worried, just as I needn't have. The love was fast and fierce.

If there was a book about adoption, I read it. I knew about reactive attachment disorder. I was on the lookout for signs of trauma, behavioral issues, and hidden disabilities. We followed the professionals' advice to the letter. How else did one follow advice?

We did the cocooning. Stayed home and kept our world small. We carried Asha around in a baby carrier. Gabe and I were the only ones who held her for months on end, the only ones to feed her and put her to bed. She needed to understand that we were her parents, so she would attach to us in a healthy, appropriate way.

For a year, I braced for Asha's regression—the anger, the sadness, the behaviors my books told me to expect. They didn't come. She attached, primarily to me but she liked Gabe too, from afar. She adored Freya, and Freya adored her back.

I also braced for my anger, my sadness. Asha was the product of my husband's affair. Her very existence should have been a painful reminder, a slap in the face. Somehow, though, the opposite was true. Asha was a living breathing embodiment of the magic of Gabe. The beauty that came from the ugliness. She was the payoff for all the pain. If I could have turned back the clock and undone things from our past, I might have—but never at the cost of Asha's existence.

41

AMANDA

(AFTER)

It's funny to watch Max let himself into the Portsea house. Usually, there's a cleaning service that prepares the house for us. When we are planning a visit, I call the service to let them know. They arrive, open the curtains, fill the fridges with groceries, put the towels out and change the sheets on the bed. They put on the heater or air conditioner. They might even light a fire. Thus, this is Max's expectation when he arrives there.

It is fun to watch him fumble for the light switches and then look around, perplexed by the cold dark space. Later, when he tries to warm up with a cup of tea, he'll be surprised to find there is no milk in the fridge. He knows that someone has to put it there, and when he really thinks about it he'll understand that, of course, no one has rung the service, but it will take a while for him to connect the dots. He is someone who has always had domestic things done for him.

He's just set down his bag when his phone starts to ring. He retrieves it from his pocket, frowns at the screen. I can tell by his body language that he doesn't recognize the number. Finally, he accepts the call, putting it on speaker.

"Max Cameron."

"Mr. Cameron? My name is Detective Sergeant Conroy and I—"

"Detective," Max says, his shoulders relaxing. "Is this about my wife?"

A pause. "Not exactly. It's a related matter. Your wife's death has prompted another inquiry that I am hoping you can help us with."

"All right." Max's voice is as cool as ever, but I can sense his wariness.

"Our inquiry relates to a business relationship between NewZ and A.S. Holdings. According to our records, A.S. Holdings provided funds to NewZ for an acquisition."

Max is quiet now. He knows better than to confirm or deny this. After several moments, he pulls out a dining chair and sits.

"Mr. Cameron, some information about this investor has come to light and we'd like to discuss it with you. We'd appreciate it if you could come in to the station for an interview."

"I'm out of town for a few days," Max says. "Is it urgent?"

For a moment, both men hang on the line.

"Anytime in the next week would be all right, I expect," Detective Conroy says.

"Right then. I'll have my lawyer call you and set something up," Max says. After a few seconds he adds, "So this is a financial investigation?"

"Our inquiry is *related* to a financial investigation," the policeman replies.

"And which department are you from?"

The detective pauses, perhaps for dramatic effect. "Homicide."

42

AMANDA

After the men broke into the house, Max stayed home for the rest of the day. That night, we lay on the bed, facing each other. I could see Max's face in the light that traveled in from the hallway. I wondered if we'd ever sleep in full darkness again. I understood the flawed logic of this, given that the men had visited the house in broad daylight, but in my experience fear was rarely logical.

Our security system had been reinstalled and two security guards patrolled the grounds. We were safe—at least that's what Max seemed desperate for me to believe. I wondered if he believed it himself.

"Who were those guys, Max? After what happened, I think you owe me that."

I expected him to fob me off, but perhaps because of the authority in my voice he didn't.

"They work for a man called Arthur Spriggs. Arthur is a business associate of mine. I met him through an acquaintance when I was looking for investors. Suffice to say, Arthur's business endeavors weren't entirely aboveboard, which was why he was so motivated to find legal ways to invest his money."

"To clean it, you mean? Money laundering?"

Max nodded. "It was ill-advised, and I knew that. But at the time I was desperate. Stupidly, I thought the relationship would end when I had enough money to pay him back. But Arthur had found the partnership fruitful and he wanted it to continue."

I remembered the phone call I'd overheard, Max trying to return money. He'd seemed so confident.

"So those men today . . ."

"Were Arthur's way of showing me that I couldn't just call off our arrangement when it suited me." He exhaled loudly.

"So what are you going to do?"

He put a hand on my cheek and looked at me. "I'm going to take care of it."

There was a hardness to Max after that. It wasn't always evident. In public, he appeared to be the same likable man he always was. He championed his charity. His business grew and thrived. But there was something harsh and implacable about him. He wasn't going to be hurt again.

43

PIPPA

Detective Senior Constable Tamil is not alone. She is accompanied by another police officer, a middle-aged man named Conroy. Tamil introduces him, but my brain is too scrambled to take in the details. Instead, Gabe and I wrap towels around the girls, which they immediately start flapping about like wings, with little regard for their dignity.

"Come in," I say to the detectives at the same time as Asha says, "Why aren't you wearing a police hat?"

"I'm a detective," Tamil says. She has the polite but baffled tone of someone who likes children but doesn't have any herself. "Detectives don't wear uniforms. But I do have a badge. Would you like to see?"

She gets out her badge and Freya and Asha look at it for a split second before losing interest.

"Why aren't you driving a police car?" Asha asks, glancing through the window at the unmarked car in the driveway. Her towel is now around her head.

"I *do* drive a police car," Tamil says. "But it's not a blue-and-white one. Mine is a police car for detectives."

"Does it have a siren?"

"Yep. But it's only for emergencies." Tamil meets my gaze over the top of the girls' heads. "Sorry to take you by surprise. We were down this way today and we thought we'd try to cover off a few last details with you, Gabe, before we finalize the suicide from the other night. If you have some time now, it will save us another trip."

"Of course," Gabe says, charming as ever. "Come on in."

We file down the hall into the living room. Asha is now holding Tamil's hand.

My mind is going a million miles an hour. First, I wonder if Detective Conroy could have been the man asking Mr. Hegarty about us, but I quickly discount it. This man is a police officer. He would know exactly where we lived. Next, I think about the wording Tamil just used. *Finalize* the suicide, she'd said. Surely she wouldn't have said that if new evidence or information had come to light.

"Why don't you have a seat?" I say. "Can I offer you something to drink? Tea? Coffee? Water?"

"We're fine," Tamil says, as they move toward the sofa.

The girls are bouncing around, thrilled by the unexpected visit. I know my role is to remove them, but I can't bring myself to leave.

"Girls," I say, "we need to speak to the police. If you and Freya go and put on your pajamas, you can have a Tim Tam each from the pantry."

The girls scamper off. Gabe and Tamil sit on the couch and I sit in an armchair. Conroy continues standing. He wanders over to the back sliding doors and looks out at the cliff. "Lovely place you've got here," he says. "What is it you do for work?"

"I'm a lawyer," I say, even though he's looking at Gabe. "Wills and estates. Gabe looks after the girls."

"Awesome." He is still looking at Gabe. "I did that for a while when my kids were little. My youngest is a teenager now. It was pretty unusual to be a stay-at-home dad back then. How long have you been doing it?"

"Just over a year."

"Bet your daughters love it." Conroy sits in the armchair opposite me, crossing his legs. "What did you do before that?"

Conroy sounds casual, friendly, and yet I sense an undertone that tells me this is more than friendly conversation.

"I worked in investor relations," Gabe says. "Back in Melbourne."

"Investor relations." Detective Conroy smiles. "I'm not from the corporate world. What does that mean exactly?"

"Well," Gabe says, "in a nutshell, I found people to give us money when we were looking to expand our business."

"'Our business'? Which business was that?"

Gabe hesitates. *Act natural, Gabe,* I urge silently. *Act natural.* At the same time, Freya appears with her pajama top stuck around her head. Her timing couldn't be more perfect.

"I'm stuck!" she cries.

I let Gabe rescue her, taking the opportunity to change the conversation to the weather.

Once Freya is unstuck, the girls run to the kitchen to get their Tim Tams and Gabe returns to the sofa. Tamil gets out her notebook and, thankfully, the questioning takes a different turn. "Okay, I'm sorry to keep coming back to this but we need to go over your statement again."

"Why?" I ask.

"Standard procedure," Tamil says. "Sometimes people remember things differently after a few days, when the adrenaline has settled."

"But it was a suicide."

"Even so, we are required to investigate all deaths with an open mind before we can rule it a suicide. So, we need to dot our i's and cross our t's."

I wonder if she's heard from Max.

"Fine," Gabe says. "Go ahead."

"All right. Let's go over what happened again. From the start."

Gabe goes over the story again, with only a little prompting from Tamil. Conroy doesn't speak at all. I wait for one of them to drop the bombshell—*We know that you worked for Max Cameron*—but neither of them mentions it.

"All right," Tamil says, after Gabe has finished. "That's it."

Gabe and I exchange a glance. *That's it?* I want to feel relieved—and I do a little—but the feeling of dread remains lodged inside me.

Tamil and her colleague rise to their feet. "Oh. Just one more thing."

And there it is. The reason for the dread.

I wonder if it gives her a perverse sort of pleasure to lull someone into a false sense of security, get them all comfortable and relaxed, and then stick the knife in. I suppose it would be quite satisfying. When they did this in *Line of Duty,* I always gave a fist pump. Not today.

"The victim's husband told us that she kept a flash stick on her key ring," Tamil says. "It was silver and her name was engraved on it. But the USB wasn't on the key ring when it was returned to him." She's looking at her notebook as she reads the description of the USB. Then she looks up. "Do you know anything about it?"

I feel blood pulsing in my face, my arms, my body. I think I might faint.

"No," Gabe says. "I didn't see any USB. But then, I didn't see her key ring either."

"I thought it was a long shot, but we had to check. All right, we'll leave you to get on with your evening."

Tamil returns her notebook to her pocket, and we file back down the hall again. As I reach for the door to let them out, the girls take their opportunity to pounce.

"Did my mummy or daddy do something wrong?" Asha asks.

Tamil chuckles. "No. I'm just asking them about something that your daddy saw."

"The lady at the cliff?"

The detective lifts her gaze to meet mine. "That's right."

"She didn't jump," Asha says seriously. "Grandma said she jumped, but it was an accident. She fell."

"Is that right?"

"Yes. My daddy said so. That's why we should never go too close to the edge. Because you can fall."

It is entirely explainable, of course. Out of the mouths of babes. What's less explainable is Gabe's facial expression when Tamil looks up at him. He is horrified. Pale. Your classic deer in the headlights. He is the very image of someone who has just been caught in a lie.

44

AMANDA

(BEFORE)

After those men broke into the house, our security increased dramatically. Cameras, alarms, keypads. I had a panic button in every room, and another to always carry on my person. Max's office was similarly set up with cameras and alarms. Everything, Max told me, was state-of-the-art.

There was also a full-time personal security guard stationed at the house around the clock, an ex-military officer called Baz. I'd been terrified of the two men who'd come to the house that day, but Baz was something else. He was the tallest man I'd ever seen, built like a rugby player, with one of those heads that flowed straight into his neck. Each of his limbs was wider than my torso and pulsing with veins. He had a mean face, huge, mangled knuckles, and a snake tattoo that crept out of the collar of his shirt. Before Baz, I hadn't known that you could feel both safe and petrified at the same time. But after a while, I started to get used to it. This level of security became our new normal.

"It's done," Max said, six months after the break-in. We were at home, in the lounge room. Max had been working on his computer, while I was editing some photographs I'd taken at the opening of the Ai Weiwei exhibit at the art gallery. We were sharing a bowl of Pringles.

I looked up from my laptop. "What's done?"

"My business with Arthur Spriggs."

He closed the lid of his own computer with a thud of finality. It was the same computer he'd been working on that day in the study, the one he kept locked in the safe.

"What do you mean it's done? What did you do?"

"The less you know . . ."

"No way, Max," I said. "No more of that. I want to know. I *deserve* to know."

A flash of something crossed Max's face. I couldn't quite place it, but it gave me a sick feeling.

"I asked Baz to return Arthur's money. In person."

"Baz went to see Arthur Spriggs?"

There was a note of disbelief in my voice. I understood on some level; Baz was intimidating as hell. But I would have thought someone like Arthur would have been used to that. I was shocked that all it would take was a visit from Baz to end this nightmare.

"No. He didn't see *Arthur.*"

Suddenly it made sense. Arthur hadn't sent his men to Max; that wouldn't have had the desired effect. He had to be cleverer than that. And so, apparently, did Max.

"He left it with Arthur's wife? Girlfriend?"

Max hesitated. There it was again—that flash. "He left it with Arthur's daughter."

A sick feeling came over me. "How old is his daughter, Max?"

A short pause. "I understand that she is two or three years old."

Baz, I discovered later, had scaled Arthur's fence and handed the little girl an envelope of cash while she played in the backyard. Her mother had ducked inside, so he waited for her to return before he left. It was important, Max said, that she saw Baz and understood what they were up against.

No harm came to the little girl, Max was clear about that, and I believed him. Then again, I'd also believed him when he said he'd never cheat on me. Goes to show how dangerous it can be, thinking that you know someone.

45

PIPPA

The Pantry is bustling. It's impressive for a weekday. Certainly, it wouldn't have been an unfamiliar sight in the middle of summer, but down here many cafés and restaurants rely on the weekend and school holiday trade from Melbourne.

I am sitting at a back table by the window, in front of a sandwich I didn't order but that I'm enjoying desperately. I haven't eaten a proper meal in days and there's something calming about a full stomach. It doesn't entirely relieve my anxiety, but it helps a bit.

"If they knew about the connection between Max and me, they would have said so." That's what Gabe said to me last night, after the police had left. "It just felt like they did because we're nervous. You don't have to worry."

Easy to say.

This morning, when Gabe had taken the girls off to preschool, he'd been an entirely different man from the nervous, shaken one of the evening before. He'd decided that the police visit was a good thing, and that the most likely scenario was that they would have closed the case by the end of the day, ruling it a suicide. Even if Max *had* been here in Portsea, Gabe said, he'd have left by now. He was probably back in Melbourne, planning the funeral. Gabe seemed so confident. I envied him.

"Be right with you," Dev says, as he sails past, holding a couple of bowls of mussels.

I don't often do wills face-to-face. I've never done one in a café while the client serves the lunch rush. But there's something about the unorthodox arrangement that I like. He has two staff holding down the fort—one in the kitchen and one serving—but when it gets busy he chips in to help.

Dev's will is one of the most straightforward I've done in a while. It almost makes me wonder why he's bothering. Of course, my official position is that everyone needs a will. Official because that's how I make money, but also because that's how I live my own life.

I made my first will when I was twenty. I did it myself, online— bequeathing my clothes, my car, and my five thousand dollars in savings to Kat. I'd also outlined my wishes for my funeral. Back then I'd wanted "Stayin' Alive" by the Bee Gees played at my funeral—I thought it would be ironic and make everyone smile. I'd amended that and most other things in my will since.

"Assets?" I say when Dev slides into the booth opposite me. I hold my fingers over the keyboard of my laptop.

Dev is single, never married, no dependents. He owns the Pantry (with a hefty mortgage), his car, and an apartment in Melbourne that is currently rented out. He has a modest amount of savings. I doubt we'll need the full hour, even with all the interruptions. I've already decided I won't charge him. Besides the free food this is bound to get me, I've learned that Dev is the mouthpiece for this entire area. If he sings my praises, it will spread like wildfire. And if everyone he talks to brings me straightforward wills like this, it will be money for jam.

"In the event of your death, what are your wishes for the Pantry?" I ask. "For example, you could have the business sold and the proceeds released to the estate, you could close it down, you could nominate someone to run it and the profits could be held in trust by the estate."

"It can be sold," he says. "Everything can be sold." A middle-aged woman in activewear enters and he waves at her. "Marg! We have raspberry and white chocolate muffins still warm from the oven."

Marg groans. "I've just been for a six-kilometer walk!" She orders the muffin.

"And who will be your beneficiaries?" I ask when I have Dev's attention again.

"My brother, Sunny."

I make a note of it, then look up. A pair of young women at the next table are watching us. Dev must have noticed too because he looks over at them. "Another coffee, Steph? Takeaway cup?"

Steph laughs in a way that makes me think she might fancy Dev. I consider him with fresh eyes. He's not bad-looking. Medium height and build. Russet-colored skin and a killer-watt smile. His most attractive feature, perhaps, is the way he pays attention to people and loves to give them what they want.

Dev calls out Steph's order to Gisele at the counter and then looks at me.

"And you, Pippa? Another coffee?"

"I'm fine. I've had too much caffeine already today. I'm a bit jittery."

"A chamomile tea for Pippa," he calls to Gisele. "For the jitters."

"Would you like to be buried or cremated?" I ask.

He shrugs. "I don't care."

"Funeral arrangements?"

Another shrug. "Whatever is easiest and cheapest."

There's something about his simplicity that I find humbling. I think about my own wishes. To be cremated, mingled with Gabe's ashes, and sprinkled over the lawn at the botanic gardens where we met and married. It felt so romantic when we decided. Now it feels silly.

"What about a letter of wishes?" I ask finally.

He raises his eyebrows and shakes his head to indicate he doesn't know what I'm talking about.

"It's for things that don't fit neatly into a will. For example, someone might include something such as 'I'd like my children to maintain an interest in the family business,' or 'My wife can keep living in the house until her death and then it reverts to the estate,' or 'I'd like 'Stayin' Alive' played at my funeral.'"

He laughs, and once again I find myself admiring his face.

"Put that in my letter," he says.

"What?"

"'Stayin' Alive.' I like it. Ironic."

"I know, right?"

My chamomile tea arrives as he laughs again.

He's done the unthinkable, I realize. I am relaxed. For several minutes I haven't thought about Gabe, Amanda, or Max Cameron. I haven't worried about the police, or the future. He really *is* good at this.

I sit back in my booth and lift the tea to my lips. I've just taken a sip when Max Cameron walks in.

46

AMANDA

(AFTER)

It's satisfying to watch the moment Pippa notices Max enter the café. It's as if she's seen a ghost. She seems the type who'd be good at concealing her emotions—heaven knows, with a husband like hers you'd have to be—but at the sight of Max, her face drains of all color.

Max hasn't seen her yet. He's come in to order a coffee. There's a Nespresso machine at our Portsea house—not that Max would even try to use it. He'd already come to the Pantry once, last night to collect some dinner. Classic Max; once he is onto a good thing, he sticks to it.

What's your plan, Max? I ask him silently.

He's dressed in his version of casual—a pair of chinos, a white shirt, a navy V-neck jumper—but instead of wearing boat shoes he's wearing his sneakers. He must be planning to do some walking. He's been to the Gerards' street twice, last night and then again this morning, but he failed to persuade the neighbors to reveal Gabe's address. Perhaps he's headed to the trail behind the Gerards' house, the one that leads to The Drop? That's how I located them too. Any local person can tell you where The Drop is. Once you're there, only two, maybe three houses have a direct view of it. I'd planned to try each of them, but I hadn't had to. Gabe came to *me*! I suspect that he wouldn't do that for Max, however.

"Just a large flat white to go," Max says to the young man who greets him at the counter. "Also, I'm wondering if you could help me."

The helpful man at the counter gives Max all the info he needs about The Drop, including a travel brochure with a map on which he draws a circle. Max is most grateful and when he pays for the coffee he adds a generous tip. He has no idea that Pippa Gerard is sitting just meters away from him. While he waits for his coffee, she gathers up her laptop and slips out the side door.

47

AMANDA

(BEFORE)

The funny thing was, in a way the Arthur Spriggs situation brought Max and me closer. We had survived an ordeal together. Faced a battle and won. We knew the other one cared and could be trusted. And it was then, after fifteen years of marriage, that our story began in earnest. More than just money. More than fidelity. More than just a transaction. It terrified me as much as it exhilarated me.

After that, Max came home for dinner on time. On the weekends, we went out, just the two of us—to movies and dinners and art galleries. We went on holidays—a resort in Bora Bora, a hike through Tasmania. For Max's fiftieth birthday, we took the trip of a lifetime to Africa. We went on safari in Tanzania in an open-top bus, we "glamped" in luxurious tents under the stars. We sat by the pool in Zanzibar. We picked out a tanzanite stone from a jeweler, and Max had it made into a necklace for me. I took photographs that would later win awards.

It felt like a honeymoon. It was the longest I'd spent with Max since we'd been married. The longest I'd spent with him ever.

"Amanda," he said one night. We were lying on our plush camping mattress, talking in the early evening. "I was wondering. Do you still worry about me finding another woman? I know that early on in our marriage it was a concern of yours. I hope you don't worry about that still."

"No," I said, realizing it had been a long time since I'd thought about this. "I don't."

The light was fading, and the tent was bathed in a gorgeous soft light. It occurred to me that it was, perhaps, the perfect moment to tell him I loved him. I was fairly sure, after all this time, that my feelings were reciprocated. And yet, even as I opened my mouth, something kept me from projecting the words.

Love had never served Max or me. Max had lost his mother and his brother—the ones he loved most. And I'd watched love slowly destroy my mother. Maybe the key to our marriage was that we didn't make loud proclamations? Maybe, for us, love was something to be whispered. Or, perhaps, never spoken of at all.

48

PIPPA

"Sorry!" I say to the car that screeches to a halt, narrowly missing me as I dart across the street without looking. Then, like a fool, I offer a wave.

The driver throws me a murderous glare as she drives away. I don't blame her. I'd do the same thing if a pedestrian ran out in front of my car. But getting hit by a car was preferable to running into Max Cameron.

I'm shaking as I jog home through the back streets. I don't think Max saw me, but I certainly didn't look back once I got out of there. I didn't tell Dev I was leaving either. He'll probably think I'm nuts. I'll have to tell him something came up. We were almost done anyway.

At home, I enter via the back door. I need to call Gabe; I need to warn him that Max is in town, at the café. It wouldn't be unusual for Gabe to turn up there at this time of day to grab some lunch.

I pull out my phone.

"Hi, darling."

I shouldn't be startled to find Mum in my kitchen. There always seems to be one family member or another here at any given time. For the first time in a long while, I feel a flush of irritation at this. "Hi, Mum. What are you doing here?"

"I was just at the shops, and I picked up some things to make soup for you and the family," she says. "Then I thought I might as well just make it here."

She's already got out a knife and cutting board and is chopping an onion. Groceries are strewn all over the counter and she's wearing my apron.

"Great."

But it's not great. I can't call Gabe with Mum here. I look at my phone, wondering if I should send him a text.

"I'm glad you're home," Mum says, as I sink into an armchair. "I've been meaning to check in with you."

I want, more than anything, to hear Gabe's voice. I want him to tell me that everything is going to be fine. I open a new message. But what do I write? The sound of Mum chopping is an annoying distraction, stopping me from being able to figure it out.

Chop. Chop, chop.

"Pip?"

Maybe I could text. Something like: *Max is here. I saw him at the Pantry.*

Chop. Chop, chop.

Maybe I should include the time he was there? I look at my watch.

The chopping stops. "Pip!"

Mum's voice cuts through the noise in my head. I look up from my phone. "Yes?"

"Is everything all right?"

"Fine. Why?"

She puts down the knife and sighs. "Because I spoke to Kat." She gives me a motherly, all-knowing look. "She said that you seemed a little . . . off." She wipes her hands on her apron, then comes and sits on the couch. "What's going on?"

It's a dangerous question. One that can induce tears in the calmest, most stable of people. Obviously no one would accuse me of being either right now.

"It's just the stress of the last few days, I suppose," I say. "Even the girls haven't been themselves. Did I tell you Asha was asking about the woman on the cliff? She asked if the woman was in heaven with her mum."

Mum winces. "It's a tough thing to understand at her age." She's quiet a moment. "Is that all it is?"

I look out the window, across the grass. A bit of police tape still clings to the moonah tree at The Drop. "No—it's this house," I say, with more fire than I intended. "I knew it was a bad idea to move here, with the cliff right there. I wish I'd put my foot down."

Mum watches me steadily. "So, it's the house that's bothering you?"

"Yes." Something feels childish about the way I say it, and I can't meet her eye. "I thought when we moved away, we'd have some peace. Thanks to this house, the drama has just moved somewhere new."

"Ah," she says. It's a loaded "ah." I can tell that she's holding something back.

"What?"

"It's just, you and Gabe have lived in a few houses now," she says carefully. "And you've had your fair share of drama at each one."

"So?"

"So . . . are you sure it's the house?" She waits a moment. When I don't respond, she continues. "Because if it were me, I'd be asking if it was something else causing your problems."

I look at her and see something in her gaze. An opinion that she'd never allowed herself to vocalize, lest she be an interfering mother.

"Like what?"

Mum opens her mouth to respond at the same moment my phone starts to ring. It's Gabe.

"Sorry, Mum," I say. "I have to get this."

I pick up the phone and Mum returns to the kitchen. She seems to be chopping even more aggressively than before.

49

PIPPA

"Gabe, there's a package for you," I called from the front door.

Both girls were at my feet, delighted by the unexpected interruption to our day. Admittedly, it wasn't so unexpected lately. The UPS man was becoming our new best friend. The packages had started arriving few months earlier. Bizarre purchases like old bottles of wine and sporting memorabilia arrived on our doorstep daily, some of them eye-wateringly expensive. Gabe always had an explanation—it was going to appreciate in value, or he needed it for some complicated reason I couldn't quite grasp.

Last week, it was a set of bikes for the family. A nice idea, except he'd ordered six of them and there were four of us (only two of whom could ride bikes). He'd brushed off the mistake, but a few days ago I sat him down and told him I was worried about the amount he was spending on things we didn't really need. He promised me he'd curb the online shopping. And yet, here we were.

"Ah," Gabe said when he joined me at the door. "That'll be the new porch light."

My heart sank. In addition to online shopping, Gabe's other recent obsession was fixing things around the house—things that, in many cases, were not even broken. First it was an apparently drippy tap. Then there was the hole in the roof that was allowing in the possums (possums that I never saw or heard). Now it was the light on the front porch—a sensor light, which I found quite helpful, but that for some reason Gabe couldn't stand.

"I might just swap it out now," he said. "It's been driving me mad."

"No. Not electrics, Gabe, it's too dangerous. I'll call the electrician."

"We don't need an electrician to change out a light, Pip!" he said, kissing my forehead. "It won't take me a minute to sort it out."

His confidence was persuasive. Maybe he was right and it was no big deal. After all, what did I know about changing lights? Besides, I had two toddlers at my heels who wanted lunch.

"All right, if you're sure."

There were worse things than having a husband who was handy, I told myself as I made toasted sandwiches. Some women would kill to have a husband who did things around the house.

The sandwiches were nearly done when the electricity cut out. From the kitchen at the back of the house, I heard the unmistakable thud of a body hitting the ground.

I'd never run so fast in my life.

When I reached the front porch, the ladder was on its side and so was Gabe, several meters away. He blinked at me dumbly for several seconds. Then he began to laugh.

I didn't understand it. He'd had the ADHD diagnosis. He was taking his medication. But Gabe was spiraling again. I could feel it in my bones.

50

AMANDA

I came home one night from dinner with some girlfriends to find the gates open and several cars parked in our driveway. They were not the prestige cars owned by most of our friends. There was a Mazda, a Subaru, and a hotted-up 1975 Ford Falcon with tinted windows—this last I recognized as belonging to Baz. It was unusual for our security guard to park in the driveway. Even though it had been years since Arthur Spriggs's men had invaded our home, unexpected guests still made me nervous. I called Max from my car.

"I'm in the driveway," I said, when be picked up. "Everything okay?"

"Fine. I've just got a few colleagues here for a meeting."

Max sounded distracted, though not alarmed. It reassured me, even though Max rarely held business meetings at home after hours. Then again, things *had* been busy now that NewZ was trying to enter the streaming sphere. It was a big undertaking that had been the focus of the past couple of years and had involved some late nights at work. It wasn't beyond the realms of possibility that Max might need to bring work home—but, still, it seemed odd.

The house was quiet when I let myself inside and I assumed Max and his colleagues were in Max's office. By this time, I'd become quite good at snooping, so I slipped into my study, which abutted the office, and put my ear to the wall.

"How the hell did you even *develop* a relationship with this contact?" I heard Max bellow, so loud that I could hear him quite clearly.

"The usual ways," came the softer, but not feeble, response. I recognized the voice as belonging to Gabe Gerard. "I know it was unorthodox, but you said to find the money wherever we could."

"Great. Did you look in dumpsters too?"

"Max, could we just focus on—"

But Max wasn't listening. "How did this get through compliance, Mei?"

"I red-flagged it when I vetted it." It was a young woman's voice now. "I couldn't verify the funds; they came from multiple holding companies on the Cayman Islands. I said it was suspicious."

"So how did it get through? Who signed off on it?"

"You did." Gabe's voice is smaller now.

Infuriatingly, the landline chose this moment to ring, and I hurried down the hall to answer it. It was a phone survey, which I declined to take part in. I got off the phone as fast as I could, then stood by the hall table thinking about what I'd overheard. They'd been talking about business, clearly; nothing out of the ordinary there. Yet the conversation had felt strangely charged. I hadn't heard Max sound so upset since . . . since the business with Arthur Spriggs, I realized.

I was still standing there when the door to Max's office opened.

"Thanks, Mei," I heard Max say, his tone polite but brisk. "Baz will show you out."

I'd almost forgotten Baz was in there. That was strange. Baz was responsible for our personal security; why would he be invited to a business meeting? I pretended to rifle through a drawer in the hall-stand while Baz walked a young woman to the foyer. He gave me a brief nod of acknowledgment on his way back to the office. When he closed the door, I returned to my study, but the voices were faint now, and I couldn't make out much of what they were saying. Eventually, I gave up and went to bed.

"That was a late one," I said when Max joined me later. I was sitting up under the covers with a novel in my lap. "What's going on?"

"I'm not sure you want to know," he said as he got undressed.

I raised my eyebrows to indicate that I did.

"All right." He finished unbuttoning his shirt and sat on the bed. "You know the streaming service we acquired a few months back?"

"Of course."

"It was very expensive. Getting the financing was tricky. For a while we thought it wasn't going to fly."

"I remember."

"Gabe Gerard managed to pull it off, though. At the eleventh hour he found an investor who came forward with fifty million dollars."

"That's right," I said, remembering how relieved Max had been. "It was a huge coup."

Max sighed. "Yes, well . . . It turns out the investor wasn't exactly the savior we were looking for."

"Why not?"

"It's a group called A.S. Holdings."

"And?" I prompted, but Max didn't continue. "So, what's the problem?"

"The problem is"—Max hangs his head—"'A.S.' stands for Arthur Spriggs."

51

AMANDA

(AFTER)

Max has a leather satchel over his shoulder and is walking with purpose. To the Gerards' house, I assume, but then he takes the steps down to the beach and heads to the rock groin that sticks straight out to sea, like a pier.

He removes his shoes. It's a romantic sight, Max walking barefoot on the rocks. In another life, I would have photographed it. The beach is quiet, apart from a few dog walkers several hundred meters away. When he reaches the end of the groin, he opens his satchel and removes the secret laptop.

Suddenly I understand what he's doing. All his secrets are on that computer: falsified paperwork, documents linking him to Arthur Spriggs. It needs to be destroyed.

He lifts the laptop and brings it down hard against the rocks. It's shocking how quickly it falls to pieces. No one on the beach pays him the slightest attention as he bashes it again and again, his face contorting with the effort. I imagine it feels cathartic.

Max had another call from the cops this morning, this time to ask if Gabriel Gerard was a former employee of his. Max replied that he had thousands of employees; he couldn't possibly be expected to remember every single one. That was interesting. It made me wonder what kind of game he was playing.

Still, the cops are smarter than either Max or I gave them credit for. They didn't simply accept that my death was a suicide, as I presumed they would—they were doing their due diligence. They'd already been keeping an eye on Max and his business dealings, but my death gave them a reason to poke into his affairs. Now, while supposedly investigating my death, they'd stumbled across another crime.

When he's finished, Max tosses the remnants of the laptop into the water and watches them sink to the bottom. Now that the computer is gone, Max is already looking more relaxed. He doesn't know that the evidence still exists—at least, he doesn't know for sure. But I suspect he has an inkling, so that final hiding place will be the next thing he looks for.

My USB.

52

PIPPA

It's midafternoon when Gabe arrives home with the girls in tow, and I'm sitting on the couch with my laptop, catching up on some emails.

Mum left half an hour earlier, having made enough soup to feed us for a week. After my phone call with Gabe, our conversation had moved on to regular topics—the girls' birthdays, Kat and Mei's baby, Dad's high cholesterol—but something about it felt forced. I was glad when she finally went home.

Mei has called twice since then, and I let both calls go through to voicemail.

"Mummy!" the girls cry, and I put my laptop aside as they scramble onto my lap. Asha's knee gets me in the belly, and it is surprisingly painful, but I ignore it and hug them both and listen to their stories about preschool. Then they tell me that Daddy has promised they can watch a movie if they're very good.

"We are very good," Freya says earnestly.

I do my best to smile. I feel Gabe's gaze on me. Like everyone's lately, it seems. I don't look at him. I can't.

Gabe sets up a couple of beanbags in front of the TV, and the girls drop into them like stones. Then he microwaves some popcorn and gives them their own individual bowls. Once *The Little Mermaid* is playing, he sits beside me.

"What is it?" he asks. "What's wrong?"

"I saw Max."

I wasn't able to tell him over the phone, with Mum here. But he obviously heard the panic in my voice, because he doesn't seem surprised. "Where?"

"At the Pantry. He was ordering a coffee."

Gabe closes his eyes, swears softly. "Did he see you?"

"No. I snuck out of there like a thief in the night." The tears fill my eyes unexpectedly and I quickly wipe them away. "Sorry. I don't know what's wrong with me."

Gabe slides off the couch and kneels on the floor, between my legs. He makes it so it's impossible for me to look anywhere but into his eyes. "It's going to be all right, Pip. I promise you."

In this cozy pod of security with our girls and the smell of popcorn in the air, it would be so easy to believe him. But I don't. This is the one thing we've come up against that actually isn't going to be okay.

"Listen to me," he says, and I do, because more than anything I want someone else to take control. I want to be a bystander. I want to be like my two little girls, staring slack-jawed at the screen, my biggest worry that my popcorn will soon run out. "I know how difficult this has been. But you didn't do anything wrong. You don't need to lie or hide from anyone. You don't need to worry about what the police will do." His face is pulsing with intensity. His cheeks are pink, and his eyes are desperate for me to hear what he is saying. "*I* was the one who lied to them, Pip. This is not your burden to carry."

But I don't believe him. I *did* do something wrong. And it *is* my burden to carry. Still, there's something about hearing him say the words aloud, knowing that he is willing to carry this weight for me. For now, it's enough.

It's not lost on me that, despite everything, Gabe is the only one who can make it better.

The girls watch another movie after *The Little Mermaid* and I lie on the couch with a novel I don't read while Gabe massages my feet. We keep the curtains drawn and, mercifully, no member of my family drops in to pay us a visit.

We order pizza for dinner and open a bottle of wine. The girls are lovely, delightful caricatures of themselves, which makes me think that Gabe must have bribed them to "be extra kind to Mummy." I'm fine with it. If my soul was ill, this is my salve. Gabe is my salve.

He puts the girls to bed single-handedly. The stories are spectacular. There are costumes, singing and dancing, and a performance with several speaking roles. The girls laugh so hard I am sure someone is going to vomit, and equally sure that they are unlikely to settle before midnight. But I'm wrong on both counts.

When Gabe emerges from their room at 8:00 P.M., I mute the television. I open my mouth to congratulate him, but he presses a finger to my lips. "Don't talk."

And so I don't. I remain silent as he kneels between my legs and removes my underwear. This is exactly what I need. To disappear into a world of me and Gabe, a world where nothing exists except *us*.

I throw my head back and bury my fingers in his hair and give in to it.

53

AMANDA

"How on earth did Gabe Gerard get involved with *Arthur Spriggs*?"

It was like a nightmare. A recurring one. Part of me was shocked to learn that Arthur Spriggs still existed. After he disappeared from our lives the last time, it felt like he was a character in a movie, like Freddy Krueger or Hannibal Lecter—someone who had been terrifying right up until the point he ceased to exist.

Max shrugged wearily. "Same way I did the first time."

Apparently, it wasn't a huge surprise that they'd crossed paths. Crooks, politicians, and oligarchs all attended the same glamorous parties frequented by people working in investor relations. The only thing you needed to earn a place on the guest list, apparently, was power.

According to Max, Gabe was a lamb to the slaughter. After all, Arthur Spriggs wasn't an idiot. He would have seen the young executive, eager to prove himself, and known exactly how to play him. Gabe forced the deal through, despite the red flags raised during the compliance process, and Max himself had signed off on it.

"It's my fault ultimately," Max conceded. "I approved it."

"Can you reject his investment?"

"It's too late. The deal is done."

"So . . . what happens now? What are you going to do?"

Max wouldn't meet my eye, which made me worry. "Same as last time," he said. "We have to be creative."

There were several more meetings at the house between Max, Baz, and Gabe after that. I didn't eavesdrop on them again. I remembered how they'd involved Arthur Spriggs's two-year-old daughter previously; I had no interest in knowing what they were planning this time.

Still, it was impossible not to notice the increase in security around that time. Baz brought on an assistant, a young guy who was almost as big and scary-looking as Baz himself, and who was stationed either outside the house or accompanying me wherever I went. For the first time in years, I had to start wearing my panic button again. And Max was always on edge, almost jumpy.

It was a Saturday night, around 9:00 P.M., when it happened. Max had been tense all evening, constantly checking his phone. When it finally rang, he leaped up and ran to his home office. I'd known this was coming. I'd been on tenterhooks for weeks, waiting for this whole episode to be over, while fantasizing that it would just go away on its own. No such luck.

I couldn't help it; I had to know. I hurried down the hall and slipped into my study to listen at the wall.

"Arthur," Max said. "I hope my team are treating you well?"

I was relieved to know that it was Arthur himself, and not his daughter, who was with Max's "team."

"I understand—and they have been instructed not to harm you," Max said. "All we need is for you to sell your shares back to me and then you will be returned to your home."

There was silence for a few seconds; I presumed Arthur Spriggs was favoring my husband with some choice words.

"You're in a van," Max said patiently. "Where we drive it is up to you. I'm hoping you cooperate, so we drive you home, after which we never have to cross paths again. If that's what you want, you're going to have to—"

Max stopped, presumably because Arthur had cut him off. After a moment, he said, "You don't seem to understand that you're not in a position to negotiate. I have no wish to harm you, but if you don't cooperate, I will."

Another silence. When Max spoke again, he sounded irritated. "Look, Arthur, we can do this the easy way, or we can do it the hard way. It's up to you."

Now the longest silence of them all. I wondered what was happening. Was Arthur calling his bluff? Surely not. But if he did . . . what did that mean? Max couldn't actually kill him. He *wouldn't*. Was that what Arthur was banking on?

When the silence continued, I found myself walking out of my study into the hall and through the door to Max's office.

Max turned to face me, but his attention was elsewhere. It allowed me to get up close beside him and put my ear to the phone.

"Fine," Max said. "Have it your way. Baz—"

"No!" I shouted, and then I heard the gunshot.

54

PIPPA

Mei calls while I'm still in bed. It's just after 7:00 A.M.—an ungodly time for most, but not a bad time to catch me. Gabe has gone for a surf; the girls are asleep. Normally I'd be in the kitchen, unloading the dishwasher and getting a head start on the day, but I haven't been able to motivate myself to get out of bed, not even for coffee. It seems as good a time as any to talk to Mei.

"Hi!" I say, settling back against the pillows. I'm glad for an excuse to stay in bed a little longer.

"You're a hard lady to catch," Mei says. "I called twice yesterday."

"I know, sorry."

I hear the girls stirring in the next room. It always starts this way, with Asha letting out a spectacular yawn. In a few minutes, she'll roll over and try to rouse Freya, who will protest for exactly three seconds. Then they'll scamper into the living room, bright-eyed and mischievous and aggressively hungry.

Mei still hasn't spoken.

"What?" I ask.

"You tell me," she says. "What's happening with Max? And don't say nothing. I saw him in town yesterday."

I curse internally. Unfortunately, Portsea is a small place. If I saw him, it wasn't really surprising that Mei did too.

"I'm worried, Pip. I know I said I wasn't going to tell Kat, but—"

"You can't, Mei. Please."

"I don't want to, believe me. She's still sick as a dog, and she worries enough about you as it—"

"What? Why does she worry about me?"

"Because you're her sister," Mei says, as if it's obvious. "And sisters worry. But now she's pregnant, I'd rather not upset her."

"Then don't!" I say. "Honestly, Mei, everything is fine. Max probably has a holiday house down here, that's all. What rich person doesn't?"

Mei considers that. "So you haven't see him?"

"No," I say. "Of course not."

"Good. Because Max Cameron is not the kind of enemy you want. He knows some dangerous people."

Dangerous. That word gives me pause. Gabe had said something similar. *Max Cameron isn't the nice guy everyone thinks he is.* I recall my night with him. The fact that I hadn't sensed his dark side makes me question my judgment—about everything.

"So Gabe's still insisting Amanda's death was a pure coincidence?" Mei says, when I don't respond.

"Yes," I say, "because it's the truth."

"All right," she says, although it's clear she isn't convinced. "But if I were you, I'd be asking Gabe a direct question: *Is there something going on that I don't know about?*"

"You've got it all wrong, Mei," I say. "And, frankly, I'm a little surprised by how quick you are to cast aspersions on Gabe's integrity. I thought you were friends!"

I hear the thump of feet on the floorboards. A moment later, two little faces peer around the doorframe. I wave at them, and they run over and jump onto the bed. But I keep the phone pressed to my ear, waiting for Mei to apologize, to assure me that *of course* she and Gabe are friends, that she would never think him capable of anything sinister.

Instead she says, "Ask him."

And ends the call.

Ask him.

I'm still thinking about my conversation with Mei as I strap the girls into their car seats an hour later. Why does she keep saying that? It irritates me, because I can't defend Gabe, and I can't understand why she is so desperate for me to confront him.

I don't need to ask him, I wanted to cry. *Because Gabe isn't the one who did something wrong—it was me!*

But of course I couldn't say this. I can't say anything at all.

I've rescheduled the girls' vaccinations for this morning before preschool, and since I didn't have a meeting this morning I decided to go to the appointment with them and Gabe. Once the girls are strapped in, I get into the passenger seat. Gabe is driving.

"Why do I have to have a shot?" Asha says apprehensively.

"Because the shot is full of superheroes," Gabe says. "The nurse will shoot them into your body, so they can be there to fight against germs. These superheroes stop you from getting sick."

The girls look doubtful.

"You can have ice cream afterward," I say.

"Yay!" the girls chorus.

I scan the streets anxiously on our way to the health center. I can't help it. Unfortunately, it's Friday, and Max looks exactly like every other wealthy fiftysomething man with a holiday home in the area. I see several men that could be him—each one causing a brief interruption to the blood flow in my body, or at least that is how it feels. But none of them is Max.

We pull up a few doors down from the health center. The girls are reluctant to get out, so Gabe heaves them both onto his back in a double piggyback. They look like a scene from a movie—the two giggling girls and their handsome father. Passersby steal looks at them and smile.

"I had an appointment for my daughters this morning, but unfortunately I can't find them," Gabe says to the woman on reception as we enter.

"We're here!" the girls squeal from his back. "We're here, Daddy!"

We are taken to a room behind a curtain and seated side by side on plastic chairs with the girls on our laps. Gabe has Freya, I have Asha. The receptionist stands nearby, poised to blow bubbles, a distraction technique to take the child's mind off the sting of the needle.

The nurse flirts shamelessly with Gabe. She's a young attractive brunette with heavy false eyelashes and penciled-on eyebrows. "Aren't you lucky having your daddy come with you?" the nurse says, ostensibly to the girls, but she keeps her gaze on Gabe. It's like she hasn't even noticed I'm here. "Had the morning off work, did you?"

"Actually, I am the working parent," I say. I hear the tight, defensive note in my voice, and I hate myself for it. "Gabe is their primary parent. *I* took time off work."

"You're the primary parent?" she says to Gabe. "That's so sweet." She removes the syringe from the plastic packet, in full sight of the girls. Asha looks horrified. I'm horrified too. The last time they had shots the motherly nurse did it surreptitiously; even I hadn't seen it coming. I feel a pang of yearning, again, for a time before we moved here.

Gabe pulls up Freya's sleeve.

"A woman fell off the cliff near our house," Asha says. "She walked too close to the edge. Normally my daddy stops people, but he didn't stop this lady."

The nurse pauses. *Now* she looks at me.

"Why didn't he stop her?" Freya asks her sister.

"I think he wasn't quick enough," Asha replies. "Or maybe he didn't like her."

"All right, little sting," the nurse says and jabs Freya, who lets out an almighty howl.

"Brave girl," the nurse says, putting a cotton bud and then a piece of surgical tape on Freya's arm.

The receptionist started blowing bubbles and one floats into my eye. I reach up to rub it and Asha chooses this moment to slip off my lap and bolt.

"Shit!" I leap up, still rubbing my eye. I push through the curtain in time to see her disappear through the door onto the street. I run after her, catching up a few doors down, where she has been stopped by a Good Samaritan.

"I don't want any superheroes," she says to the man in chinos, a white shirt, and a navy jumper who has stooped down to her level.

When he sees me, he stands upright.

"Hello, Pippa," he says.

55

PIPPA

"Hello, Pippa."

Max looks so ordinary, so safe. The kind who would stop to help a woman in a broken-down vehicle, and who would champion women's rights, while also expecting a home-cooked dinner when he got home from work. Despite this, I feel intimidated. It's something to do with his presence. His sense of self. The way he is, already, the one in control.

I'm instantly cold—that horrible, clammy feeling you get when you're about to vomit. There is no running away now, no sneaking off. Asha watches us curiously but silently, perhaps not wanting to draw attention to herself in the hope that I'll forget she's meant to be having her shot.

"Hello, Max," I whisper.

I glance back at the health center. I can't decide if I want Gabe to come out or stay where he is. I feel stunningly unprepared for this conversation, which I realize is absurd. For all my panicking, my overthinking, my terror, I hadn't stopped to consider what I might say if I came face-to-face with Max. How I could even look him in the eye.

As it turns out, I *can't* look him in the eye, so instead I focus on his shoulder.

"I think you know why I'm here, Pippa. But I'll give you the benefit of the doubt and explain. My wife Amanda passed away this week. Took her own life, I'm told, by jumping off the cliff behind your house."

I should act surprised to hear this, I know, but I can't find it in myself to feign shock.

"A strange coincidence, don't you think?" Max continues. "That she chose to jump from that particular cliff?"

Max waits now—a good strategy, because I only last a few seconds before I start talking.

"She said she'd seen a video." Now, finally, I look at him. "Why was there a video?"

Max sighs. "That was unfortunate. We have CCTV of the entire office, for security reasons. I asked them to turn it on the night you came in because I thought Gabe might end up joining us and I didn't know what to expect. After . . . what happened . . . I asked security to cut the footage. I didn't mean for them to send it to me. She found the video on an old laptop."

It's probably not that important in the scheme of things; still, I'm glad to have an answer to this question.

"But while the footage explains why she came here," Max went on, "it doesn't explain why she jumped."

"I'm sorry," I say. "I wish I understood the inner workings of a suicidal woman, but I—"

"That's the thing," he says. "Amanda wasn't suicidal when I last saw her. In fact, in our twenty-five years of marriage, she never seemed suicidal. So, it's hard for me to accept that, even after discovering this video, she'd suddenly choose to jump off a cliff behind the home of one of my former employees. Surely you can understand why I'm perplexed by this."

I take a few seconds to consider this. "Well," I say, "I guess the video must have affected her more than you think. And The Drop is a well-known suicide place."

"That's true," Max says. "But I've since discovered that Gabe didn't tell the police he knew Amanda. If this truly was a coincidence, why would he conceal that?"

He fixes me in his gaze. I understand its intention is to intimidate me. It works breathtakingly well.

"I just want to know what happened to my wife, Pippa." There's the tiniest quaver in his voice here. I notice, suddenly, that he looks thinner and paler than the last time I saw him.

"Mummy," Asha says, "do I still have to get my superheroes?"

"Yes, baby," I say, taking her hand. To Max, I say, "I'm sorry, I need to go. We have vaccinations. I wish I could help . . ."

"You can," he says. "I'd like you to ask Gabe to call me."

His hands are tucked into the pockets of his chinos, but he draws one out, holding a business card between his fingers. It reminds me of the last time he did this, all those years ago. "Give him my card."

I take it. Nod. What else can I do?

"I'm staying down here for a few days," he calls over his shoulder as he walks away. "Maybe longer. Depends how long it takes to get to the bottom of things. Tell Gabe I'll look forward to hearing from him."

I remain where I am until he disappears around the corner.

Amanda wasn't suicidal. Max is wrong about that; Amanda *must* have been suicidal. Because if she wasn't . . . what had my husband done?

"Pip!" Seconds after Max disappears down the street, Gabe and the receptionist join me. "I was wondering where you two had got to." To Asha he says, "Come on, poppet, the nurse is waiting. The sooner it's done, the sooner you can have ice cream."

The receptionist takes Asha by the hand and leads her back to the health center, distracting her with a discussion on the relative merits of vanilla and chocolate.

"I saw Max," I say to Gabe.

"What?" He stares at me. "Just now?"

I nod. "He said Amanda wasn't suicidal."

I watch Gabe's forehead crease as he takes that in. "Well," he says after a beat, "we have evidence to the contrary."

I hand him Max's card. "He wants you to call him."

"I bet he does."

"He knows you didn't tell the police that you knew Amanda. So, he has that over us."

Gabe swears under his breath.

"What are you going to do?" I ask.

He's staring down at Max's card, lost in thought. After what feels like a lifetime, he says, "I guess I'm going to call Max."

56

PIPPA

Gabe's moods continued to ebb and flow. I was getting used to it, as much as one could get used to living with constant uncertainty. He was better, I found, when he had something meaningful to consume his attention. More often than not, that meant work. I was okay with this. If he was going to direct his hyperfocus somewhere, work was as good a place as any.

His latest project was a challenge. His company wanted to get into streaming, and for that they needed money—lots and lots of it, and as the head of investor relations it was up to Gabe to find it. He worked day and night. I never asked too many questions about his work. The truth was, I had only the most rudimentary understanding of what Gabe did, and when he talked about it I understood less rather than more.

What I did understand was that with every project, Gabe worried that he wouldn't get the finance together in time. It was practically a prerequisite for any acquisition; an investor would drop out at the last minute, or there'd be a price increase, or some other crisis that would send Gabe into a tailspin. I'd come to realize that the drama of this was part of the fun, so I didn't worry too much when, days before the streaming deal was due to take place, he started the usual talk about how he might not be able to get the money together.

"This is different, Pip," he said when I'd reminded him that this happened every time. (He also said this every time.) "It's *really* different."

Indeed, he was working incredibly hard. On top of the late nights there seemed to be a lot of hushed phone calls and clandestine meetings. There was even a meeting one Saturday night. I remember it, because it was raining and Gabe had gone out in his waterproof boots. I'd joked that this was not what I'd expected an executive job to entail.

He didn't arrive home until four or five in the morning. When I got up the next day, I saw his boots outside on the rack, upside down and freshly cleaned. I remember being impressed that he'd thought to clean them at that late hour. Unfortunately, he hadn't thought to wipe his muddy boot prints from the laundry floor. As I dropped to my knees to do it myself, I noticed that the dirt and mud was tinged with something else. It looked a lot like blood.

The next day, I called Dr. Ravi.

It wasn't just the bloody boot prints, which Gabe explained away. (A dead animal on the road, he said.) It was everything else. The compulsive online shopping. The fact that he'd recently told me he wanted to start an Uber service on the moon. I'd laughed, but he stayed serious. Lately I found it difficult to tell when he was joking. The line between normal and not normal had always been so thin for Gabe; sometimes I didn't know if I was talking to a genius or a madman.

I'd been having my doubts about Gabe's ADHD diagnosis. Yes, there'd been a brief period when he'd seemed to improve, but those days were long gone.

"Thank you for your call, Pippa," Dr. Ravi said. "But before we chat, I need to be clear that I can't talk specifically about Gabe or anything he has divulged to me, as it would breach doctor-patient confidentiality."

"I understand," I said. "But I'm not sure who else to talk to."

"What's been going on?"

I told Dr. Ravi about the compulsive spending, the Uber on the moon. I told him everything else I'd stored up, details that seemed insignificant on their own but were worrying when presented side by side. The fight I'd overheard between Gabe and a workmate, in which Gabe had accused his colleague of spying on him. The poetry he'd written about grief, and how it was the only path to true spiritual enlightenment. How he sometimes cried because he was so happy, and it frightened the girls.

When I finished talking, Dr. Ravi was silent for a long time. Finally, he said, "I agree that sounds concerning, Pippa."

There was something so gratifying about hearing that, after thinking for so long that I was making a big deal out of nothing, I felt a lump in my throat.

"And he's been taking his medication?"

"Every day." I swallowed. "I've checked."

I could hear Dr. Ravi tapping at his computer. "I'd like to see him, today if possible." He paused. "I see he missed his last two appointments. He didn't even call to cancel. Do you think you can persuade him to come in?"

"I don't know," I said. But I did. I already knew he wouldn't come. Why would he? According to him, he'd never felt better.

The tears started to flow now. They filled my throat and blocked my nose until it felt like I was drowning.

"Unfortunately, I can't do anything if I don't see him myself," Dr. Ravi said. "Unless I have reason to suspect that Gabe is a danger to himself or to others. Do you think that's the case, Pippa?"

"No," I said. "He's not dangerous."

But then I thought of that bloody boot print, and I wondered if I'd told the truth.

57

AMANDA

(AFTER)

Max has only just got the heating going when his phone rings. He takes a seat in an armchair before answering the call.

"Max Cameron," he says.

Gabe is at home, pacing the living room. Pippa is sitting on the couch watching him. Her hands are steepled in the prayer position. I wonder if she's actually praying.

"Max. It's Gabe."

Max is as impressed as I am by how quickly Gabe called, but he waits several moments before responding. It is, I assume, a strategy designed to unnerve the other man. Judging by the look on Gabe's face, it is successful. "Gabe. Thank you for calling."

"Pippa said you wanted to talk to me."

A number of emotions are evident in Gabe's voice. There is the hot tone of protectiveness for his wife. Irritation that he has been put into the position of having to make a call he doesn't want to make. Also, fear. Max holds the cards here, and Gabe knows it.

"Pippa is correct," Max says. "I want to know what happened to Amanda."

Gabe stops pacing. He looks through the glass sliding doors out to The Drop. "I assumed the police would have told you."

"They did." Max's voice is slow and careful. "But it's extraordinary what the police don't know."

He lets that hang there for a moment. I'd forgotten how good Max was at creating an air of tension to give himself the upper hand.

"Look," Gabe says. "I'm really sorry about Amanda. I can't even imagine what you are feeling. But I don't have any information that you don't already know."

"You'll forgive me if I don't believe you."

"It's true. Honestly, it was as much of a surprise to me as it was to you that Amanda came here. I didn't even *recognize* her at first." Gabe pauses, changes tack. "She told me she knew what had happened between you and Pippa. She'd found a video on your computer. There was nothing I could do."

Max rubs his temple with two fingers and drags in a breath. "All right," he says. "Now tell me what really happened."

"That is what really happened," Gabe says, but with a little less conviction.

"Bullshit." Max's voice is strained. Powerful, and yet threaded with something vulnerable. His chin, I notice, wobbles. "My wife wasn't suicidal, Gabe. She would never have taken her own life. She knew how much suicide has taken from me already."

"I'm sorry," Gabe says.

"Fine," Max says through gritted teeth. "I'll take my questions to the police. I'm sure the fact that you and Amanda were previously acquainted—and that you are a former employee of mine—will be very helpful to their inquiry."

Now Gabe is silent. It is a strangely intense war between two strangely vulnerable men. A frightening prospect given that, in my experience, vulnerable men are the most dangerous.

"You could," Gabe says. "But you haven't. Which makes me think you don't *want* the police to look too closely into what happened. Why might that be, Max?"

Pippa stands up, moving closer to Gabe. Her hands remain steepled. Gabe doesn't look at her. He looks like he's almost enjoying himself now.

"You have no idea what I want," Max says coldly.

"Then tell me," Gabe says. "You're the one who called me. What do you want?"

"I told you: I want to know what happened to *my wife*," Max snaps, his emotions betraying him. He stops, takes a deep breath. When he continues, his voice is more controlled: "But since you seem reluctant to enlighten me, let's talk about something else. . . . I know she had a USB with her—why don't you tell me about that?"

Gabe sinks into the armchair. "Not much to say. The USB had the footage of you and Pippa in your office. Amanda brought it to show me because she didn't think I'd believe her."

Max closes his eyes. "Then what happened?"

Gabe rubs his forehead. "She was upset. She talked about how important fidelity was to her. Then . . . she jumped."

Max sits forward in his chair, so his head is almost resting on his knees. His face is scrunched up in an effort to restrain his emotion.

When Max doesn't reply, Gabe continues, "I didn't tell the police that Amanda and I were acquainted because I knew it would look bad. Especially after how things ended between you and me before I left Melbourne. But that's what happened."

Max is quiet for so long that Gabe has to ask if he's still there. I think Max is going to once again demand to know what really happened, but instead he switches gears. "Where is the USB now?"

A pause. "I have it."

Max sits up straight. I'd seen enough to know that the USB contained evidence of things that could destroy him, send him to jail. "I need it back," he says.

"You can't have it," Gabe replies.

Max is incredulous. "Excuse me?"

"You can't have it." Gabe's thinking on his feet, clearly. But once he says it, I can see that he warms to the idea. "I'm keeping it, in case you decide to tell the police about my connection to Amanda."

"Gabe," Max says, his voice quieter now. "I think you'll find—"

"If what is on the USB is so valuable, it will be in your interests to keep quiet. I'm sorry, Max, but it's the only way I can protect my family."

I watch Max's hand curl into a fist. "I'd urge you to reconsider, Gabe."

"I won't," Gabe says, though he looks less confident now. There's no mistaking the menace in Max's voice. And yet what can he do? He dropped the USB into a crevice between the rocks—he has nothing to give Max. He could confess that, but it would mean losing his one bit of leverage.

"Funny," Max says, "I thought you knew who you were dealing with."

"Is that a threat?" Gabe asks.

Silly boys. They're both so scared. Both talking such big talk.

"Unfortunately," Max says, "it's a promise."

Max ends the call and bangs his head against the headrest of the armchair. I can practically see the thoughts swirling in his head as he considers how to proceed, weighs up various options. Max is good at assessing risk. Excellent at devising contingency plans. It is a passion of his. But even I can see this situation has him stumped.

When he mulled over business decisions in the past, even tricky ones, he always seemed so *alive*. He practically buzzed with energy. It has occurred to me that this is what happens when genetics combine to hit the sweet spot. He had just enough magic to make him brilliant, but not so much that it sent him mad—unlike his brother.

But today, Max looks as close to mad as I've ever seen him.

Part of what is holding him back is that he still feels affection for Gabe, even now. He understands that Gabe is trying to protect himself and his family. He understands that Gabe, despite his brilliance, can make very bad decisions. His empathy for Gabe is what makes this so hard.

After several minutes, he picks up his phone. He doesn't want to do it. He knows it's the wrong thing to do. But he does it anyway.

"Baz," he says, "I have a job for you."

58

PIPPA

"What happened?" I ask the moment Gabe hangs up the phone.

I am on the couch, clutching a cushion to my chest as if it is a giant stress ball. I heard Gabe's half of the conversation, obviously, but I need to know what Max said. The idea that this is not my burden to carry is so preposterous to me now I almost laugh. How could I not share it with Gabe? He is my husband. For God's sake, Gabe *is* me.

Gabe is standing at the back door, looking out over the ocean.

"Gabe?"

Still, he doesn't respond. He ponders. Breathes. I have a sudden impulse to punch him in the face if he doesn't answer me immediately.

"*Gabe!*"

This snaps him out of it. He looks at me blankly, as if he'd forgotten I was here. "What?"

"What happened?"

"Sorry," he says. "Max didn't believe me when I told him Amanda jumped. He said if I didn't tell him the truth, he was going to the police." He turns back to the view. "But then he started asking questions about the USB, and he seemed to forget about the police."

I squeeze the edges of the cushion. "And?"

"And it occurred to me that I could use it as insurance. To stop him going to the cops."

"But you don't have it."

"No. But he doesn't know that. The important thing is that he *thinks* I have it."

He moves away from the back door and sinks onto the couch beside me. He still looks troubled.

"But he must have been upset when you said you wouldn't give it to him," I say. "Surely he's not just going to accept that?"

"He wasn't happy. But he's a pragmatist. He'll understand that we have to protect ourselves."

I'm not so sure. Would Max just let it go? I think of what Gabe said to me the other day. *Max Cameron isn't the nice guy everyone thinks he is.* I think of what Mei said. *Max Cameron is not the kind of enemy you want. He knows some dangerous people.*

"He's worried the USB will fall into the wrong hands, Pip. But it won't. It's gone. Which means Max is safe from whatever is on it . . . and we're safe from Max."

"But are we really safe? If Max is the guy you said he is, surely he's going to try to get it back?"

Gabe tucks a strand of hair behind my ear and smiles at me. It is supposed to be reassuring, but it misses somehow. I get the feeling that he's as concerned as I am.

The next question that slips out of me takes me by surprise. Yet

I must realize the weight of it, because it comes out so softly even *I* can barely hear it.

"There's nothing else, is there, Gabe? Nothing you're not telling me?"

"*No*," he says. I can see the sense of betrayal in his eyes. "There's nothing."

He puts his arms around me, and we drift into silence—Gabe in his world, me in mine. I try not to focus on the fact that I'm not sure I believe him.

59

AMANDA

(BEFORE)

Max and I both reared back as we heard the gunshot.

"Baz, Jesus. No!" Max cried. "I didn't give instructions to shoot. I said not to harm him! What are you doing?"

I put a hand on Max's arm. "What is it? What happened?"

But he didn't meet my eye, and he shook his head to silence me.

"Baz," he repeated. "Are you there? What just happened?"

Max listened. His eyes closed. "Shit. *Shit.*" He walked over to the wall and rested his forehead against it. Then, again: "Shit!"

Baz must have continued talking, because Max was silent for a while, just nodding. Finally, he said, "All right. Yes. Call me when it's done."

He ended the call, walked around his desk, and collapsed into his chair. It took me several minutes of pleading to get him to say anything at all.

"What happened?" I asked, kneeling by his side. "Tell me, Max. Please."

"It was an accident," he said at last. "A miscommunication." He had a faraway look in his eyes. I suspected he was in shock.

"But I don't understand. What kind of miscommunication? Baz is a professional. How did this happen?"

Max didn't meet my eye for the longest time. When he did, there was something in his gaze. It looked a little like responsibility. Or guilt.

"Baz didn't shoot him," Max said. "It was Gabe."

60

PIPPA

(NOW)

"What are you looking for, Daddy?" Freya asks that afternoon at the beach. It's cold but sunny and the girls are playing on the sand in their tracksuits, with buckets and spades. I sit beside them on a towel, pretending to be interested in their banter, while utterly consumed by my own thoughts.

"*Daddy!*" Freya repeats. "What are you looking for?"

Gabe is on his hands and knees on the rocks, peering into the nooks and crannies. Since his phone call with Max, he's become obsessed with finding the USB. He has fishing wire with magnets attached, which he intermittently drops into holes and then pulls out again. So far, he's pulled out two bottle tops, a five-cent coin, and a foil chocolate wrapper. He's so focused on his search that he still doesn't hear Freya's question.

"Daddy just dropped some money," I say. "He's trying to find it."

The girls look appalled. They recently discovered the value of money when Dad gave them two dollars each to buy treats at the corner store. An important lesson in fiscal management, Dad said, as they considered the price of gummy bears versus Kinder Surprises. Also a royal pain in the arse, given that they now ask the price of every item on the shelf at the supermarket, and whether that is more or less than two dollars.

"I'll help," Asha says, picking up her bucket and moving to the foot of the rocks. I watch as she starts jamming her chubby little hands into the crevices between the rocks.

"Keep looking, Daddy," Freya says supportively. "You'll find it!"

I don't share Freya's confidence. These rocks would take a crane to move, and they are stacked at least six high. Something as small as a USB would likely have slid down a crevice to the bottom, particularly given all the rain we've had. It would be like finding the proverbial needle in a haystack. I have to say, I won't be upset if it doesn't turn up. Perhaps it's the fact that I feature on that USB, but I take great comfort in knowing it's buried under the rocks. That is, I think, the perfect place for it.

But Gabe appears to feel differently.

After nearly an hour, I get up off my towel and go sit beside Gabe on the rocks. "It's not the end of the world if we don't find it, is it?" I ask.

It's not, as far as I can tell. Yet since Gabe's phone call with Max, and despite his assertions to the contrary, I can't help but feel that I'm still missing a piece of the puzzle.

"No," Gabe says. "It's not the end of the world. The important thing is that Max thinks we have it."

"So why are you even looking?"

"I'd just like to know that it really is gone. That it won't show up unexpectedly in a year's time."

"If it does, it's Max's problem, not ours."

Gabe shrugs, but a flicker of something crosses his face. It looks a little like fear.

61

AMANDA

(AFTER)

It's a sweet little beach excursion the Gerard family is on. Such a handsome family, out at the beach with their buckets and spades. They look like they wouldn't have a care in the world.

But I'm starting to realize it's a rare family that doesn't have a few problems. The Gerard family certainly have their fair share of troubles. Mental illness, infidelity, an illegitimate child, and now, criminal behavior—packaged up as a happy family day at the beach. It's just so interesting.

Perhaps the most interesting thing is that, as Gabe and Pippa sit on the rocks, agonizing over their future, they fail to notice that their darling little girl has found herself a shiny silver piece of treasure. One with my name engraved on the side. She decides not to tell her parents what she's found lest they make her return it. Instead, she pops it into her bucket and sprinkles sand over it, quick as a flash.

She's her father's daughter, that one.

62

AMANDA

"Gabe Gerard shot Arthur?"

Max sighed. "Yes."

"But why was he even *there*?"

A look of shame crossed Max's face. "He wanted to be there. He said it was his mistake that got us into this mess and he wanted to ensure that we got out of it."

"And you let him?"

Max didn't respond, but his face said he understood his error.

"Your judgment of him is skewed, Max," I said.

Max looked weary. "It's a little too late for this, Amanda."

I let out a breath I didn't realize I was holding. "So what happened?"

"Apparently, he meant to shoot *near* Arthur, to scare him. He grabbed Baz's firearm as if it were an episode of *Law & Order*. I don't know what came over him." Max rested his head in his hands. "This whole thing is a nightmare."

Baz dumped Arthur Spriggs's body in the scrub by the beach. He did a good job; it took the cops nearly a week to find it. When they did, Arthur's underworld connections meant the investigation went off in the wrong direction. The case was mentioned briefly in the papers and that seemed to be that. But Max was haunted by it.

Gabe lost his job, obviously. For a moment I'd worried Max wouldn't let him go, but thankfully he did what was necessary. Apparently, Gabe didn't take the news especially well. He begged Max to reconsider, which I thought was rich of him. He got off easy, compared to us. Now, not only did we have a shady investor in the company, its boss had just been murdered! This made extricating ourselves from the investment that much harder.

"We'll get out of it," Max said. "It's just a little more complicated now. And it will take a little longer."

"And Gabe?"

Max threw up his hands. "He moves on with his life, I guess."

"Hopefully far away from us," I said.

For a while, it looked like that was exactly what he did. But our involvement with the Gerard family didn't end there. Sometimes I wonder if that's exactly what Max wanted all along.

63

PIPPA

I've been in the supermarket for nearly an hour. Usually, I find the supermarket soothing. The rows of goods lined up and labeled and in their proper places, adjacent to similar and complementary items. The oranges and apples and bananas arranged in pleasing color-coded piles. The little baskets for weighing produce. The music playing through the speakers—Smooth FM—which almost always features a Lionel Richie song.

Today, though, I am not soothed. I attribute that to the fluttery, nauseated feeling in my belly I've become accustomed to this past week. Today, it's worse than ever. And I have the bizarre sensation that someone is watching me.

I glance up from my shopping list suddenly. The faces around me are all familiar. Preschool mums, neighbors, people I've met at the surf club. But the sensation remains. As I stand at the deli counter ordering ham, as I reach for the yogurt, as I squeeze an avocado—I feel it. It's unnerving. I watch a young mother hand her baby a peeled banana. The baby throws it on the floor. Nothing at all out of the ordinary. Everything is exactly as it should be.

I mean, it isn't ridiculous to think someone could be following me, is it? Max, for instance. Isn't it *probable* that he is keeping an eye on us? Or, if not him, one of his "people"? Someone like Max is bound to have people.

What if someone breaks into our house? I think suddenly. If Max is so desperate for the USB, it would be the obvious thing to do. He wouldn't find the USB, of course, but who knew what would happen to the house . . . and anyone in it. I think of my family, the way they drop in without warning, sometimes letting themselves in the back door. Someone could be conducting surveillance on the front, think the coast is clear and then head inside only to find Mum in the kitchen making soup, or Kat and Mei popping by for a cup of tea. I must warn them, I realize. But what would I say?

"Pippa!"

The voice comes from behind me. I spin around, gasping loud enough that the woman with the baby turns to look.

It's Dev from the Pantry. "Are you all right?" he asks.

He's carrying a woven shopping bag. Leeks and celery peek out the top. We're in a supermarket at 3:00 P.M. Never has there been a less threatening encounter. And yet my heart is racing. I put a hand to my chest, draw in two slow, deep breaths. What is wrong with me?

"Fine," I say. "Just too much . . ."

"Caffeine?"

I laugh. "Yes." If only that's all it was.

"I'm glad I ran into you. I wanted to apologize for keeping you the other day."

"Oh no," I say, realizing that I never got in touch with Dev to explain my sudden departure. Was that only the other day? It feels like a lifetime ago. "*I'm* sorry for running off. I just saw the time and remembered I had somewhere to be. You were busy serving and so I slipped out. I meant to text you. I will get in touch when I've finalized your will, though." I haven't even started on it yet. "It's been a bit busy this week. There'll be no charge."

Dev raises a hand in protest, but I raise my own hand. "I insist. You can pay me in fries. And by spreading the word of my services among your customers, if you feel so inclined."

"Well, I can certainly do that."

"Then it's a deal." I smile. "Anyway, I'd better get this shopping finished."

"Yes, me too." He steps out of the way of my shopping cart. "See you."

I feel a little better after this exchange. I'd let myself get carried away, I understand now. There is no need for me to be jumpy. It's just the events of the past week, I tell myself. It would put anyone on edge.

I finish my shop, go through the checkout, then wheel my shopping trolley into the car park. It's when I'm loading my groceries into the boot of my car that I glimpse him in my peripheral vision. A man so tall and wide that he must be some kind of bouncer or bodyguard. It would have been frightening even if he hadn't been walking directly toward me, which he was.

I grab three bags at once, and an apple rolls from one onto the ground. I leave it. Because suddenly he's beside me. He smiles, but it only makes him look even more menacing. I notice he has a tattoo of a snake on his neck.

"Whoops," he says, picking up the apple. He hands it to me. "Dropped this."

"Thank you," I whisper.

He's silent for a moment, as he assesses me. There's something not right about his gaze. "You're not nervous, are you? People are often nervous when they see me. But I'm an old softy really. Why don't I help you with this?"

Before I can object, he is reaching into my trolley. I stand there in silence while this huge, menacing man handles my groceries. There's something about the fact that he can do this in broad daylight, with people all around us, that feels more terrifying than a midnight break-in.

When the groceries are in the car, he hands me my handbag. "Here you go. It's important to return things to their rightful owner, don't you think?"

I take the bag from his outstretched hand.

"Hope you bought strawberries," he says, almost as an afterthought. "Asha's favorite, right?"

He holds my gaze, his expression serious now. When he is satisfied that I've got the message, he nods, and walks away.

64

PIPPA

(THEN)

When Asha turned three, Gabe didn't show up to her birthday party.

Things hadn't been great between us. Gabe had been so preoccupied with work that I'd barely seen him—and when I did see him, he was buzzing with the frenetic energy of someone whose mind was elsewhere. I'd come to accept I was powerless in this; I couldn't help him. But could I leave him? It felt impossible. He was the air I breathed. As difficult as life could be with him, it had to be better than life without him. Didn't it?

It was a Friday afternoon. Kat had offered to host the party at her place because her walls were painted in shades of blue and green that went perfectly with the Under the Sea theme, and Mum had decorated the house with sea creatures and sparkles and made the girls the most adorable matching squid costumes the world has ever seen. I'd attempted a mermaid cake but changed it to a sea urchin once I'd realized the level of difficulty.

I'd invited the eight little three-year-olds from my mothers' group, together with their parents—though it was mostly the mothers who could make it. Gabe had promised he'd try to be there by three, but he was nowhere to be seen. At 3:31 I tried calling and texting, but his phone was switched off. When I called his office, the receptionist acted strange. She put me on hold for quite some time, and when she returned she just said, "No, he's not here. Sorry."

I'd told everyone he was on his way, just stopping for ice, which wasn't the wisest cover because it meant that Dad didn't bother to get ice and we spent the afternoon sipping warm drinks and glancing at the door.

"Do you think he's got into an accident?" Mum said eventually.

"No," I said. "I'm sure everything's fine."

But I wasn't sure. I imagined him at a bar. Perhaps with a bartender. The truth was, Gabe could have been anywhere. With anyone.

Why hadn't I forced him to go to the follow-up appointment with Dr. Ravi?

An hour and a half later, we ended up cutting the cake without him. I remember the hot flush of irritation, combined with an icy undercurrent of dread. Where was he? *Had* he got into an accident?

"Is everything all right with Gabe, darling?"

Mum and I were in the kitchen, cutting slabs of urchin cake and placing them in turquoise napkins. I could see how difficult it was for her to ask. Mum, who'd had her own interfering mother-in-law, prided herself on never interfering in her children's marriages. The fact that she was asking made me suspect I hadn't hidden our troubles as well as I'd thought.

"Yes, of course."

"Good," Mum said. "Good. Because I did wonder if . . ." She

trailed off, but then she frowned as if deciding that she was just going to go ahead and say it. "It's just that he can be a little up and down, can't he?"

She didn't look at me as she said it, which was how I knew she was really worried.

"I don't know you what you mean."

She looked at me then, placed a hand over mine, and said, "I think you do."

It's hard to describe the humiliation of realizing that, after pretending harder than you've ever pretended, no one believed you. It was like dressing up in high heels and lipstick to get into a nightclub only to be told, in front of a long line of other clubgoers, that your ID is clearly fake. I felt so exposed. If Mum knew, who else did? Did Dad? Kat? What about our guests, standing around awkwardly waiting for their cake? Did they know what was going on too?

Eventually I pretended to take a call from him, and then said loudly how sorry I was that I didn't get his message, and did he need me to come home? When I ended the fake call, I told people he'd come down with a terrible stomach bug and was at home in bed. I said that he'd texted, but I hadn't seen it. It was clear Mum didn't buy it, and I presumed that Dad didn't either. As for the guests, I had no idea. But what else could I say?

Later, when we'd cleaned up, I packed up the car and took the girls home. Gabe still wasn't there. I put the leftover sausage rolls and cake in the fridge, fed and bathed Asha and Freya, and then put them to bed. Still no Gabe. I found homes for the new toys Asha had received. Then, when there was nothing left to do, I went to the garage for a couple of suitcases and began to pack.

I'd go to my parents' house to begin with, I decided. I'd been working part-time for the past year, but I'd be able to increase my hours and put the girls in childcare for another day. Even if Gabe didn't pay child support, we would survive—financially, at least. I just wasn't sure I'd be able to survive emotionally without him.

I had filled one suitcase when he walked in the door. He was missing his suit jacket, and his shirt was untucked. His knuckles were raw, and his sleeve was covered in blood.

"Oh my God. What happened to you?"

He looked around, as if surprised to find someone home. But his surprise quickly turned to annoyance.

"Work," he said. "It's bullshit. I'm practically running that place. No one else can do what I do, no one else spearheads the campaigns. I'm sick of working for someone else."

He was speaking fast. Almost too fast for me to understand what he was saying. It could have been alcohol or drugs, or it could have been the voices in his head.

"What happened to your hand?" I asked.

"I'm done. I'm starting my own company and I'm taking the clients with me."

"Did you hit someone, Gabe? Is that what happened?"

He nodded. He kept nodding. I didn't know if he was nodding at my question or something else, something inside his head.

"I need to go back to the office," he said suddenly.

"I think you need to go to the doctor," I said. "Why don't I call—"

"I have to go, Pippa!" His face was red, his eyes bulged. He looked like an entirely different man—a stranger. I let him go. I just wanted him out of the house.

I waited a few minutes; then I got out his boss's business card. I'd thought many times about calling him. I'd had the card for years now. Sometimes I got it out and just looked at it. In the past I'd worried that by calling I might get Gabe into trouble. But his behavior at home had been so erratic, it felt likely that he'd been the same at work. I reasoned that if his boss knew he was unwell, he might be more forgiving of Gabe's behavior. More than that, I hoped that his boss might be able to convince him to seek help when I couldn't.

"Max? It's Pippa Gerard. Gabriel Gerard's wife."

I was worried he wouldn't remember me, but he did.

"Where is he now?" Max asked when I told him briefly what was going on.

"He said he was going to the office. Who knows if he is?"

"Why don't we start there?"

There was something about the word "we" that undid me. I agreed to meet Max at the office and called Mum to come and look after the girls.

She came straight over. I didn't give her much by way of explanation, and she didn't ask, which proved that she had a much better understanding of our situation than I'd realized. I wasn't sure why I was surprised. Mum was a nurse. She'd been there for the ADHD diagnosis, the surprise grandchild. Of course she'd notice the erratic behavior!

And so I drove to the NewZ headquarters.

But Gabe never showed up.

65

PIPPA

"Gabe? Can you give me a hand with the shopping bags in the car?"

We're in the kitchen, and I've just set two bags on the counter. The girls are in the living room, playing with Lego, but they're being unusually quiet, and after Asha's recent comments we can't be too careful of little ears.

"Sure."

Gabe follows me back to the car. I wait until we're in the garage, standing in front of the open boot, before I say, "A man approached me in the supermarket car park."

The color drains from Gabe's face. "What?"

"I was putting the bags in the car, and he came up and insisted on helping. He was enormous. Clearly some kind of thug. He had a tattoo on his neck."

Gabe frowned. "What kind of tattoo?"

"A snake. Why? What difference does that make?"

He shakes his head. "What did he say?"

I stare at him for a second. "When he'd put all the grocery bags in the boot, he gave me my handbag and told me he needed to return it because it's important to return things to their rightful owner."

Gabe closes his eyes.

"Then"—I clear my throat, which is suddenly dry—"he said something about strawberries being Asha's favorite."

"Fuck," Gabe says.

"I'm worried that he'll send that man to our house. What if the girls are here? You need to call Max, Gabe. Tell him we don't have the USB."

He hesitates. "I'm not sure that's the right move."

"The right move," I say, my voice rising, "is whatever protects our children from danger, Gabe!"

"All right," he says. "I'll take care of it."

"How?" I ask.

The look on his face says he doesn't really know.

66

AMANDA

(BEFORE)

"We will never know the number of lives we have saved."

Max was standing on the podium in his dinner suit, somber-faced and commanding. All eyes were on him, and not just because he was giving the speech. All eyes had been on him since the moment he arrived. They always were.

We were at a black-tie dinner. We didn't go to many of these anymore; Max generally delegated them to younger executives. The only ones we did attend were the fundraisers for mental health and suicide prevention—and even then, he'd just pop in, do his part, and duck out again.

Tonight, Max had been complaining of a sore neck before we'd got here, and he'd taken a muscle relaxant. We joked that he would slur his way through his speech, but he sounded as impressive as ever.

"We *do* know that because of your generous donations, we have been able to provide counseling for thousands of men and women. People who might not be here today if it wasn't for your generosity."

I was seated to the side of the stage, having joined Max for the early part of the evening—the handshaking and photographs. After his speech, though, his obligations were fulfilled, and we were free to leave.

"What now?" I asked him.

He draped his jacket over my shoulders. "Lovely night for a walk."

Indeed it was. We strolled out into the mild night air, waving away the waiting car. Baz followed a short distance behind us. Since Arthur Spriggs's murder, we'd upped our security again. Now we had a guard at the front gate as well as at the door. We even moved into our penthouse apartment in the city for a while—it had a private elevator and only one entry point, which made it easier for Baz to see who was coming and going—but when a few weeks passed without incident, we felt safe enough to move back home. Still, I knew the whole matter weighed on Max. He might have been ruthless when it came to business, but he had never meant for anyone to die. If Gabe hadn't jumped in, I doubted he'd even have hurt Arthur very badly.

"But what's done is done," he'd said. And so it was. We all just needed to move on.

We walked to a boutique restaurant, where we ate mussels and drank pinot grigio. Over dinner, Max told me he'd had a difficult day. Gabe Gerard had showed up at the office in a state, unaware or refusing to acknowledge that he'd been let go. Apparently, he'd had some sort of episode, yelling and screaming and throwing furniture around.

"What did you do?"

"I wasn't there." Max sighed. "Someone called security. When I heard about it, I drove around and tried to find him, but he was long gone."

"You drove around looking for him?" My tone gave away my surprise.

Max shrugged. "He's clearly unwell."

"Clearly," I said. "But you don't drive around looking for every person who has an emotional breakdown, do you?"

Max looked at me for a long moment, as if contemplating something. Then he reached out and took my hand. "I need to tell you something. But first, there's something I want to show you."

I had to admit, I was intrigued as he led me along the river. It was a beautiful clear night, and the stars were out. We walked in silence as Baz maintained a respectful distance. After several minutes we came to a bridge running over the river, and here Max stopped.

"You see that bridge?" he said. "That's the bridge my brother jumped from when he was seventeen."

I knew Max's brother had taken his own life, of course. I'd heard Max tell the story countless times during fundraising events. But Max had always said that Harry overdosed on pills and their father found him.

"I know," Max said. "It's not the story I tell. But when I started the foundation, I knew I'd have to retell the story of Harry's death over and over, and I didn't think I could do that to myself. So I made one up. That way, it feels like I'm talking about another person. I don't know if I'd get through it otherwise."

I nodded, reluctant to speak in case I broke the spell. Max so rarely spoke about his brother, and he never did so unprompted. There was something so fragile about it. I was almost afraid to breathe.

"Harry was a golden boy," Max continued. "You know the type?

The kind of kid that actually glows. He was so good-looking. Whip-smart. Creative. And charming!" This part, like the information about the bridge, was new and pure—not the broad strokes he normally painted Harry with: "a straight-A student," "full of potential." I knew without asking this was the real story, the real Harry. "Everyone loved him. Teachers. Girls. No one had a bad word to say about Harry. I adored him too, of course." Max's eyes were misty now. "I must have been around eleven or twelve when I started noticing that something was different about him. I don't even know how to explain it. It was little things. He'd talk a bit too fast. Or he'd jump from one topic to the next without any discernible connection. It was like his brain worked faster than everyone else's. He knew what was going on in his head but no one else did."

Max was gazing out across the water. I squeezed his hand.

"He felt everything more than other people, you know? Some days he carried the weight of the world on his shoulders and he didn't understand how others weren't carrying it too. One night I got home and found a letter on the kitchen counter. He said he couldn't take it anymore. It was too much. He'd decided to jump off this bridge. There was more in the letter, but I didn't read it until later. Mum and Dad weren't home, and we didn't have mobile phones back then. I jumped on my bike and pedaled here as fast as I could. I was at this very spot when I saw him jump." He pointed to the ground where we stood. "I screamed out to him as he fell."

"Max." I held him tightly around the waist. "Oh, Max. I'm so sorry."

He wiped at a rogue tear that trickled down his cheek. "Gabe reminds me of him. He's similarly troubled. And similarly gifted. I guess I just got it in my head that if I took him under my wing and gave him . . . I don't know, a chance to channel his gifts . . . he might be all right. He might not go the way Harry did. But I was wrong."

Another tear fell. He tried to laugh it off. "Shouldn't have had that muscle relaxant or the second glass of wine."

"You're allowed to be emotional," I told him. "Muscle relaxant, wine, or not."

We found a bench and sat there for nearly an hour. And Max told me things he'd planned never to tell anyone. Things that shocked me, things that made me want to weep. Things that made me understand.

"Anyway," he said, "I think Harry would have been pleased that his brother married someone so perfect for him."

The beauty of the moment was not diminished by the fact that he didn't say the words *I love you.*

"Should we go home?" I suggested, and he nodded.

Then his phone began to ring.

67

PIPPA

I am putting away the last of the groceries when Kat throws open the back door.

"Aunty Kat!" the girls cry in unison.

"Hello, poppets!" She smiles at them, but as soon as her eyes find mine, I know something is wrong.

"I just need to speak to Mummy for a second," she says to the girls. She avoids Gabe's gaze entirely. To me she says, "In private."

I haven't seen Kat like this in a long time. Her mouth is tight and tense, as if she can't move it properly.

"All right," I say nervously. "The bedroom?"

Kat nods. She follows me there in silence and closes the door behind us. I feel like I've just been summoned to the principal's office. Tension radiates off her.

"What is it?"

"I was just at the Pantry. Everyone was talking about the fact that it was the NewZ owner's wife who jumped at The Drop."

My heart sinks. I sit on the bed, cross my legs. Then I uncross them again.

"Why is this the first I'm hearing about it?" Kat asks. "Do Mum and Dad know?" When I don't respond, she adds, "Do the *police* know?"

"It's complicated, Kat."

Kat comes closer, squatting so her eyes are level with mine. Her bump is starting to show now and it looks uncomfortable. "*What's* complicated?"

"It . . . it was a coincidence," I stammer.

"Pretty big coincidence."

"Gabe didn't recognize her. He didn't find out until afterward."

Kat frowns at me. "So, the police know then—that Gabe used to work for Max?"

I hesitate.

Kat throws up her hands. "For God's sake, Pip!"

I could explain. I could give her the excuse that Gabe and I have been reciting to each other and to ourselves for days. *It wouldn't look good. The police wouldn't understand.* But now, in front of Kat, it feels weak.

"It would have looked bad!" I say. "You know it would."

"Because it *is* bad! If Gabe didn't tell the police, it means he has something to hide."

"No. That's not true."

"Is he taking his medication?" Kat asks.

"Yes—I've checked."

"So, you're worried too, then? You must be if you've checked."

I close my eyes, breathe deeply. "I always check. The doctor recommends that someone does." I open my eyes. "Look. He didn't do anything. But if we tell the police, they'll think he had something to do with it. And now that Max—"

"Wait!" Kat's eyes widen. "You've been in touch with Max Cameron?"

"Yes."

"You need to go to the police, Pip. You need to tell them about Gabe's connection to Max. If Gabe's done nothing wrong, he has nothing to hide."

"Why is everyone assuming that Gabe is the one with something to hide?" I explode. "Why doesn't anyone consider that it could be me?"

This stops Kat.

I take a breath. "Amanda came here because she found a video— of me and Max."

Kat's jaw drops. "You mean . . . ?"

I nod. "It was before we left Melbourne. But Amanda only just found out. That's why she came here. She jumped because of *me*, Kat."

Kat sinks onto the bed.

"So you can all stop pointing your fingers at Gabe; he didn't tell the police because he was trying to protect me. *I'm* the bad guy this time."

"But why don't you just explain that to the police? It's not as if you pushed her."

"Gabe kept it a secret because he didn't want me to blame myself. But if he goes to the police now and admits he lied about knowing her, and given his history with Max, it would look terrible for him. It'd seem like he was guilty."

Kate's forehead creases. "He lied to *avoid* looking guilty?"

"No. He lied to protect me."

She stares at me for a long moment. "That doesn't make sense."

"Yes, it does. He didn't want me to—"

"What is it going to take for you to see what is happening here, Pip?" Kat cries. "What is he going to have to do? You've supported him through affairs. An illegitimate child. His career disgrace. A mental illness. What next?" She rakes a hand through her hair. "We're all worried sick about you, Pip. Me, Mei, Mum and Dad. We've been worried for years. Why do you think we all moved up here when you did? Why do you think we're always at your house?"

This stops me. "Because . . . we're a close family."

"No. No, Pippa. This isn't about us being a close family. This is about you. You've supported Gabe through a lot. Someone needed to support you."

It takes me a second to grasp this. But it's too much, too fast.

"You said this move would change everything," Kat plowed on. "For a while, I thought you might have been right. Now this. At some point, you're going to have to accept that it isn't the illness—it's Gabe. How long are you going to live like this?"

"He's my *husband*," I say softly. A pathetic response, I know, but the only one I have.

Kat stands suddenly. "Fine. But I can't support you anymore. Not when you keep acting so damn stupid." She opens the bedroom door.

"What if it was Mei?" I yell after her. "Would you stay with her? Support her?"

Kat pauses in the doorway. Suddenly she doesn't look angry anymore. She looks tired.

"I'd want to," she says. "But she would never let me."

68

PIPPA

Max Cameron was waiting for me by the automatic doors in the reception area of the huge skyscraper that housed his media empire, NewZ. It was late, and apart from the security at the front desk, the foyer was deserted.

"Pippa," he said, when he'd let me in. "It's good to see you. I'm sorry it's under these circumstances."

He was dressed in a dinner suit, minus the jacket. I felt embarrassed to realize he must have left an event to meet me. I also felt flattered.

"Thank you for meeting me."

"Why don't you come up to my office and we can make a plan?" Max said. "If Gabe shows up, security will ring me immediately. I also have my personal security detail driving around the neighborhood, on the lookout. In the meantime, if you're willing to talk about it, I'd like to understand better what has been going on with him."

I noticed a slight slur to Max's voice and wondered if he'd been drinking when I interrupted him tonight. Even so, he was reassuring. He had his personal security looking for Gabe? It made me wonder why I hadn't called him earlier.

"You saw Gabe tonight?" Max asked, as we took the elevator to the thirty-fourth floor.

"Yes. An hour or so ago. He seemed pretty . . . I don't know. Drunk? Out of it?"

Max nodded. He didn't seem surprised.

"Was he like that at work today?"

The doors slid open and we exited the elevator. "I didn't see him today. But according to reports, yes, he was in a bad way. I have to say, I'm worried about him, Pippa."

"He's been working hard lately," I said, my instinct to play down his behavior so deeply ingrained I couldn't help it. "He might be a bit burned out. Maybe he blew off some steam, had a few drinks."

Max watched me for a moment. I got the sense that he wasn't buying my excuse for Gabe's behavior. In a way, I was glad.

"I want to show you something," he said, leading me down the hallway. We stopped outside a large boardroom. The wall was glass, and I could see without entering that it had been vandalized. Chairs were strewn around the floor. There was a giant dent in the wall. The pieces of a conference phone were scattered across the large oak table.

It took me a moment to understand why he was showing me.

"Oh my God," I said, as realization dawned. "*Gabe* did this?"

Max nodded. He didn't need to say anything else after that. It was true that sometimes a picture was worth a thousand words. I saw the damage to the wall and recalled Gabe's bloodied hand. My own hand went to my mouth.

Max touched my shoulder. "Come on, let's talk in my office."

He led me into a huge corner office with floor-to-ceiling windows, polished concrete floors, and an enormous L-shaped desk. In ordinary circumstances I would have been impressed, but tonight it barely registered. All I could think about was Gabe. My husband was seriously unwell. I couldn't hide it anymore. I couldn't defend it or make excuses. I couldn't do anything . . . I didn't even know where he was.

We sat in armchairs in front of a glass coffee table.

"Do you think he might have gone out with some colleagues?" I asked. "He often goes out drinking with them when they're working on a project."

A strange look crossed Max's face. "Pippa, you do know that Gabe doesn't work here anymore?"

I stared at him. "What do you mean? He was at work today."

"Yes, he came in today. But I let him go a couple of weeks ago. When he came in today, he was very upset that he'd been let go and he wanted to speak to me. I wasn't here, unfortunately. As you can see from the state of the boardroom, he wasn't happy."

It took me several seconds to understand. "You fired him? But . . . why?"

Max chose his words carefully. "I'm guessing it won't be a surprise to you to hear that while Gabe was a valued employee at NewZ, he has also displayed some worrying behavior."

I didn't reply, but the expression on my face must have revealed something, because Max continued.

"Things came to a head a couple of weeks ago, with the streaming deal. There was a problem with one of the investors, and it was a big problem. I could see Gabe didn't take it well. I should have followed up with him. I'm so sorry."

I didn't respond; I was still reeling from this new information. Gabe had lost his job a couple of weeks ago and never told me?

"This is a personal question, Pippa," Max said gently, "but I need to ask: Has he ever been violent at home? Has he ever hurt you or your daughters?"

"*No.*" Even the idea of it shocked me. Then I remembered Gabe's face tonight. So red and angry. "But things have definitely escalated lately. Tonight, when he came home . . . he frightened me. It's the first time I've felt like that."

"Does he have a diagnosed condition?"

"ADHD," I said. "But I—I'm not sure that's what's wrong with him."

"I have to agree," Max said. "I'm not a psychiatrist, but what happened today seemed more like a kind of psychosis. Is that possible?"

"*Anything* is possible." I felt tears on my face and realized I was crying. I stood and walked to the window. This was it, I realized. If Gabe was this far gone, there was no one in the world who could help him.

"You've done an extraordinary job managing this, Pippa," Max said, joining me at the window. "But this is more than any one person can handle. Gabe needs professional help, possibly as an inpatient. There's no shame in it. And if insurance doesn't cover the out-of-pocket costs, I'd be happy to cover them personally."

It was extraordinarily generous of him. But I found it hard even to think about out-of-pocket costs when I didn't know where Gabe was. I imagined him wandering around the city. Maybe he'd found a bar to drink in. Maybe he'd found a bartender? Later, he'd be full of apologies, and I'd be full of doubt. *He didn't mean it! He was ill.* Then he'd go to see Dr. Ravi, maybe get a new diagnosis, and we'd start all over again.

As all of this settled over me, I let out a sob. Max didn't really open his arms, but I fell against him and rested my head against his chest. He widened his stance and became a warm, solid wall. I wanted to disappear into it. Bury my head. Make it all go away.

"What do I do, Max?" I cried.

He put his arms around me. There was something about it. For so long I'd felt like I was alone, carrying the secret of Gabe's illness. Suddenly there was someone else, someone who truly seemed to care.

"It's all right," he said softly. "We'll sort this out, I promise."

He was so authoritative. I *believed* it. It made me imagine what it must be like to be married to someone like Max. Someone you could count on. Someone who didn't create drama but, rather, helped you sort it out. It was *intoxicating*.

I stepped back and looked at him. It may have been the fact that he was giving me exactly what I'd been craving from Gabe for so long, but it was as if I saw him anew. He even *looked* a little like Gabe. I'd always thought the line between attraction and desperation was thin. I was desperate for comfort. I *yearned* for it. It did something to me. I lifted my chin and kissed him.

It came over me then, all at once, like a frenzy. A *need*. Was this how Gabe felt, I wondered, with the bartender? I pulled off my T-shirt, my bra. I stepped forward and pressed myself against him. It wasn't about Max, I knew that, even then. It wasn't even about me. Like everything else in my life, the entire fucking thing was all about Gabe.

69

PIPPA

Gabe doesn't say it aloud, but judging by the next few days, our new plan is to never leave our house. We don't take the girls to pre-school. We don't go to the park or the beach. We don't even set foot outside. We start employing rudimentary security measures that we haven't bothered with in the past, like locking windows and security doors. We even figure out how to use the alarm, which is something that has been on our to-do list since we moved in. We don't discuss our reasons for any of this, because that would involve Gabe admitting he was worried. Instead, we do it by silent agreement.

For me, it isn't a huge break from my routine. I work, conduct my Zoom meetings, play with the girls. They cope well to begin with. Once, as I walk past their room, I hear them pretending they are at the beach, and Asha acts as if she has discovered treasure. I wish I could escape to an imaginary world so easily.

Gabe is a different story. Staying indoors has never suited him.

He needs to be active, to move his body. He's trying to hide it, but I can see he's barely reining himself in.

By the fourth day, even the girls have had enough.

"I want to go to preschool," Asha says.

Gabe and I look at each other. Since my encounter in the car park, it has been quiet. No word from Max. No indication that he plans to go to the police or attempt to retrieve the USB. But, then again, we haven't been anywhere.

"How about we play outside in the sandpit for a bit?" Gabe offers by way of a compromise.

The girls, starved of any such fun for days, accept this and burst outside before he can change his mind, excitedly chatting about the treasure they will discover out there.

For a while, I stand at the window and watch them. The sandpit was built by Gabe and Dad shortly after we moved in; they cleverly designed the wooden cover so that it can be folded in half to become a bench seat. Gabe does this now and sits facing the cliff as the girls get busy with their buckets and spades.

Kat's words echo in my mind. *If Gabe didn't tell the police, it means he has something to hide.* I don't get it. Why was everyone so quick to blame Gabe? They *love* Gabe.

At least, I'd thought they did. I remembered Kat saying, *Why do you think we all moved up here when you did? Why do you think we're always at your house?* How had I missed that? And if I'd missed that ... what else am I missing?

There's one final thing Kat said that I keep thinking about— perhaps more than anything else. *How long are you going to live like this?*

It's the question I most desperately want answered. And I'm starting to realize that the only one who can do that is me.

70

AMANDA

(BEFORE)

"Just the two of us, the horizon, and all these lovely staff," Max said with a laugh, as he touched his champagne glass to mine.

It was Christmas, and once again we were on a yacht in the Whitsundays. It was idyllic. I'd never seen water so clear or sand so white. And I'd never seen Max so relaxed. For a week, he didn't so much as check his emails. We snorkeled and swam. I took photographs. We sat on the deck and drank wine. We fished. One night, we rowed to shore in a dinghy and our captain cooked freshly caught tuna on a makeshift barbecue. We ate it on the sand while drinking white wine.

"Do you ever wish that you had been pregnant that time?" Max asked out of the blue.

I knew the time he meant. I was surprised to hear that Max remembered it too. Or, if not surprised that he remembered it, I was surprised that he'd thought about it, reflected on it, since.

"For a while I did," I admitted. "When I saw a baby, or when my friends' children were little and they were entirely consumed by them."

Max was listening to me so intently. There was something pained about his expression, and it hit me suddenly that this was something he'd been carrying all these years. Maybe I'd even seen that pained expression in his eyes on those odd occasions we were in the company of a newborn baby.

I saw the apology he was about to offer, so I made sure I got in first. "But now I see what a gift it has been, just the two of us, spending our lives together. And I'm grateful for it. Truly."

I was. Of course, if we'd had children, I'm sure we wouldn't have regretted it. We probably would be sitting here surrounded by our family, talking about how empty our lives would have been without them. But we would have been wrong. Our lives were not empty. Even with all that remained unsaid between us, as I sat there with Max, it was hard to imagine any alternative reality in which I would be more content, more fulfilled.

And still the sadness remained on Max's face. "You always asked so little of me, Amanda. I should have given you so much more."

I smiled. "You gave me what I asked, remember? Fidelity. That was the deal."

Max smiled back. His eyes were both sad and happy.

"Darling," he said, "it was such an easy thing to give."

71

PIPPA

(NOW)

I stay in my office for over an hour while Gabe is outside with the girls in the sandpit. When I finish my work, the house is quiet. After days of being cooped up in the house, it is strange. I close my computer and go to the kitchen, wait for the kettle to boil, make a cup of tea. I'm jiggling the tea bag in the water when I hear the toilet flush, and then Gabe walks into the living room.

"Bathroom," he says by way of explanation, but I'm already opening the glass doors, scanning the yard for the girls.

The sandpit is empty.

The spike of adrenaline is instant. My face becomes hot. My mouth becomes dry. My vision blurs at the edges.

I look beyond the fence toward the bushes and the moonah trees. Toward The Drop . . .

I see the man first—the giant man from the car park. He's bent over, talking to my little girls. As he stands upright, my stomach lurches. The size of him next to the tiny girls makes my blood run cold. They're so close to the cliff edge. He could pick one up in each hand and in a heartbeat they'd be gone.

"Gabe," I say in a strangled voice.

And then I run faster than I ever have in my life.

72

AMANDA

It's funny how bad things sneak up on you when you least expect it. It's almost as if the universe wants to maximize the utter shock and despair. For a year, Max and I had been happy. Gabe and Pippa had moved away, and the drama with Arthur Spriggs had settled. Max was still working, but he was winding back—handing over more things to the executives and coming home earlier and earlier. We'd started to talk about retirement.

"I've been thinking about it," Max said. "It's time for a life change. I think we should move overseas. Maybe to Europe. We can sell the business and start over."

"But how can we sell the business without exposing the investment from A.S. Holdings?"

"I don't know yet, but I'm going to set up a meeting with the accountants to see what's possible."

It was on that day—the day the accountant came to our

house—that I found Max's secret laptop on the floor of the walk-in wardrobe, next to the open safe. I hadn't seen it in a while; I'd almost forgotten it existed. Max had probably come in to check something and then forgotten to put it away.

For over a minute, I just stared at it. After years of coveting this computer, or at least its contents, I suddenly felt reluctant to touch it. Max and I had been so settled. What if I discovered something I didn't want to know? What would I do then?

Still, I found myself closing the door of the wardrobe and kneeling on the floor. I gently turned the screen to face me. A spreadsheet was open, one I couldn't make heads or tails of—but then spreadsheets were always like gibberish to me. I minimized it and opened the email inbox. That was where the interesting stuff would be found—or it was in the movies, at least.

But this wasn't the movies. Most of the messages were years old and appeared technical—about servers and systems. There were a few from Arthur Spriggs, which caught my eye, though the contents of these messages was disappointingly dull. More recently, I found emails from Baz and other members of the security detail.

To my relief, all the names in the inbox were male. I was about to pack it in when I noticed an email from someone by the name of Stef.

I clicked on it.

Consider it done.

An innocuous enough message, but I scrolled down anyway. It turned out Stef's full name was Stefan, and he was the head of security at NewZ. Now I thought of it, I might have met Stef the day Arthur Spriggs's men broke into our house—a stocky intense little man, who Max insisted was very good at his job.

Evidently Stef was the type never to start a new email thread; he just replied to the last message he'd received, even if it was about an entirely different matter. Annoying trait, I imagined. As I scrolled down, I came across quotes for security systems, information about alarms, policies for security passes. Most of the messages originated from Stef, and Max's replies were brief, along the lines of "Sounds good," "Well done," "Great job."

I was about to close the computer when I came across a message from Max to Stef.

> *Hi Stef,*
> *Need a quick chat about CCTV footage from my office last night.*
> *Max*

I scrolled up and saw that Stef had replied a few minutes later.

> *Sure. Call me anytime.*

Then an hour and a half after that:

> *As per our discussion, please confirm that the attached is the section you would like deleted.*

One minute later, a message from Max to Stef.

> *That's it. Cheers.*

I looked at the email. There was no attachment.

I sat back on my haunches. Why would Max want to delete

footage from his office? Try as I might, I couldn't think of a scenario that would explain it.

I glanced over my shoulder. Max could walk in any time; I didn't
have time to search the computer for it. Instead, I got out my keys
and stuck the USB into the computer. Once the flash drive in-
stalled, I clicked "All Programs" and then "Backup." Once I was
done, I replaced the computer exactly where it was on the floor, the
spreadsheet maximized on the screen. If the footage was on this
computer, I was going to find it.

73

PIPPA

I race toward The Drop with Gabe on my heels. The girls call and wave. The man turns to see us running toward him, then sprints away at a speed I wouldn't have thought possible for someone so enormous. Gabe and I each seize a girl.

I clutch Freya so tightly she cries out. "Mummy! Stop that."

In Gabe's arms, Asha is also protesting. But we don't release them until we are all back inside the house and the sliding door is closed and locked. I close the curtains too.

When I'm sure we're safe, I drop to my knees. "What were you doing out there?" I try not to shout but am only partly successful. I grip Freya's little hand. "We've told you you're *not supposed to go near the cliff.*"

The two of them look both defensive and guilty.

"But we were with a grown-up!" Asha says triumphantly, hopeful that this loophole will get them out of trouble. "We're allowed to go there with a grown-up."

"*No!*" I say. "No, Asha. You're allowed to go out there with Mummy or Daddy, or Nana and Papa, or Kat or Mei. Not with any other grown-up. Definitely not with a stranger."

She frowns crossly. "But he was super nice! He had jelly beans."

"And he had a picture of a snake on his neck," Freya adds. "His name was Ralph."

Both girls are smiling. I am shaking.

"The man's name was Ralph?" I ask, thinking this might be useful to tell the police. But, then, we can't tell the police about this, can we?

"No, silly," Asha says, laughing. "The *snake's* name was Ralph."

Freya slides her hand from my grip. Asha tries to do the same with Gabe, but he holds her tight. "What did he say to you? You need to tell us everything, do you understand?"

"He was a very big man," Asha says, after a moment's thought. "Even bigger than you, Daddy."

"I thought he was a giant," Freya adds.

"Me too!" Asha says.

They don't seem the least bit intimidated. It's as if they've had a visit from Mickey Mouse. I can't decide if I should be relieved or if this makes it more chilling. I notice, suddenly, that Asha is holding a small piece of lined paper, the type that you tear out of a notebook. "What's that, Asha?"

I reach for it, but Asha yanks it back.

"The giant man gave it to me. But he said I had to give it to Daddy." She hands it to Gabe. "He said he might come back and visit again, to make sure you got the message."

Gabe looks at the note for a second, then closes his eyes. I snatch it out of his hands and read it.

Last chance to play nice.

74

AMANDA

(AFTER)

Max is standing at the window, looking out over the vast, blue ocean. It's obvious to me he's thinking about Baz, and the note he's instructed him to give the little girls. Max may be a hard-nosed businessman in a lot of ways, but he isn't cut out for the criminal life. He never wanted anyone to get hurt—not even Arthur Spriggs. He certainly doesn't want anything to happen to Pippa, or her little girls.

He is so lost in thought that the sound of his phone ringing startles him. He turns and sees it on the dining table.

"Max Cameron," he says, lifting it to his ear.

"Mr. Cameron, it's Detective Sergeant Conroy. We spoke the other day."

If Max is rattled to hear from the police, it's not apparent. He seems calmer than the last time they talked. As if he's in control again. "Yes, Detective. I believe my accountant has set up a meeting with you for tomorrow, correct?"

"That's right. But there is another matter I wanted to discuss with you. It concerns a former employee of yours—Gabriel Gerard. I understand he was the person responsible for recruiting A.S. Holdings as an investor?"

"If you say so," Max says neutrally.

"According to our records, Mr. Gerard was let go shortly after Arthur Spriggs, of A.S. Holdings, was murdered." He lets that hang there for a moment. "What's most interesting is that Mr. Gerard was also the last person to talk to your wife, Amanda, before she jumped off the cliff."

Max doesn't respond. It's hard to tell if this is strategic or not.

"This isn't a surprise to you?" Detective Conroy asks.

"I didn't say that."

"I see. Well, I must admit we are a little curious as to why Mr. Gerard never mentioned that he was a former employee of yours in his statement to police. Which makes me wonder . . ."

"Wonder what?" Max's question is tinged with frustration. I have the impression he wishes Detective Conroy would dispense with the theatrics and just spit it out.

"It makes me wonder if Mr. Gerard had more to do with your wife's death than originally reported."

"I'm sorry, Detective," Max says. "The other day you said you were investigating the murder of Arthur Spriggs?"

"I am. But there is a clear overlap here. Mr. Gerard was fired from your organization for bringing a criminal investor on board. A criminal who was murdered. A year later, your wife is found at the bottom of a cliff outside this same employee's home. You'll understand our interest, I'm sure."

Again, Max opts for silence. I wonder what is going through his mind.

"Listen, Mr. Cameron," the detective says finally. "I get it. It's clear that you and Gabriel Gerard have dirt on each other. But in these kinds of situations someone always talks. If that person is you, your journey through the courts will be looked on a little more favorably. If it's not, that benefit will be offered to Mr. Gerard. The choice is yours."

Detective Conroy waits. I wait. Max will not be hurried as he weighs up his next move. Eventually, he lets out a long sigh.

"Fine," Max says. And he starts to talk.

75

AMANDA

It took over an hour to go through the files that I'd imported onto my USB from Max's laptop. I loaded them onto my own computer and went through it all in my study. Max was busy with the accountant, totally preoccupied, but I kept the screen facing away from the door just in case.

I thought it would be simple to find it. I searched file by file. I found some interesting stuff, no question. Invoices made out to Arthur Spriggs's company. Spreadsheets and profit-and-loss statements from Max's early years in business—ones he was so desperate to hide he kept them on a laptop locked in a safe. I found letters from lawyers pertaining to individuals who needed to be silenced. Reports from detectives who'd undertaken surveillance jobs. But no video. I couldn't decide if I was annoyed or relieved.

Suddenly I remembered something Max had told me once about hidden files. I opened a Google browser, typed in "How to find hidden files," and Google produced some very straightforward instructions. And just like that, there it was. A video. It was four minutes long, saved by the date.

It worried me, I'll admit, that Max would leave incriminating emails with Arthur Spriggs where they could be easily found yet hide the contents of this video. What did that mean? As my mouse hovered over the file, I registered the date. It was the night he'd taken me to the bridge his brother had jumped from. The night that Max had been called away . . . by Pippa Gerard.

I remember the way Max's face had changed when he answered the call.

"Of course. I'll meet you at the office."

When he'd explained why he had to go, I understood. He was apologetic, of course. He called the car around and asked Baz to see me home.

He got home a couple of hours later. I roused as he slid into bed.

"Everything all right?" I asked.

I couldn't remember if he responded, but I remembered that he'd fallen asleep with his arms around me that night, and we stayed like that until morning. That was the image in my head when I clicked on the file and the grainy image appeared on the screen. It showed Max in his office, standing next to a woman I dimly recognized as Pippa Gerard. He appeared to be hugging her. Then they shifted. Pippa lifted her chin. Her hands moved down his back. And she kissed him.

I reached for my wastepaper basket and vomited.

76

PIPPA

(NOW)

I follow Gabe as he stalks to the bedroom.

"What are you doing?" I say to him. "Are you calling Max?"

He holds a palm up, silencing me. I remain in the doorway, my gaze darting back and forth between him—pacing with the phone pressed to his ear—and the girls, whom I will never take my eyes off ever again.

"Max," Gabe says after a couple of seconds. "Yes, my four-year-old daughters passed that message along. What kind of person would—"

Gabe is quiet, so I assume Max has cut him off. The hand holding the phone is shaking—whether in fear or anger, I don't know.

"In that case, you might as well come and get it," Gabe says.

I stare at him. Come and get it? The USB? But we don't have it!

"Will you be coming in person or sending one of your thugs?"

Gabe asks. "Fine. Give me half an hour to get my family out of the house. I assume you'll understand if I don't want them around?"

"What the hell are you doing?" I say when he hangs up.

"I'm meeting Max," he says. "To give him the USB."

"But you don't *have* the USB." I steal a glance at the girls, sitting openmouthed in front of the television. They haven't moved a muscle.

Gabe walks to the window, looks out. "Take the girls to your parents' house, Pip. Stay there until I let you know it's safe to come back."

"Not until you tell me what you're going to do."

He turns and looks me in the eye. "I'm going to fix it."

77

AMANDA

(BEFORE)

Max was still in his office with the accountant. Down the hall, my whole world had fallen apart. The image would forever be burned into my mind. Pippa kissing Max. Pippa taking off her top and pressing herself against him. That's where the video ended. Part of me was glad I didn't have to watch any more than that. If I had, I was sure I'd be sick again.

The ache of it was physical. I'd heard people talk about having a sick feeling or a heaviness in their belly when they were heartbroken, but this wasn't just in my belly—it was in every single cell. *Max* was in every single cell. It's one thing finding out your husband is unfaithful when you are primed for it. Expecting it. But after all I'd done to avoid this exact situation—the years of eavesdropping, the spying—I'd been caught unawares. How could I have been so stupid?

I desperately wanted to make sense of it. Was it a chance

encounter? An affair? As far as I knew, Max hadn't anticipated Pippa's call on the night in question. It had come out of the blue. Pippa had claimed to be worried about her husband's mental state, I recalled. Was that the truth? Or was it all part of a ruse to get Max to come to her?

And was Max in on the ruse?

I was still staring at the screen when Max stuck his head into my office. I stared at him anew, changed somehow in the wake of what he'd done. He looked different to me. Like an impostor. A wax statue of my husband.

"We have to head to the office for a couple of hours," he said. "I'll be home for dinner, though."

I nodded. Smiled. I might have waved. It all felt robotic. But Max didn't seem to notice. Funny to think that this was the last time I ever laid eyes on him.

After he was gone, I looked back at the screen. Did he love Pippa Gerard? Was that what this was about? Pippa and Gabe had moved away very soon after the night of the video. To Portsea—a lovely spot. We had a beach house there ourselves, which we used for a month each summer. Max said he was glad Gabe was able to make a fresh start. Was he also glad because it meant he didn't need to live with the guilt of his affair with Gabe's wife?

Only a week or two ago Max had showed me an article about how Gabe had earned himself a reputation as a "suicide whisperer," talking to people who came to the cliff outside his house, convincing them that they had something left to live for. I thought it was a lovely full-circle moment. I'd been happy for him. Now I was sad for him. Sad for me.

I needed answers, and I wasn't going to get them from Max.

I picked up my computer, carried it to the dining room table, and left it there, open, where he would see it. Why bother with a note when this would tell him everything he needed to know? Then I removed the USB.

Now, I needed to speak to Pippa.

78

PIPPA

It took me a couple of minutes to realize that Max wasn't responding to me. I'd been too wrapped up in my own rebellion, throwing off the shackles of the perfect wife. But gradually I became aware of Max's stillness, and I stepped back and looked up at him.

"I'm sorry, Pippa," he said. "I hope I didn't give you the wrong impression. But I love my wife."

I was mortified, but Max seemed even more embarrassed than me. He could barely meet my eye.

"I'm so sorry," I said, hurriedly retrieving my bra and T-shirt from the floor. "I'll leave now."

"I'll call security and let them know you're coming down," he said, when I was dressed. Polite to the end.

I traveled down in the elevator alone.

I was almost home when I received a phone call from Max's

security guard saying Gabe had returned to the NewZ offices. He'd been in a highly agitated state, and Max had called an ambulance. I was stunned that, after everything, Max was still helping Gabe.

I turned the car around and drove to the hospital.

79

AMANDA

(AFTER)

As Max talks to Detective Conroy, a sense of peace washes over him. I feel it too, even though I'm still not sure where I am, or what I'm doing here, on this strange threshold between the universe and beyond. What I do know is that while I've been in this liminal space, I've discovered things that most people never get to see. Things which have altered my perspective on the messiness of humanity.

It's as if, while living your life, you view the world through a straw. You see only the tiniest sliver, all of it from your own perspective. Other people have their motives, their backstories, their feelings, but you don't know that unless they share them with you, and even then there's every chance they're lying or prevaricating. What strikes me most now is the *audacity* of people, walking around with such certainty while armed with only the scantest information. I'm ashamed to say I was one of those people.

But in death, you see everything. All perspectives, all motives, all backstories. It's overwhelming at first, wading through it all. Not to mention horribly unsatisfying. With perspective, you lose glorious things like self-righteousness, self-pity. You still feel deceived and hurt, but they swim among other, more compelling emotions, like understanding, and empathy, and concern. Emotions you don't necessarily want to feel for those who have caused you pain.

Of course, of particular interest to me is Max's infidelity with Pippa Gerard. In death, I can see the moment it happened, as well as everything that led up to it. The context is unsettling and, frankly, irritating. It takes away my white-hot rage and replaces it with a whole spectrum of feelings, ranging from betrayal to compassion.

I see that, like me, Pippa is a woman who loves her husband deeply. A woman who has put up with more than she should have for the sake of her marriage. A woman who, among other things, took in her husband's love child and never once resented that baby for her father's wrongdoing. A woman who made a bad choice on a desperate evening when she attempted to seduce Max, but who isn't overall bad. If anything, in the context of her own marriage, I can almost understand it. There's only so many times you can be hit before you decide to hit back.

In death I discover that Max's intention, on meeting Pippa that night, was pure. I discover that, on top of the emotion he was feeling, the wine and pain medication created a perfect storm for Max. But the most interesting thing I discover in death is that I misunderstood what happened after the video stopped. In death, I see the whole scene unfurl. And instead of breaking my heart, it brings me such immense joy, I feel like my feet might lift off the ground and take me all the way to heaven.

80

PIPPA

The girls protest as I pull them from their beanbags.

"We were watching *In the Night Garden*!" Asha cries. She wriggles out of my grip and plonks back on the beanbag. "The Pinky Ponk has just arrived!"

"And the Pontipines!" Freya adds.

I grab a tote and throw in some snacks, spare clothes for the girls, and their teddies.

"But we're going to Nana and Papa's," I say with forced cheerfulness.

The girls are torn. I watch their little faces as they weigh up the premature ending of *In the Night Garden* against the likelihood that their grandparents will shower them with treats. It's a significant dilemma. I can almost see their little minds whirling.

My mind is whirling too. Max is coming here. Gabe has promised him the USB. When Max finds out he doesn't have it . . . I don't know what's going to happen.

Or do I?

"You need to go, Pip," Gabe says. "It's been fifteen minutes."

He's strangely calm. It's almost enough to calm me. Almost. We each strap a girl into her car seat and close the door, and then I meet Gabe in front of the car. "Gabe, are you sure . . . ?"

"Don't worry, Pip. Leave everything to me."

He kisses me and pushes me gently into the car. The girls are arguing before we even get out of the driveway, and I'm glad because it drowns out my thoughts.

It's okay, I tell myself. *Gabe's got this.*

"Asha!" Freya whines. "It's my turn."

"But it's my special treasure!"

"Mummy," Freya cries. "Asha's not sharing."

I turn out of our street. "Share, Asha."

"But it's mine!" Asha says.

I glance in the rearview mirror to see what they're arguing over this time. And that's when I see what Asha is holding. It's tiny and silver.

I slam on the brakes and pull over to the side of the road.

"Where did you get that?" I say, leaning between the front seats to snatch it from Asha's hand. I examine it closely, seeing the name engraved on the side. AMANDA CAMERON. I look back at my daughter. "Asha?"

"At the beach," she says. She's part sulky, part nervous about getting into trouble. "I found it in the rocks when Daddy was looking for money. But it's mine!"

"Why didn't you tell me?"

She blinks. Shrugs as if to say, *Why would I?*

I sit for a moment, trying to figure out what to do. Should I go back? No, not with the girls in the car. I'll drop them off and then return home with the USB. *It'll be fine*, I think. *Now, everything will be fine.*

"Dad!" I call through my open window when I pull into Mum and Dad's driveway and see Dad in the front yard, pulling weeds. "Can you mind the girls for an hour or two?"

Without waiting for a response, I fling open the car doors and start getting the girls out.

"Hi, sweetie." Dad stands upright. "Sure. Everything all right?"

"Fine. It's just . . . I have a meeting and Gabe isn't feeling well. I won't be long."

"Slow down, Pip," Dad says. "A meeting's not worth giving yourself a heart attack."

He gives the girls a high five and they disappear inside, probably looking for Freddo frogs.

"I know. But it's an important meeting. I'll be as quick as I can."

I start to get into the car, but Dad stops me. "Pip, wait."

"What?" I say impatiently.

Dad looks uncomfortable. "Are you sure you're okay? You haven't been yourself these past weeks. And it's not just me who thinks so. It's Kat and Mei, and your mother. In fact, you seem an awful lot like the old Pippa that I thought we'd left behind in Melbourne."

"I'm fine." I squeeze the USB in my hand. "It's just a bit hectic right now, Dad."

"Your life is often hectic," Dad says. "At least, it has been since you met Gabe."

I almost laugh. There goes another family member, turning on Gabe.

"Dad—" I start, but he continues over the top of me.

"Listen, Pip. I want you to know that while we love Gabe, we have grave doubts about his ability to be a loving and supportive partner to you. It's just one thing after another with him, and you always end up hurt. He's so volatile; we just don't know what he's capable of."

He says it loudly and all in one burst, as if he doesn't want to lose his nerve. It silences me.

We don't know what he's capable of.

But I do, I realize suddenly. I do know.

Gabe is planning to kill Max. The realization hits me with blunt force. How else could he fix this, without the USB? Why else would he want us all out of the house?

I glance at my watch. It's been half an hour. "I'm sorry, Dad—I have to go."

I reverse the car out of the driveway and, with a screech of tires, accelerate down the street.

I know what I have to do.

81

PIPPA

"We believe that Gabe has bipolar disorder," Dr. Sullivan said.

I was sitting in a vinyl armchair in a small room off Gabe's ward. Gabe had been admitted as an inpatient to the psychiatric facility, after having what his new psychiatrist explained was a psychotic episode. Since then, he'd been sedated, poked, prodded, and questioned. An endless trail of medical professionals had been in and out. I'd been by his side, or just outside his room, the whole time.

"Bipolar?" I said. "Gabe is *bipolar*?"

"We believe so, yes."

"But what about the ADHD?"

"A misdiagnosis," Dr. Sullivan said. "Or, perhaps he has both—that's not uncommon either. ADHD and bipolar disorder share many symptoms, but the delusions and paranoia and psychosis Gabe experienced are not associated with ADHD. And given the extended periods of mania he has experienced, I am confident bipolar is the correct diagnosis."

It takes me a minute to digest this. "Do you think he's had it his whole life?"

"These days, most people are diagnosed in their teens or early twenties. But it can be missed. And it's clear you've been propping him up for a long time, Pippa."

A thought hits me, so strong and powerful it takes my breath away. "Our daughters! Will this . . . I mean, is it hereditary?"

"There is a genetic link. If one parent has bipolar disorder, we see an increased risk of it in a child. If both parents have it, the chances increase again. But many children of bipolar parents do not have the disorder. My advice would be to keep an eye on your daughters and have them assessed if you have any concerns."

Of course I was thinking of Asha. She was her father's daughter. And as it wasn't beyond the realm of possibility that her biological mother might also have had bipolar disorder, or another mental illness, I'd be keeping a very close eye on her.

"The good news is that, with medication and therapy, the prognosis is good. Especially as he has such wonderful family support. I have every confidence that he will lead a full and productive life, Pippa."

I latched on to this. Clung to it. Perhaps stupidly, after everything that had happened, I felt hopeful. Now that he was receiving proper treatment, I told myself, I'd have Gabe back. The real Gabe.

"Let's start again, Gabe," I said, a couple of weeks later. I'd spent much of that time at Gabe's side, learning as much about bipolar disorder as I could.

Gabe was still in the hospital, but the new medication was

starting to take effect, and I could see glimpses of the old him. Now that he had been diagnosed, life would get better, I was sure of it. And a fresh start would help him along.

"We could move out of the city—maybe down the coast? You can have some time off and take care of the girls, and I can grow my client list like I've been meaning to."

We started looking at homes right then and there on our phones. Only a few days later, we fell in love with the cliff house.

There was still the matter of what happened between Max and me. It bounced around in the back of my mind constantly, a bizarre little flashback that felt like a dream. It was the kind of thing that, under the circumstances, I could have kept to myself. We were moving away, starting again. Max was unlikely to mention it. Besides, nothing even happened. Max stopped it before it started.

And yet.

I was surprised to realize there was a part of me that wanted to hurt Gabe. While I accepted that he'd been unwell, it didn't change the fact that he'd hurt and betrayed me. For my own self-respect, it felt important to even the score. Then I could put everything behind us, for good.

So, while he lay in the hospital bed, I told Gabe what had happened in Max's office. Except this version had a different ending.

82

PIPPA

The house is quiet. I race from room to room, throwing open the doors, as if expecting to find Max and Gabe sitting in a bedroom together, but they are nowhere to be found. I'm about to lose hope when, through the back sliding door, I see them outside.

They are standing at The Drop, close to the edge—precariously so. Just as on the day of Amanda's death, the wind is wild. Both men stand unnaturally tall, their legs wide, their shoulders back. Max has his back to the cliff, Gabe faces it.

I throw open the door. "Hey!" I shout, loud enough for my voice to carry through the wind.

They both turn to look. The color drains from Gabe's face.

"Pippa, go inside," he says as I make my way across the lawn and let myself out the gate.

"No."

Max's gaze moves to me. He's wearing a navy woolen coat over his clothes, brown leather driving gloves, heavy boots. I am in a T-shirt and jeans, but I don't feel the cold. I feel acutely aware of how deserted it is—midweek, midafternoon, outside of school holidays. There's no one around. The houses on either side of ours are week-enders, empty today. Anything could happen and there would be no one but us to see.

"Gabe just explained that he got rid of the USB." Max has the kind of careful blank expression that I imagine would be useful in business meetings.

"It's true," I say. "He dropped it into the rocks the day after Amanda died. But I have it."

Gabe's head snaps to me. "What?"

I hold it up. "Asha found it at the beach." I keep my gaze on Max. "But if I give you this, we want our life back. More importantly, we want to know that our daughters are safe."

"You have my word," Max says.

"Wait!" Gabe cries. "You can't just hand it over. What's stopping him from going to the police the moment he leaves here? Or what if he forgets to call off his thugs? Pip, he had our *girls*!" Gabe's voice cracks.

"For the record, I would never have let any harm come to . . ." Max stops suddenly. It's almost as if he's lost track of what he was going to say. His gaze drifts to Gabe and it becomes softer. "Baz was instructed not to scare them, just to leave the note."

"We have to trust him, Gabe," I say. "What choice do we have? Whatever dirty secrets you have on here, Max, are all yours."

I hand him the USB. Max takes it, and for a moment everyone is silent. I half expect Gabe to make a grab for it. Perhaps he would have? But after a few seconds, Max drops the USB and crunches it under the heel of his boot. Then, while we watch, he pushes the remnants of the USB over the cliff with his foot.

"I told you I'd destroy it," Max says to Gabe. "I also called Baz before I left home and told him I had resolved things between us. And I have no intention of speaking to the police. All I want is to know what happened to Amanda. She died suddenly, in very strange circumstances which I know almost nothing about. The only way I'll ever find out what was going through her head in the lead-up to her death is if you tell me."

"She *jumped*," Gabe says. "She was devastated. She said your relationship was based on trust and fidelity. Since you slept with Pippa, she didn't feel obliged to keep our secrets any longer."

Max's eyes move to me. "Amanda believed I'd *slept* with Pippa?"

Max stares at me. I force myself to hold his gaze. It's the very least I can do. The only thing I can offer him. But I feel like I might die from the shame. "I told Gabe that's what happened. I'll never forgive myself."

Gabe turns to look at me. "You didn't sleep with Max?"

I shake my head.

"All right," Max says. "What happened then?"

"Like I said, she jumped."

Max isn't convinced and the men argue for a moment, but I tune out, stuck on something Gabe said.

Since you slept with Pippa, she didn't feel obliged to keep our secrets any longer.

"What did you mean, Gabe?" I say. "When you said Amanda didn't need to 'keep our secrets' anymore?"

Gabe frowns, shrugs. "Did I say that?"

"Was Amanda going to reveal something about Max?" Then I think of the word "our." "About *you*?"

Gabe's face colors. I stare at him as realization dawns. I am an idiot. Amanda didn't jump. *Of course* she didn't! Kat was right. Gabe didn't tell the police about his connection to the Camerons because he had something to hide. He wasn't protecting me—he was protecting himself!

"Tell him, Gabe," I say to my husband. "Tell him what happened to Amanda. The truth."

Gabe looks uncomfortable.

"Tell him," I repeat, louder this time. And, finally, Gabe does.

83

AMANDA

(BEFORE)

I'd only been standing at The Drop for a couple of minutes when Gabe came out. It had been a miserable afternoon, windy, rainy, cold. The sun was preparing to set. The surge of adrenaline that had brought me this far was starting to ebb and I felt light-headed and exhausted. But I was determined. I wasn't prepared to lie down, helpless, as my world collapsed around me, like my mother had. I was going to find out the truth. I wouldn't let Max's shame become mine.

"Can I help you with anything?" Gabe said.

I turned at the sound of his voice. I'd forgotten how handsome he was. Breathtakingly so. His voice was warm and friendly. It was little wonder people decided life was worth living after a few minutes with him. He approached me slowly, holding up his hands, as if to say *I come in peace,* stopping several meters back from the edge.

"I'm not going to jump, if that's what you're worried about," I said, realizing this was the reason for his caution.

Gabe looked puzzled at this declaration. There was a short silence as he scrambled to understand. "I'm glad to hear it."

"You don't recognize me, do you?" I said. I wasn't offended; why would he? We'd only met a couple of times. Besides, I wasn't particularly memorable. Not in the way he was. Or Max.

He came a couple of steps closer, peering at my face.

"Amanda Cameron," I said. "Max's wife."

Now he knew. Immediately he became wary, even took a small step back. "Of course! Amanda . . . What are you doing here?"

"I read the article about you. That's how I knew where to find you. But actually, I'm looking for your wife."

"Oh." Gabe took a moment to process this. "May I ask why?"

"Because I just discovered video footage of her and Max in his office. Pippa was half undressed."

"Footage?" Gabe's face expressed his shock and disbelief, which I expected. It was part of the reason I'd brought the USB. But then he said, "Max filmed it?"

I stared at him. "Wait—you knew about this?"

"Pippa told me. It happened over a year ago, before we moved away. But I had no idea it had been filmed."

And there it was, the confirmation. I hadn't realized how much I'd been hoping that it was all a misunderstanding. That when the footage stopped, Max stopped too. My head began to spin.

"I'm sorry," Gabe said, softer now. "You must be upset."

I laughed. "Upset? Max is the great love of my life. The only thing I ever asked of him was fidelity." I threw up my arms. "It's bad enough that he would betray me at all, but to do it with . . ."

It was because I was so upset that I nearly said it. But I stopped myself. How ridiculous that was . . . even while freshly wounded by Max's betrayal, I couldn't repress my instinct to protect him.

"I've spent my life keeping his secrets. Protecting him. And for *what*?" I held up the USB. "This contains the contents of his secret computer. I could send it to the media. Or the police! I could ruin him! Maybe I will . . ."

Gabe, I noticed, was watching me warily now. "I'm not sure that's a good idea, Amanda."

"Why not? Why shouldn't I?"

"Amanda." Gabe took a step toward me. "Take a breath. Take a minute to think about this."

"Max didn't think twice before he betrayed me!"

I was talking a big game. It felt amazing. Suddenly I felt powerful— like I had control in a situation where I'd previously had none. But I knew, even then, that I would never turn over the USB to anyone. No matter what Max had done, I couldn't do that to him. Loving and protecting him had become part of my DNA.

Gabe's stance had changed now. Rather than the calm neutral man who'd appeared on the cliff, he appeared almost . . . predatory. It prompted a realization. The type that comes out of nowhere and hits you forcefully. Of *course*. Max wasn't the only one who could be hurt by what was on this USB. There was information on here that would incriminate Gabe. By the look on Gabe's face, he'd realized this too.

He lunged for the USB.

For a moment, we both had it. I pulled it toward me, and Gabe pulled it back. I gripped it tightly and leaned back, all my weight in my heels. I really thought I had it. Then Gabe ripped it free, and suddenly I was falling.

Gabe tried to help. He lunged forward, his arms outstretched. He almost caught me. Then he stopped. He held his palms up flat; he stood upright. Perhaps he thought it was too late? Or perhaps he'd realized that if I went over the cliff, everything became simpler? I guessed I'd never know.

And so I plunged to my death. It's probably a cliché, the fact that I was thinking about Max as I fell. Even though he'd betrayed me, I felt proud that, as I fell, I was taking Max's biggest secret with me to the grave.

It served Gabe right that now he'd never know it.

84

AMANDA

(AFTER)

When Max told me about Gabe, it was late, and we were having one of our cheese platters. I don't know why he chose that particular time to tell me. Perhaps it was because Gabe and Pippa had moved away and it felt safe to say it out loud. Maybe it was because, by that point, we'd never trusted each other more. At least that's how it felt to me.

"A few months after Harry died," Max said, "a young woman named Marina came to see my dad and stepmum. She was a girlfriend of Harry's, apparently, although not one they'd met before. That wasn't so strange; Harry had a lot of girlfriends. Anyway, she told them she was pregnant."

Max was sitting in his armchair, holding a glass of red wine, but his gaze was far away. I sat forward and put my own wineglass on the table.

"My parents were very wealthy, as you know, and Marina

was . . . not. This is all secondhand information, of course; my parents only told me about it years later. They said she had no proof that the baby was Harry's, and with Harry dead, she had no way of getting a DNA test to prove that it was his. It was determined—by my father, I guess—that she was angling for money. They sent her away.

"It took me a year to track her down after they told me. That was before the days of social media. By then, Gabe was a teenager. I met Marina at a café and proposed we do a DNA test now. We could use my DNA to determine whether Gabe and I were related. I don't know why I bothered, though; from the moment I saw his photo, I knew that Gabe was Harry's son. The fact that he was already showing signs of mental illness made it even more obvious." Max stared into his wine, lost in the memory. "I wanted to meet him, of course, but since my parents had refused to acknowledge his existence, he wasn't interested. According to his mother, he didn't even want to know our names.

"I offered financial support, and Marina accepted it. When she died a few years later, I quietly paid off the mortgage on her house so Gabe could keep living there. But it wasn't enough. I should have done more."

"Did you reach out to him?" I asked. "Suggest a meeting?"

"My lawyers attempted to connect with him on my behalf, but he wouldn't speak to them. So, I kept an eye on him from afar. When I discovered he'd become a landscape gardener, it was easy. I hired him to do the garden, and then I sat out there and struck up a conversation with him." Max smiled. "He was a shining light, Amanda. So much like Harry. I couldn't stop staring at him. It was like watching Harry if he'd lived. I offered him at job with NewZ on the drop. I couldn't resist.

"Gabe had all of Harry's magic. He had his darkness, too, but I told myself it wasn't as bad in Gabe. I thought if I offered him a career, gave him a sense of purpose, it would help. I even spoke to his wife, Pippa, at the Christmas party and told her to call me if she ever needed anything.

"Gabe had a picture of his daughters, Asha and Freya, on his desk. They are the most darling little girls; I can't even describe it. I took a photo of the photo." He shook his head. "Freya is a dead ringer for my mother. And Asha, she has that cheekiness, you can just see it, even in the photo. I saved the picture and sometimes I would log on just to look at it. The sight of their little faces . . . often it brought me to tears."

I thought of the time I'd seen Max looking at his computer, all misty-eyed. It all made sense now. He was looking at Harry's granddaughters. His great-nieces.

"Why didn't you tell Gabe the truth about who you were?" I asked.

"I planned to, once we'd developed a relationship. I almost did, once. We were in my office, and he started talking about his wife and daughters. Conversation moved naturally to extended family, and I managed to ask about his father." Max sighed. "I'll never forget the look on his face when he told me how his father's wealthy parents had turned his pregnant teenage mother away. I thought it was the most disgusted a person could look. But then he told me about his uncle, who apparently became aware of his existence when he was a teenager. He talked about how his mum had made him do a cheek swab, which had confirmed that we were, in fact, related. He said, 'Can you believe that? He'd only just discovered I existed, and instead of asking to see my face, he asked to see my DNA.'" Max sighed. "That was the moment I knew that if I wanted to have my nephew in my life, I would have to keep our connection a secret.

"When Gabe moved away, it was hard. I still worry about him every day. The same way I would have worried about Harry, I guess."

He looked up, meeting my gaze for the first time since he'd started talking. "This is why I decided never to have children, Amanda. The mental illness that runs through our genes has taken so much from me. First Mum, then Harry. As soon as I'd confirmed Gabe's existence, I promised myself I would look out for him. But I wouldn't have children of my own. I couldn't risk losing someone else I loved to this. It would have broken me."

For a moment we just sat in silence, as I pondered everything he'd shared. Then Max said, "I've never told anyone about this, Amanda."

"Your secret is safe with me," I replied.

And, as it turned out, it was.

85

PIPPA

"She said you were her soulmate," Gabe says.

The three of us stand together by the cliff edge as Gabe recounts Amanda's last moments.

"She said that?" Max asks.

Gabe nods.

Max takes a moment to absorb that. As his eyes grow misty, a desperate sadness washes over me. For a moment I think he might cry, but instead he takes a long deep breath and says, "Then what happened?"

"She was going to take the USB to the media or the police. I tried to convince her not to do that. I was thinking of what would happen if it got out. From what she said, there was some stuff on there that—"

"That would have been damaging to you," Max says.

"Yes."

Despite the fact that I'd suspected this, it's still a shock to have it confirmed.

"I tried to grab the USB." Gabe inhales slowly. "But she held on to it. We struggled and I managed to pull it out of her grasp. The momentum of it sent her flying backward and she went over the edge."

Max closes his eyes, and sighs.

"I didn't mean for her to fall," Gabe says, emotional now. "I tried to grab her before she went over. But I . . . I couldn't."

My instinct is to believe him, but I'm not sure I trust my instincts anymore. As for whether Max believes him, it's unclear. When he opens his eyes, his expression is hard to read.

"Thank you," he says finally. "Thank you for telling me."

Max steps forward so quickly, Gabe doesn't see it coming. As he wraps his arms around Gabe, he closes his eyes and squeezes them tight. He holds Gabe for a moment; then he pulls back. As he does, he locks eyes with Gabe, and something passes between them that I don't understand. I'm not sure even Gabe understands. But there's something powerful about it. I can't look away.

In the near distance, I hear the crunch of feet on gravel, the soft lilt of laughter. Walkers approaching. Gabe and I take a step back, and Max looks out toward the ocean.

"And this is where it happened?" Max says. "This is where Amanda fell?"

"Yes," I say.

He is very close to the edge I realize as the walkers appear on the path behind us. I'm about to tell him to move back when he says, "She was my soulmate, too."

Then he steps off the cliff.

86

AMANDA

One thing I've learned about happy endings is that they don't always look the way you'd expect. In some cases, a happy ending involves the couple walking off into the sunset together. In others, a happy ending is when, after years of lying to themselves, a couple goes their separate ways. I like to think that's what will make Gabe and Pippa happiest. I just hope they know it too.

I watched Max's final interaction with Gabe. I traveled through every emotion with him, *felt* every emotion. The bewilderment at Pippa's lie. The anger at what Gabe had done. The sadness of what he was leaving behind. In the end, what I felt most from Max was love. Love for me. Love for Harry. Love for Gabe. Funny how love can remain, despite everything.

Max had confessed to the money laundering and the murder of Arthur Spriggs on the phone to Detective Conroy. He attributed the guilt and stress of this as the main contributor to my death by suicide. He maintained that Gabe had no involvement in any of it. It was the last chance he'd be able to give his nephew, he reasoned, so he had to take it. For Harry.

He'd left the house before the police arrived to arrest him. Now, they'd never get the chance.

So, here we are. Finally, it makes sense, what I've been doing here—stuck in this strange space between life and death. I've been waiting for him; the love of my life.

And now it's time to go.

87

PIPPA

ONE YEAR LATER

"Are they twins?" the woman at the park asks me, as I tandem-push the girls on the swings. She's been looking at them for a while, trying to figure it out.

Asha beats me to the answer. "No," she yells from the swing, her little legs pumping hard. "Just sisters. Our birthdays are six months apart."

"I'm older," Freya chimes in from her own swing.

"I came out of my first mum's tummy and then she died," Asha adds cheerfully. "This is my other mummy."

I smile and shrug at the woman, who is clearly bamboozled by this abundance of information. After a minute, perhaps just for something to say, she says to the girls, "Well, you do look alike."

"We look like our dad," Freya says. "Mummy, can we have a snack?"

I didn't bring snacks. In the past this would have been unheard

of, but lately I've been much more relaxed about that kind of organization. I look at my watch. "Daddy will be here soon. Maybe he'll
bring some?"

"There he is!" Asha shrieks. "Daddy! *Daddy!*"

I glance to my right just as Gabe leaps the low fence into the
playground and jogs toward the girls with his arms outstretched.
This is how he always greets them after a few days apart—at a running pace. As if he can't stand one more second apart from them.
The girls leap off their swings in unison; the feeling is clearly
mutual.

He's even more tanned than the last time I saw him. He must
have spent the past few days surfing around the clock. He seems to
have come straight from the beach now, as his hair is wet and pushed
back and he's dressed in board shorts and a white T-shirt and sandals.
I notice several women ogling him as the girls leap into his arms and
he props them on either hip. They wrap their arms around his neck,
their legs around his waist.

"Hey," Gabe says to me.

"Hey," I reply.

It's strange greeting him like this, even a year on. I'd be lying if
I said I didn't feel sad about it sometimes. There are many things
I miss about being married to him—watching him be a dad to our
girls most acutely of all. But I *can* breathe without him. This is
something that has surprised me.

The other surprise is that there are so many things I *don't* miss
about being married to Gabe. The constant worry. A feeling that the
ground could shift under me at any moment. The heightened state
of awareness I lived in for years, thinking it was excitement rather
than recognizing it as anxiety. I still don't know if Amanda's death
truly was an accident, nor do I know what was on the USB that

was so threatening to Gabe. Nor do I have to know. Because Gabe's problems are no longer mine. Gabe is Gabe. And I am me.

What I do know is that the bipolar disorder wasn't responsible for his actions. In the past, I'd always found it hard to visualize the line where his illness ended and his free will began. Now I see it. His illness hadn't lied to me. His illness hadn't covered up his mistakes and said that it was for my sake. That was all Gabe. Which meant we were done.

The police discovered the connection between Gabe and Amanda, of course, and Gabe was re-questioned about it. Initially, it seemed as if they suspected Gabe of playing a role in Max's death too, but the walkers had put that idea to rest; they had seen Max step over the edge while Gabe was several paces away.

In the end, it was Max's own statement to the police before his death, asserting that Amanda had been suicidal, that exonerated Gabe.

Gabe and I were both baffled by this, until a few days after Max's death, when Gabe received a message from Max's lawyer explaining their familial connection. The letter included the DNA test Gabe had done when he was fifteen years old.

It explained a lot. The way Gabe had got his job with Max. The fact that he managed to keep his job despite his ups and downs. It also made me realize what Max had been going to say when he told us that Baz was never going to hurt the girls. Of course he wasn't. They were Max's flesh and blood.

Asha and Freya were named sole beneficiaries of Max's estate, with the money to be held in trust until they turn twenty-one, at which time they will become wealthier than any person has a right to be. They don't know this yet, and I have no intention of divulging it anytime soon. I plan to give them the most normal childhood

I can. After the turbulence of their first four years, it feels like the least I can do. If Gabe is upset to have been denied an inheritance, he's showed no sign of it—and I do know that Gabe had never been particularly motivated by money. And, after what Max sacrificed for him on the cliff, he only speaks about his uncle with gratitude. Which adds to my belief that, in dying, Max took the fall for something else that wasn't entirely his fault.

"Ah, here's Nana," I say, as I spot Mum walking toward us.

Gabe and I haven't formalized our custody arrangement, but I've made it clear he is not to spend time with the girls unsupervised. I want Gabe to be part of their lives, but that doesn't mean I trust him. Sometimes it is Mum or Dad who accompanies the girls. Sometimes it is a friend's parent on a playdate in the park. Sometimes it is me. So far, Gabe hasn't objected. He understands he's got off lightly. Besides, for all of his troubles, he loves his daughters. He'll take any access to them that he can get.

"Nana!" Asha cries, launching herself at Mum.

"I'll have them back to yours by five," Gabe says to me.

I wave until they disappear around the corner (once, apparently, Asha turned around to give me one last wave and I'd already left, and I won't ever hear the end of that).

Once they are gone, I leave too, wrestling with that strange, untethered feeling I always get when I walk away from my girls. It's temporary, I know this, usually lasting only until I walk through my front door and become my alter ego, the person I get to be when I'm without them now.

Sometimes, I hang out at the Pantry with Dev, drinking coffee and chatting. We've been spending more and more time together, and while it's nothing romantic yet, I've come to enjoy his company in a way I hadn't expected to. A few weeks ago, he made me a three-course meal at the Pantry after it closed, and it was one of the nicest evenings I can remember in a long time.

Occasionally I will FaceTime Kat and Mei to see my gorgeous nephew, Ollie. Kat and Mei moved back to the city just before Ollie was born. Mei had more work opportunities in Melbourne, and Kat wanted to support her. Before they left, Kat told me that it felt strange to be moving away from me, but for the first time she knew I would be okay. Perhaps for the first time, I knew that too.

We moved out of the cliff house a few months ago. I couldn't live there anymore after everything that happened. I bought a cottage a few streets back from the beach, and Gabe bought his own cottage around the corner. There is a lot of coming and going between our two houses. Forgotten toys being brought back and forth. Once, when the girls wanted to ride their scooters to Daddy's without Mummy (there were no roads to cross), we even stood outside our houses on our phones so we could confirm that there were always eyes on them.

In short, Gabe is still a part of our lives. But he's not my whole life. He's not *me*. Not anymore.

I have reached my house. My cottage is small, just two bedrooms, a living room, a galley kitchen, and a sunroom, but it is quaint and charming and full of character. I'd planned to spend the afternoon reading a book and drinking coffee, but suddenly I have a better idea.

I hire a board from the surf club and spend the afternoon falling off it. Turns out I don't need someone holding my board and pushing me onto the wave—I can do it myself. Several times, as I ride the wave, I have that glorious, blissful feeling . . . like I'm flying. It's even better than the feeling I had the day Gabe took me surfing. Because it teaches me that Gabriel Gerard isn't the only one who can make magic. I can make magic too.

Acknowledgments

You know you're onto a good thing when you tell people your new book idea and they enthusiastically cheer—"Yesssss. I'd read that."

That was the response I received when I announced I'd decided to write a book about marriage and murder. It was during the protracted 262-day Melbourne lockdown, and my girlfriends and I had started a WhatsApp group to chronicle our daily marital misgivings—Christian's urgent need to mow the lawn every time there was homeschooling to be done, Sam's repeated failure to put his undies in the laundry basket instead of beside it, the whisper of the air entering Stew's lungs as he had the audacity to breathe. Suffice to say that by the time I floated the book idea, there was no dearth of suggestions of how the murder might take place.*

But while *The Soulmate* started as an exploration of how we might like to murder our husbands, it quickly morphed into something else. An exploration of the bad and good sides of marriage. What we bring to it. What it brings out in us. I like to think of it as a murderous love story. Unconventional, of course, but that's what I do.

As always, I owe a debt of gratitude to the people behind the scenes, most importantly my editor, Jen Enderlin, whose belief in me boggles my mind on a daily basis. Also to the team at St. Martin's—Katie Bassel, Erica Martirano, Brant Janeway, Olga Grlic, Kim Ludlam, and Christina Lopez, who, after so many books together, I think I can call my friends. Also to the team at Pan Macmillan Australia, specifically Alex Lloyd, to whom this book is dedicated as thanks for always incorporating my down-to-the-wire changes (and, it has to be said, bribery for always incorporating my future down-to-the-wire changes), and the wonderful Clare Keighery for her publicity magic. And enormous thanks, as always, to my literary agent, Rob Weisbach, who always has my back (and also my front and my sides).

To my sensitivity readers, who helped me form a credible understanding of bipolar and the eroding effects it can have on relationships, this book is infinitely better because of you.

To Amy Lovat, my assistant and soon-to-be fellow author—as sad as I am that you are far too talented to be my assistant forever—I can't wait to watch you fly.

To my writing gang—Jane Cockram, Kirsty Manning, Lisa Ireland, and Kelly Rimmer—one day I'll write a book about you guys and I legitimately can't decide who will get murdered. Most likely it will be the man in Big W who came up to our signing table, asked if we were famous, and then decided not to buy a book. That poor bugger is going to have a painful literary death.

To Kerryn Merrett, my friend, another soon-to-be author and police detective, who constantly reminds me that not everything that happens in *Line of Duty* is real. I respectfully disagree about *Line of Duty,* and if you keep telling me Steve Arnott isn't real, we may have a problem on our hands. Still, thank you for everything.

To my friends and family, who provide me with endless book fodder. Keep being the gloriously dysfunctional humans you are. And to my readers, who have embraced my very peculiar brand—funny books about family and murder—because of you, I get to keep writing my very peculiar books. For that, I am forever in your debt.

*No husbands were harmed in the making of this book (fine, Christian did suffer an elbow to the ribs one night while I was "asleep" but no long-term damage was done).

About the Author

Mrs Smart Photography

Sally Hepworth has lived around the world, spending extended periods in Singapore, the United Kingdom, and Canada. She is the author of *The Secrets of Midwives, The Things We Keep, The Mother's Promise, The Family Next Door, The Mother-in-Law, The Good Sister,* and *The Younger Wife.* Sally now lives in Melbourne with her husband, three children, and one adorable dog.